For Lynda

British Columbia is not so much a place as a state of mind.
Jean Barman, *The West Beyond the West*, 2007

"We get a massive earthquake every 300 to 500 years around here, and we're due. They're super bad. When it comes, it's a monster. A full-rip nine."
Patrick Corcoran, Coastal Hazards Specialist, Oregon Sea Grant, 2011

FULL RIP NINE

A Story of Political and Seismic Upheaval

BY

PETER CHARLES HEAP

PROLOGUE

November 26, Copper Queen Mine, British Columbia

James clambered up the rough, rock-strewn trail that wound through the trees. He concentrated on keeping his footing. Breaking an ankle was not an option. He felt vulnerable enough out here by himself as it was. Working his way along the steep path, he struggled to tamp down the fear and maintain his focus.

The climb was taking more out of him than he expected. Recently he had run less and less. Work always seemed to get in the way. His endurance was down. He hated to admit it, but the years were taking their toll as well.

Every half hour or so, he stopped to take a drink of water and look back towards the valley floor. He had come a long way up through the pines and, as he stood straining to catch any sounds of pursuit, he was glad of a jacket. The air was crisp in the shadow of the trees.

He emerged past the tree-line into full sun and followed the dusty trail across a slope and along to a ridge. From here, he looked ahead to see the path snaking across the far hill and out of sight up to the left. He checked again to see if anyone was following him, but the path was empty. The fact he could see no one did nothing to reduce his level of anxiety.

All he could see was an eagle circling lazily on the thermals. He was surprised at how much height he had gained in the last two hours. He started down and across the saddle before heading farther up the mountainside.

When he reached the point at which the path disappeared, he was able to look ahead and see a tumble-down collection of mismatched wooden structures perched precariously on the spur of a rocky outcrop – the abandoned mine site. He set off, uncomfortably aware that the ground fell away sharply to his right. A stumble at this stage would be dangerous.

An hour later, he trudged up to the first building, the terminus for a tramline that had taken men and ore down to the valley. The platform and the buildings above it were made of weathered grey wood. None of it looked very stable, but he crawled cautiously up onto the catwalk, which led to a rickety flight of stairs. From there he looked back down for thousands of feet and across at a range of mountains capped with snow. The sun might be bright, but the air was cold.

Except for his footsteps and the sound of the wind whistling through rusting cables, the place was silent. James stared into the void. He was alone, he was scared, and he couldn't shake the feeling that this whole trek into the wilderness was a futile gesture. There was no guarantee, after all, that the young woman he was searching for was anywhere nearby. All he had was hope and a rumour of her future plans – not much to go on.

As the sun sank behind a neighbouring mountain and the temperature dropped, James made camp in a small shed that seemed marginally less porous than the rest. Darkness fell early, and he was exhausted. He laid out the tarp and the sleeping bag after a cold meal. He was fast asleep within minutes.

He awoke to a painful jab in the ribs from a gun barrel. Momentarily he could make out several shadowy figures standing over him. Then a large boot descended on his chest. His ribs cracked and the air left his chest in a rush. A light shone directly into his eyes. He couldn't speak and he couldn't move – he was trapped!

"You have exactly thirty seconds to tell us who you are and what you're doing here" came a low voice. "If we don't find your explanations convincing, you're going back down this mountain a whole shitload faster than you came up it."

I. ORIGIN STORY

CHAPTER 1

May 10, Toronto

A striking man in his mid-thirties stood on the edge of the packed platform at the Bloor and Yonge subway station in Toronto. Piercing grey eyes surmounted a full black beard. He ignored the morning rush-hour crush around him and looked inward to a peaceful place, away from the noise and the heat. The breeze of the oncoming train hit his cheek. He readied himself for its arrival. The next moment, he felt a strong push in the small of his back. His last thought as he looked up from the track at the driver's horrified face was regret. He had so much left to do.

From the back of the screaming, heaving crowd, a heavy-set figure slipped away. He wore a Blue Jays jacket, a matching cap and a large red bristly moustache. Moments later he emerged from the nearby washroom, clean-shaven and wearing a beige suede coat. He walked up the stairs to the street and spoke briefly into a cell-phone as he emerged onto Bloor. He passed the police cars converging on the TTC station. A block away, he tossed the phone into a Dumpster.

Joe was not especially bloodthirsty, but this particular job had given him some satisfaction. His old friends in Special Forces would appreciate the help.

CHAPTER 2

May 25, Ottawa

J ames woke with a start. The hotel room was still dark, the bed warm. The person beside him slept peacefully, a slender arm draped across his chest. Her tangled auburn hair spread across the pillow. Her lingering perfume filled his head with memories of a night full of scotch, banter and, finally, a hot slithery descent into lust. Under other circumstances, James would have been content, even happy. Unfortunately, he was in the wrong hotel room at the wrong time with the wrong person – his boss, Anne Richardson, the Premier of British Columbia.

They had met many years earlier at Yale Graduate School. Their first encounter had been over lunch at the Hall of Graduate Studies. It was early in the fall term when James had seen her advancing across the flag-stoned courtyard, tall, lithe, long hair flowing, jeans compellingly tight. He was sufficiently impressed that he missed his footing and dropped a pile of books. Anne smiled faintly as she strode by. Despite this unpromising beginning, James was overjoyed to find her later the same day examining the menu posted outside the dining room door.

"Do you eat here often?" he said, writhing inwardly at the cluelessness of this opening gambit.

"Only if I'm trapped in this part of campus at mealtime," she replied. "Would you like to know my sign now, or should we reserve that for later in the conversation?"

Fighting to extend the exchange, however disastrous so far, James fell back on the standard enquiry about what subject she was studying. Relenting somewhat in the face of his social ineptitude, she smiled and told him her major was Asian Studies.

They continued chatting stiffly as they made their way through the cafeteria line and then went to sit together at the end of one of the long tables that filled the fake-baronial dining hall. Much to James's annoyance, Anne seemed to know almost everyone who subsequently came through the door. The men in particular insisted on stopping for a word. The table soon filled up with people intent on engaging Anne and totally ignoring James. Half an hour later, he gave up. He bussed his tray and wandered out. Anne didn't seem to notice his departure.

Three days later, James sat in the same cafeteria glumly picking away at an undistinguished shepherd's pie. Anne had not shown up again for lunch or dinner. James assumed that she was going to some trouble to avoid running into him. He could hardly blame her. His performance had been unfortunate, even by his own low standards.

A tray slid onto the table beside him. He looked up to see Anne settling in. He tried to control the idiotic grin that he knew was consuming his face.

Anne smiled back. "Actually, I decided the conversation was worth putting up with the food for. How have you been?"

James couldn't recall having spoken to Anne much at all when they first met, but he was greatly relieved that she had reappeared. This time he managed to be reasonably charming and, after a very long meal, they agreed to meet that night for a movie. Within days, it became clear that they would be fast friends. On top of which, they were incapable of keeping their hands off each other.

James' memories of the next eighteen months were a

vivid kaleidoscope of joy and pain. The relationship crashed and burned several times, but always the two of them found a way back. Both of them had major independent streaks, and neither found compromise a natural approach to overcoming differences.

Then, during one of the many periods when Anne and James were at odds, he had left university abruptly. His departure came on the heels of a series of conversations with one of his professors. This patrician refugee from the Kennedy Administration regaled his small seminars with tales of Camelot while sporting a succession of violently-coloured silk pocket handkerchiefs in his jacket pocket.

James found the professor engaging, if somewhat arch, and he had been pleased when the silver-haired academic invited him for coffee after class. Coffee led to lunch, and then one day, over hamburgers in Mory's, James and the professor were joined by a nondescript representative of one of the US government's lesser-known intelligence agencies. The professor made his excuses, and James was left alone in the white clapboard retreat with a rumpled bureaucrat.

After a slow start, the conversation turned to the opportunities available in the shadow world to an ambitious young man with impressive analytical skills. Flattered by the attention and intrigued by initiation into a parallel reality whose existence he had always suspected, James viewed the prospect of slipping away from the routine of graduate school with no regret.

As a condition of his new employment, James was forced to cut off all contact with his former life. In later years he came to recognize the brutality of the rupture. At the time, simply leaving town had seemed convenient, a method of avoiding yet another difficult scene. If he thought about it at all, he probably assumed he and Anne would pick up again in a few months' time. In fact, he was not to see Anne again for two decades, not until six months before the last provincial election in BC, when she made a successful run at the party leadership and he was a key aide.

James stared at the ceiling and wondered at how two quite intelligent people could deal with their feelings so haphazardly. For his part, he regretted his decision not to keep in touch with Anne, especially once he was no longer part of the intelligence world. He had never met anyone as smart and as empathetic as Anne. Then, more recently, despite the opportunity once he had started to work with her again, he had never chosen to speak to her directly about their earlier time together. He recognized, of course, that his track record for opening up to other people was far from exemplary. He had many acquaintances and few friends, and a succession of women had simply walked away after frustrating months or years of polite reticence on his side.

Those relationships came and went, like an itch that needed to be scratched. He missed the girls when they left, but he became adept at ensuring that the break-ups were never his fault. He was deliberately truthful about his lack of desire for permanence. He was also open about the fact that he was often dating more than one woman at a time. Being straightforward provided him with a kind of armour that the succession of angry and upset women could not penetrate. Besides, most of his jobs required 24/7 focus. He couldn't afford the pull of family obligations.

James might have had a limited emotional range, but he was not stupid. He knew that, at his age, the chances of establishing significant friendships, let alone meaningful romantic ties, were diminishing by the year. What he did not know was whether he was prepared to take action to change these circumstances.

As James slipped out of bed, Anne mumbled something he didn't catch and rolled over. As quietly as possible he eased the door open and, clutching most of his clothes, trotted warily down the hall. Once safely in his own room, he collapsed into a chair. He tried to take stock. How had he managed to end up in the premier's bed? Oh right, now he remembered. As usual, it was all the feds' fault.

CHAPTER 3

May 4, Victoria

T he federal announcement had been unexpected. The prime minister had never been keen on First Ministers' Conferences. In fact, he had held only one previously in his tenure, to reassure Canadians about a rapidly deteriorating international financial situation. Despite that meeting's generally positive outcome, the prime minister had never been tempted to hold another such conclave. Why give premiers any more free airtime? All they did was use it to demand more unconditional federal money to solve problems they should have dealt with themselves.

Until now. In BC, the e-mail had come in to Alessandra Barbieri, the premier's peppery deputy minister, from the federal clerk of the Privy Council. The gist of the message was that the PM felt strongly that the desultory national debate over pension reform had wandered on long enough. The PM was inviting the premiers and territorial leaders to Ottawa in three weeks' time. The objective of the meeting was for heads of government to agree on ". . . a set of principles to guide officials in the search for a renovated national pension regime that would be equitable geographically and inter-generationally, while remaining actuarially sound." Provincial jurisdiction would, of course, be respected, but the time for concerted pan-Canadian action had, in the prime minister's view, finally arrived.

This message was greeted by surprise and a measure of disbelief in Victoria. It was true that the PM's remote style had pulled his party down in the polls lately. He needed to be seen to be taking action. His government had responded ineffectually to an economy that had been going sideways for several years. The feds seemed incapable of providing leadership inside the country and paralyzed by an unstable situation internationally.

More urgently, in the past year, the demographic fault lines in the country had been revealed in a variety of ways. On one side, the swelling ranks of retiring baby boomers were becoming increasingly nervous about the financial prospects for their declining years. From their perspective, the feckless young people reclining on couches at home or noodling away at dead-end service jobs could hardly be trusted to maintain the social safety net on which the boomers would increasingly be reliant.

On the other side, a network of young people based largely in urban Canada but driven by a potent alliance of disenfranchised native youth and radicalized Quebec university students was building a web-based campaign attacking their elders for selfishness and ignorance. This polyglot alliance saw cutbacks in social programs and education funding, as well as cuts to EI and possible increases in pensions, as direct attacks on youth. At the heart of their sometimes obscene social media campaign was a demand for respect.

An especially disturbing phenomenon started to emerge at odd locations across the country – flash-mobs aimed at older people. Called together on a moment's notice via Twitter, crowds of teenagers and twenty-somethings gathered at intersections and started to jeer anyone who looked much over thirty, picking on the frail elderly in particular. Chanting and menacing, the groups often reduced older pedestrians to tears, forcing them off sidewalks and sometimes bowling them over. Social media spread support for the self-proclaimed young "wrinkly wranglers."

Mainline commentators expressed outrage at such behaviour, but the momentum behind these attacks seemed to be growing. Young people felt burdened with debt, condemned to flipping burgers and generally ignored. They saw a clear societal bias in favour of the boomers. They were quite prepared to aim their anger at the nearest targets. They knew that the chances of being caught were low.

As the inter-generational tensions within Canadian society multiplied, the flashpoint turned out to be the otherwise mundane and technical topic of pension reform. The politically sophisticated student groups in Quebec started the ball rolling with a concerted attack on the Quebec Pension Plan. Their basic argument was that society was spending too much money on old people. The overly rich Quebec pension system, coupled with all the funding going to the elder-dominated health care system, was guaranteeing that government investments in job generation and education would not be made. In an interesting twist, these Quebec groups reached out across the language divide to counterparts across Canada and galvanized the debate on Anglophone campuses.

The Quebec government, backed by the full might of the French-language commentariat, condemned a movement they characterized as self-serving and ungrateful. After all, Quebec university and college fees were easily the lowest in Canada, and the heavily subsidized daycare system was a model for all. How dare these kids claim that the needs of children and youth were being ignored?

The rapidly rising tide of inter-generational resentment caught the feds by surprise. The "grown-up" backlash against the flash-mob assaults was undeniable, especially in some Western Canadian cities, where the involvement of First Nations youth added an uncomfortable racial element to the mix. For the most part, adult urbanites wanted the police to come down hard on these kids, and the sooner the better. Provincial governments were hesitant to provide direction to the police forces. The cops just felt caught in the middle. They knew that once they started swinging truncheons, they would face a larger, not a smaller, problem.

Then the inevitable happened. In Regina, a flash-mob surrounded several older shoppers and backed them up against a department store window. The plate glass gave way and shattered inwards in a welter of shards and blood. Three older women were badly cut, and when a pair of policemen tried to make arrests, the flash-mob turned on the police. Before long, a battle was raging across the main intersections of the city. Police reinforcements arrived. More young people rushed downtown. Tear gas floated across demonstrators, shoppers and business people alike. Only a downpour drove the crowd off the streets, leaving behind dozens of people arrested and more sent to hospital.

Reaction was swift from one end of Canada to the other. Media sympathy was clearly on the side of the injured seniors. In addition to the expected calls for order to be restored, the federal government came under severe criticism for not dealing with the broader problem of intergenerational equity. The prime minister reacted by attacking the "small groups of radical, irresponsible youth" and hinted darkly that foreign-inspired elements were prompting the recourse to violence. He also directed his communications and justice ministers to conduct an immediate enquiry into the misuse of the internet to subvert public order.

The prime minister's response was generally seen as inadequate. A sustained assault in the House and on the op-ed pages left the impression that he was losing control of a volatile situation. In the meantime, the flash-mobs continued to appear at irregular intervals across the country. Shop-owners began to complain that business was being harmed as older people became nervous about shopping.

After two or three weeks of pressure, the prime minister capitulated. Invitations to premiers to discuss pension reform were the upshot. The message from the prime minister focused on the technical issues related to pensions, but the follow-up calls from the Privy Council Office indicated that the feds looked on the meeting as an opportunity to deal with the larger equity-related questions as well.

* * *

When Barbieri called together the usual suspects to discuss a BC reply, the consensus around the table in the Legislature's heavily panelled Oak Room was that the meeting was likely to be unproductive in the extreme. On the one hand, apart from anything else, it seemed unlikely that a meaningful discussion of the inter-generational divide could occur if only one side were at the table. On the other hand, it would be difficult for premiers to refuse a direct prime ministerial call to deal with what appeared to be an emergent situation, so not attending did not appear to be a realistic option.

James slipped into the Oak Room, a short stroll from his office on the second floor of the West Annex, where premier's office staff hung their hats. He had decided to sit in on Barbieri's meeting, although normally the minutiae of Canadian federal–provincial diplomacy left him cold. He was happy to take time away from his day-job as the Premier's main political adviser, however, and he wondered if the Ottawa meeting could be used for their own purposes. As Barbieri brought matters to a close with a call for briefing material, James held up his hand.

"Does this Ottawa trip give us an opportunity to make our case with the feds about the resource auction?" he asked. "We've been taking no end of flak from them, but we've never been able to explain in any detail what we had in mind. Could we do this around the margins of the fed–prov meeting without drawing too much attention to ourselves?"

"I think you can assume that if we do a sidebar on the auction, someone will notice," came a voice from the end of the table. "The Ottawa Press Gallery has been starved for a major First Ministers' meeting, and they will be all over it. As long as you don't expect your resource auction idea to blush unseen, sure, we could see if the feds would be interested. I don't think you send the premier to this briefing, though. Send a minister to take the abuse, if there is any."

This comment came from Barbieri's ADM for Federal–Provincial Relations, Victor Campbell, a grizzled veteran of inter-jurisdictional combat. Victor's general world-view, on the basis of several decades of fed–prov work for a succession of governments, was that, if things could go wrong, they would. That being said, Victor knew all the players across Canada and gave consistently practical, if usually discouraging, advice.

"Let's talk to the premier about it, Franklin," said Barbieri, as she rose and headed for the door. "If she wants to do it, Victor can set things up. And by the way, if the answer is yes, you'd better come along. You'll love Ottawa in May – all mud and a bit of ice."

CHAPTER 4

May 4, Victoria

L ater that day, as he often did when he needed to think something through, James took his concerns about the resource auction and the Ottawa trip to his resident expert on BC history, Alastair Reid.

The old man sipped his scotch. He and his visitor looked out through leaded windows at a spectacular view that was disappearing slowly in the fall twilight. They sat in the high-ceilinged library of an Edwardian mansion situated at the top of the affluent Rockland neighbourhood in Victoria. The room was lined with huge floor-to-ceiling bookcases, a tribute to the owner's omnivorous literary tastes. Beyond the tidy houses of Fairfield on the slopes below, the two could see the Straits of Juan de Fuca, and the Olympic Peninsula in the distance.

"You're a disgrace, James. Despite my best efforts, you know nothing about this government and even less about the province. For the life of me, I don't understand why you were hired. If I weren't such an innocent, I would assume that you had attained your position on the basis of an unwholesome personal relationship with the premier."

James responded from deep in an armchair. "Isn't that why I'm here? To further my education? And to provide you with regular infusions of single malt, of course."

Alastair maintained his accusatory tone. "I realize that you were born in Vancouver, but you didn't stay long, did you?"

"That was hardly my fault," James said. "We had no money. My mother was a very bright woman, but she had a low-paying job as a departmental secretary at UBC. The fact that she was smarter than most of the professors who lorded it over her understandably made her resentful. I never knew who my father was, but I always suspected he was a married academic. Anyway, when the chance came up for a full-ride track scholarship at the University of Oregon, I jumped at it. Besides, my mom and I weren't getting along at the time. It was a golden opportunity to get out on my own. The only problem was that she died while I was away at school..." His voice trailed off.

"We all have sad family stories. Mine would curl your hair. The point is, clearly your background in relevant British Columbia history is deficient." Reid paused to refill his glass. "I think what annoys me most about you and your optimistic friend, the premier, is your stubborn refusal to acknowledge this province's dark heart."

"Your Scots Presbyterian upbringing makes the story much too easy to tell. It's all about original sin, isn't it? In our case, the sin of first contact."

"You can be as flippant as you like, young man, but that doesn't alter the fact that when the transplanted Brits who took this place over became bored with ransacking the province's natural resources, they systematically oppressed every non-white minority in sight."

"That's one way of looking at it, but I'd remind you that most of those 'transplanted Brits' were in fact from Scotland, your nineteenth-century ancestors. There's plenty of guilt to go around."

Although James had heard versions of this harangue before, he always learned something from this dyspeptic eighty-five-year-old. Alastair might be trapped in a wheelchair, but his memory and his sense of historical injustice remained intact. He possessed an encyclopaedic knowledge of the primary sources of British Columbia's history, having spent most of a long, productive career in the Provincial Archives.

"Your problem is that you have almost no direct experience of this province outside of the bourgeois confines of Kitsilano. I, on the other hand, grew up in BC's mighty forests. Did I ever tell you about my whistle punk days?"

James tuned out as Alastair recounted his short but eventful career in logging. As the familiar story of how Alastair ended up in a wheelchair ebbed to a close, James roused himself and nodded sympathetically. After a respectful pause, he drew the conversation back to the resource auction.

"Is the premier right when she says we need radical change? Surely we could be tipped over the brink just as easily as propelled forward. Why would BCers want to take this big a risk?"

Alastair swirled the scotch around in his glass. He turned on the table lamp beside him before responding.

"Well, over the years, the economy has suffered from recurrent boom and bust cycles that hit the folks working in the smaller resource communities especially hard. To some degree, though, we've gotten used to the arrival of bad times. I'm not certain people here find that prospect all that scary – we always seem to recover."

Alastair swivelled around and fixed James with his direct gaze. "But I think there's more to it than that. BCers generally live on the edge of things. The Europeans who came here felt isolated from the rest of North America and far from their homelands. In addition, this country represented a last chance. If people couldn't make it here, they were out of options. California is full of "last chancers" too, for many of the same reasons. As a result, West Coast culture generally has a strong crazy streak running through it. That's one reason why, with all due respect to your friend the premier, a complete political novice can come out of nowhere, condemn the *status quo*, and win an election based on little more than Scotch mist and coupons."

"I guess it's also true," James said, ignoring the shot at his boss, "that, as a relatively young society, at least in non-aboriginal terms, the people of the coast have been quick to embrace the new and the innovative. We haven't had many traditions to overcome."

"That's probably the case," Alastair said, "but I've come to the conclusion that literally underlying the unsettled feeling here is the realization that natural disasters are never far away."

Alastair rolled himself over to one of his large bookcases and pulled out a quarto-sized volume. "If you've got time, let me read you a story."

James refilled their glasses and settled in. Alastair's deep voice soon filled the room.

The smoke from the driftwood fire blew into the faces of the children listening intently to the elder's quiet words. His lined face was lit by the setting sun. The elder spoke through the rhythmic break and suck of the waves hitting the pebbled beach they sat on. Sometimes it was hard to hear, but his steady, reassuring voice wrapped the children up in a story they had heard before, but which they all loved. They huddled closer to the fire, tucking their hands into their sleeves as the cool sunset wind lifted off the sea.

"This all happened long ago in a village much like this one," he said. "Just like ours, the village sat on a long beach, backed up against the forest. Just like ours, the village was quite isolated. Except for the occasional trading trip, the people of the village rarely saw strangers.

"The people of the village lived well. They took salmon, shellfish and seaweed from the sea; they took berries, venison and timber for their houses from the land. The families in the community all had tasks and honours to share. The sea, the land and the people were one.

"As he flapped over the village in the form of a raven, the Creator saw that the people lived in peace and harmony and was content.

"Then one day, a wise woman who lived alone at the edge of the village had a dream. In that dream the raven came to her with a terrible warning.

"'Some people,' he said, 'are taking the great gifts I have given them and are misusing them. They fight among themselves, and they strive for domination. They have forgotten the covenant they made with me when I gave them the sea and the land, and they live selfishly and without honour. The earth,' the raven said, 'must be cleansed of all those who disrespect it.'

"The wise woman was frightened by this warning. She begged the raven not to destroy her people. She pleaded with him to remember that her people maintained the terms of the covenant and lived together in peace and harmony. She asked what she might do to save the village she loved.

"The raven considered the wise woman's words. He knew, of course, that she was telling the truth about the village, because often he flew over it and saw that all was well. Still, the raven's heart was black with rage about the behaviour of the rest of humankind, and he was determined to set an example that would never be forgotten.

"'Hear me,' the raven said to the wise woman. 'Humankind has forfeited my regard, and humankind is one. All must share in the just punishment for the wrong actions of the few. Nevertheless, I know that what you say about your village is true. I am prepared to spare its people – but only if you are willing to take their penalty on yourself.'

"The wise woman bowed her head. She remembered the laughter of the children, the warm comfort of the dances, the clear eyes of the fishermen and the feasts prepared by the women. She could not stand by and see all this destroyed. Even in her fear, she rejoiced that she seemed to have the power to cause the raven's wrath to pass by her people.

"'Tell me what I must do,' she said simply.

"'In three day's time,' the raven directed, 'you will tell the villagers that they must move up into the hills with all they can carry. If they do not heed your advice, they will be caught in a great wave which will wash the coastline clear. As for you, after you have sent your people to safety, you must wait by the shore for my judgment.'

"At this point, the wise woman awoke to find nothing changed. She wondered about the raven's message and even doubted the truth of her dream. Nevertheless, despite her misgivings, in three days she called the people of the village together. She told everyone about the message from the raven. Many of them also had doubts about the meaning of the dream, but the wise woman had always given them good counsel in the past, so after a short debate, they set off uphill with all they could carry. Despite the urging of her friends, the wise woman did not go with them but remained on the beach, watching them trudge away.

"Just as the people of the village reached higher ground, a huge sea creature churned up the ocean and sent massive waves crashing against the shore. When they returned, their village had been spared, although the trees on either side were knocked flat. It looked as though the whole coast except for their home had been devastated.

"Although they searched for her all day, there was no trace of the wise woman. The people were saddened by this loss but took comfort from the fact that the wise woman's warning had saved the whole village.

"Then, on their first night back, a wonderful thing occurred. The villagers noticed that a new light hung over the village. It did not twinkle like the other stars but shone steady and strong. Clearly, the raven had rewarded the wise woman by taking her up into the sky and making it possible for her watch over her beloved village forever. The people still missed the practical advice the wise woman had given them, but now they all knew that they could take inspiration from knowing that she would never really leave them."

The elder finished his story, and the little group sat silently in the growing darkness watching the fire die.

There was a reverent hush as Alastair finished reading. "So, what did you think? Not bad, eh? Even the First Nations here seem to have a clear sense of the temporary nature of things."

"Very nice, but why do I think there's more to this than a pretty story?" said James.

"Well, in fact, it turns out that this isn't an indigenous myth at all. This book and the stories in it were manufactured by a Protestant missionary who travelled through coastal communities in the late-nineteenth century. The book was a fundraiser, intended to support the establishment of residential schools. Some would argue that books like this deserve to be burned, considering the cultural appropriation involved, and the purpose of the fundraising."

Alastair rolled back to the centre of the room. "I just wanted to remind you of something that you should have figured out for yourself by now. Nothing in British Columbia is as it seems."

CHAPTER 5

May 17, Seattle

Ten days after his successful mission in the Toronto subway, Joe sat with a woman at a plain table in a nondescript room in a small motel near Seattle's airport. He had met her several times to receive assignments. He never felt comfortable around her. In his line of work, he was not easily spooked, but this woman had a wild streak that made him nervous. It was her eyes. Sometimes they looked right through him: the eyes of a stone-cold killer.

"Colonel Johnson wanted you to know that he was very pleased with how things went in Toronto," she was saying. "Very quiet and efficient, just the way we like things done."

"Our friend made it easy," Joe said. "He took the same subway every morning. Careless. Actually I was more worried that the horsemen might have had a tail on him, but we didn't see them."

"The colonel's agency contacts are pleased as well," the woman went on. "The Canadians probably would have picked him up eventually, but we needed him out of play sooner. We also wanted to send a message – just because you're not in the States doesn't mean you're safe."

Joe knew all this. But why had he been summoned to Seattle? "So what was so important that we needed to meet?"

"We have a different sort of assignment for you this

time," the woman responded. "We want you to travel to Victoria and Vancouver and to familiarize yourself with the cities. The colonel is convinced that political developments are going to mean that the foundation will need to be operational up there fairly soon. When the time comes, we want to make sure that you're comfortable in that setting. You've done that sort of thing before; it shouldn't take you more than a week or two to get the lay of the land."

Joe nodded. "You know, I've explained to the colonel that I prefer short-term jobs. My wife's not well. I need to be around home."

The woman smiled. "If you have to go back a couple of times, that's fine. Just so long as you're ready to go within a month or so. By the way, the colonel asked me to tell you that he spoke to the administrators at the Citadel. I'm sure your granddaughter would have had no trouble gaining entry, but he wanted to ensure that they understood what a good candidate she was."

Joe's face lit up. "She's a pistol, all right! And she's had her heart set on that school. Please thank the colonel for me. Tell him not to worry about north of the border. He can rely on me." He got up and walked out of the room.

Alison Colette watched Joe leave. Once again she was impressed by her boss's attention to detail. Joe was already one of their most reliable agents, but providing one more reason for him to be utterly loyal would do no harm at all.

CHAPTER 6

May 26, Ottawa

A t eight o'clock, James walked into the small hotel meeting room that served as the temporary BC headquarters in Ottawa and made himself as inconspicuous as possible by sitting in a chair along the wall. He avoided catching Anne's eye.

In his early fifties, James still had the build of a distance runner. He was a touch under six feet tall, wiry and slender. His thick brown hair belied his age. His pale, hazel eyes turned green at moments of stress. Unless he chose to draw attention to himself, people often failed to notice that he was in the room. At an earlier job, a wit had proclaimed that James raised diffidence to an art form. James himself would not have contested this judgment. He valued his ability to fade into the background. He found safety in the role of observer and relished the opportunity to intervene on his own terms.

The premier was sitting at the head of the table, a cup of black coffee beside her. She looked extremely cheerful and disturbingly fresh. Certainly more so than her finance minister, who sat beside her looking grumpy as well as jet-lagged.

Ministers of Finance generally kept out of the ordinary run of federal–provincial meetings. They and their officials considered that the only such meeting worthy of their time was the annual get-together with counterparts that formed part of the budget cycle in December. Otherwise, they ran the world and left the inter-jurisdictional bickering to others.

On this occasion, however, since the resource auction secretariat rested in his ministry, and since this initiative was demonstrably the most important one for the provincial government, the premier had prevailed on the finance minister to come along for the purpose of explaining to the feds the rationale for the auction idea.

The minister of Finance was a pudgy, cerebral-looking Victorian named Rupert Smith. He owed his position to two main characteristics. With his bald head and accountant's glasses, he looked every inch the Finance man. Second, and more importantly, he was the party's one MLA from the provincial capital. The only problem with his appointment was an awkward additional attribute – he was both stupid and vain. He proudly traced his lineage from the second premier of BC, Amor de Cosmos, conveniently ignoring the fact that this worthy had died insane.

Smith was an aggrieved man. From the perspective of the Ministry of Finance, the resource auction initiative was a gigantic gamble. No provincial government had ever tried anything remotely close to what they were proposing to do now. Informed commentary was likely to be devastating. The scale of the proposal was large enough that the average voter was liable to be doubtful at best, terrified at worst – assuming they understood it at all. The idea hadn't even originated with Smith's ministry, although his people had been lumbered with implementation. No, it had apparently sprung from the fertile mind of the premier herself.

When Richardson first outlined the proposal to a small committee of ministers, she had seemed so convincing. The meeting took place in the Cabinet Chambers overlooking Vancouver Harbour. For once the subject matter kept attention in the room instead of on the view outside.

"What we're proposing," the premier had said, her eyes shining, "is shock therapy, not just for the government but for the whole province. The challenge we face is how to mobilize the province's amazing resource base so that British Columbians can enjoy the quality of life they feel entitled to. Or to put the question in terms of what government delivers: how can we pay for a full set of social programs over the long term as the population ages and the government's revenue flows veer erratically from year to year?"

"And the answer to the question," a skeptical minister asked, "is that well-known free-market instrument, a public auction?"

"Exactly," the premier responded. "Instead of doling out resource rights piecemeal, we package up all the provincially owned resources and auction exclusive rights to their exploitation to the highest bidder, domestic or foreign. Payment would be made to the Provincial Treasury in the form of a guaranteed revenue flow over twenty-five years."

Anne pressed on into the frightened silence. "The sectors we cover will include minerals, oil and gas, and forest products, but basically we're talking about any resource where we have clear jurisdiction – so probably not fish, for example."

"Second, if access rights to some or all of the resources in the package are not exercised within ten years, all rights revert to the provincial Crown. This should reassure folks who think we're totally losing control over the land-base. We'll retain ultimate regulatory jurisdiction, of course, no matter who holds the resource extraction rights. We can still enforce environmental standards, for example. We're not giving up and walking away from our responsibilities."

The premier moved on, undeterred by the quiet apprehension around the table. She wondered fleetingly whether she should have mentioned the possible reaction of actual voters. Suddenly this crazy scheme had taken on some reality for a group of ministers facing re-election fairly soon. "The reserve price for the auction is twice the provincial government's average annual natural resource revenue over the past twenty-five years for the first ten years, renegotiable for the last fifteen. This should work for both us and the successful bidder. It gives us all the ability to adjust to changes in the international economy over time."

Anne could tell that references to "revenue numbers" were causing some eyes to glaze, so she pressed ahead. "Half the take from the winning group will flow to general revenue, half to a heritage fund for future investment. The idea is to smooth out revenue flows, hopefully at a higher level, not to trigger an artificial torrent of expenditure that would destroy fiscal discipline, overheat the economy and drive a skills shortage. We have no intention of becoming another Alberta."

"The final point may be the most important, though." Anne looked around the room, seeking out each minister's eyes in succession. "The successful bidders must include BC firms as partners as they develop their projects. We'll have to administer this provision carefully, so as not to drive away prospective bidders, but a key message overall is that we're aiming to generate jobs in BC as well as social programs."

After a short pause, everyone had wanted a say. The element of risk involved was breathtaking. But the government was becalmed, and something dramatic was required. The discussion that followed Anne's brief summary had been heated but, in the end, she talked them all around, even Willem de Groote, the man Anne had defeated for the leadership, and the man who everyone expected would pick up the pieces if the premier stumbled.

And now he, Rupert Smith, the minister of Finance, a power in the government in his own right, was being sent off like an errand boy to convince a bunch of supercilious feds that this wasn't the silliest thing they'd ever heard of. At least Colin would be there with him. Smith personally had only the dimmest sense of how this all might actually work, and Colin was so good about details.

Victor Campbell, the fed–prov ADM, opened proceedings. "Minister, as you know, your meeting with federal Finance is scheduled for nine o'clock, ahead of the opening of the First Ministers' meeting at 10:30. It should be fairly straightforward. You describe our approach, he listens – all pretty pro forma."

The premier smiled across at Smith. "We all know how persuasive you can be, Rupert. Firm but reasonable; that's the ticket. You can tell me how it went before I go over to First Ministers."

Smith looked less than enthusiastic but dutifully heaved his bulk out of the chair and went on his way with his deputy minister in tow. James watched them with foreboding. As long as Smith kept his mouth shut, he was no liability. Sending him into a situation in which he would have to speak coherently for an extended period of time, however, was asking for trouble, even with his able deputy minister, Colin Jordan, there to support him.

A week or so earlier, Jordan had come over to James's office for a late-afternoon chat. He laid out his many concerns about the auction idea and confessed that he was considering whether he should resign. He saw his own professional reputation at stake. James had managed to talk him back off the ledge but knew that Jordan was still not convinced. At James's suggestion, the premier had taken the time to call Jordan in and make a personal appeal for support. The premier could be very persuasive one-on-one. Colin had agreed to stay on, at least for the moment. Both James and the premier knew, however, that the resource auction initiative was on life-support, even within the bureaucracy.

After Smith and Jordan left, Anne led the group through a quick review of the FMC agenda items. Then everyone dispersed back to their hotel rooms, some to phone home, others to catch some needed rest.

CHAPTER 7

May 26, Ottawa

On the other side of town in the storied old Langevin Block, which sat smugly across from Parliament Hill, federal officials were putting the finishing touches on preparations for the FMC. All the various scenarios had been reviewed, the briefing notes vetted and the logistics confirmed. There was not much room for error in any federal central agency but, for the sleep-deprived inmates of the federal–provincial part of the Privy Council Office, the pressure was especially intense. An FMC was a performance without a net, right out in front of a national TV audience. Any screw-up would be immediately pounced on, and blame would swiftly be assigned.

And rather unusually, British Columbia had come up in the lead-up to the conference. In common with most central Canadian commentators, the Ottawa crowd had watched with disinterest the fledgling BC administration feel its way through its first year. From the banks of the Rideau, Richardson's surprising election victory looked like yet another inexplicable development in a region that usually defied understanding. When the erstwhile academic sent her ministers across the provincial landscape searching for new ideas, the level of federal disdain mounted steadily.

One of Anne Richardson's campaign planks had been

a pledge to increase BC's clout within the federation. This promise had piqued the curiosity of one or two officials in the federal–provincial bowels of the Privy Council Office, but only the most raddled political junkies in Ottawa paid much attention to BC affairs on a daily basis. So when Richardson gave a televised speech to the province announcing a resource auction, there was both shock and outrage in Ottawa that the premier could move in this way without first talking to the feds. This was not a case of increasing provincial clout; it was a case of significant intrusion into federal jurisdiction. That was an intolerable affront.

If a province wanted to make questionable decisions about managing its resource base, that was by and large its own business. From the high-water mark of the 1980 National Energy Program, when the federal government had attempted to impose its will on the oil and gas industry, Ottawa had steadily backed away from trying to regulate the country's natural resources directly. The provinces ran the show for the most part, but federal authorities became involved when provincial or national boundaries were crossed.

The international aspect was of particular concern to the feds. Richardson's plan for an auction that might attract bidders from a range of countries was a clear attempt to act in an area of federal jurisdiction. Ottawa's instinct was that this attempt would have to be rebuffed.

The morning after the speech, the issue had come up at the prime minister's early morning briefing. Opinion was divided over the premier's intent, but no one questioned the need to respond promptly and strongly.

"That young lady simply has to be brought to heel," said Prime Minister Massey in his Upper Canada College drawl. "I'm willing to believe that she has no idea what she's doing, but we can't do nothing. If BC gets away with this, some serious province like Quebec or Ontario might feel inspired. The precedent is what concerns me, not the substance. The chances that the Chinese or the Japanese might actually play ball are remote, but I don't care. Let's knock this on the head now!"

The PM turned to his grizzled chief of staff. "What have we got on Richardson?"

The chief of staff made a show of riffling through a thin file in front of him. "The problem, Prime Minister, is that the premier hasn't been in politics all that long, so we don't have a track record to draw on. We're doing some quick research on what she might have said or done while she was at UBC, but it may take a day or two to find what we need. In the meantime, I think that at least a couple of ministers should make public statements calling into question her judgment. We can hold you in reserve until later. After all, we'll be seeing her at the First Ministers' Conference in May. You can always demolish her then in person."

"I'm sure I can, George," the PM said testily, "but I want her taken down a peg or two right away, not in three months. Can't we suggest that one of the more plugged-in columnists point out how inane her ideas are? You know the thing – 'She's out of her depth, doesn't understand how business is conducted, liable to do damage to Canada's international standing and the good order of the federation.' I can't imagine it will take much urging to get someone to go to print. This is such a silly idea."

And with that, the meeting passed on to more important subjects. But on that basis, a campaign of derision began to roll out of Ottawa. Multiple federal ministers attacked the resource auction with varying degrees of outrage. One or two commentators took on the BC government too, putting the auction in the context of a long line of coastal craziness. *Newsworld* featured a series of editorial cartoons that had poked fun at a succession of BC premiers over the years, culminating in the latest crop lampooning the auction. Even a tame Maritime premier felt moved to suggest that the BC approach would never be taken there, and to question the advisability of this challenge to national unity.

In some quarters in Ottawa, however, Premier Richardson's speech was not dismissed as an idiosyncratic aberration. In a quiet corner of PCO, a brief call was placed to the agency charged with monitoring phone and e-mail traffic across the country. Whatever skeletons there might be in the premier's past, from here on, she, her immediate colleagues, and her family would be watched and listened to carefully. Surprises could be career limiting, and the officials in PCO and PMO had no desire to be the bearers of bad tidings. The PM's temper was notoriously short when it came to receiving bad news.

CHAPTER 8

May 26, Ottawa

A n hour or so after the BC delegation meeting, James'
phone buzzed. Jordan was on the line to confirm the
worst.

"I just debriefed the premier on how the meeting with
the federal ministers went. I thought you'd like to hear what
happened first-hand," said Jordan. "That was a major-league
uncomfortable meeting."

"Make it quick. I'm on my way to join the premier and
Victor for the drive down to the convention centre. How bad
could it be?"

"Well, at least the meeting didn't last long. We walked
in, and the federal Finance minister was nowhere in sight.
Instead, there were the Industry and International Trade ministers, loaded for bear. My minister was already upset that his
opposite number had bailed on the meeting, but he started in
on the standard spiel anyway. After five minutes, Hogan, the
Industry minister, cut him off, told him they'd read the premier's speech and didn't need his summary, thanks. Hogan and
the Trade guy then went up one side of Smith and down the
other. They accused BC of mismanaging its resources, naively
opening the door to foreign interference and ignoring clear
areas of federal jurisdiction. They went on to say that BC can
expect to face open and harsh federal criticism until it backs

down. Racicot, the Trade minister, was especially offensive and personal. He called the premier an uninformed Pollyanna and told my minister that he should start reviewing his c.v. now, because he was going to need it soon."

"Jesus, what did the minister do?"

"After Racicot made his c.v. crack, he sat there for a moment. I don't think he could believe what he was hearing. I couldn't either, for that matter. Interestingly, there were no federal officials with the two ministers. I assume they wanted full deniability. Anyway, our minister did exactly the right thing. He got up and walked out. God knows what we do now. When I told the premier about all this, she was seriously pissed off, but I think she still plans to attend the PM's conference. I suspect she'll want to talk to you and Victor about next steps. Good luck!" Jordan finished. "I'm going to stick with my minister and watch you guys on TV in some bar."

Five minutes later, James piled into the back of a Town Car with Victor Campbell and an incensed premier.

"That meeting with Rupert is the most outrageous thing I've ever heard," she fumed. "I've talked to Rupert, thanked him for his restraint in not decking one of those idiots, and told him we'd pick our spot and then get our own back someday soon. I never thought I'd actually do it but, effective this moment, we're starting our very own enemies list. Those bastards!"

James and Victor waited for the next tirade, but there wasn't one. Richardson stared out the window for a moment and then spoke to the driver.

"Pull over here, please. I'd like a word with my officials. Why don't you get yourself a cup of coffee, and then we'll be on our way."

The driver looked confused, but the premier was clearly determined that he should leave the car, so he got out into the cold slush, pulling out his cell-phone as he went.

"Okay, Victor, this is where you earn your big bucks," the premier said. "What can we expect the feds to do next, carpet bomb the Leg? I knew the prime minister was a control freak, but this looks over the line, even for him. Should I bother to show up for his damned meeting? I'd be quite happy to tell this guy to take us straight to the airport instead of the Conference Centre."

Victor looked even sadder than usual. "Premier, I wouldn't blame you for going home, but I don't think we should rise to the bait. Obviously, the feds wanted to send you a message, and God knows it was plain enough. I don't think the PM will want to rain on his own parade, however. For now he's probably going to let matters lie. Unless you raise the issue publicly, I would expect Massey to stay quiet. My guess is that the feds believe that, with a warning that harsh, we will just back off."

James cut in. "Victor, you know these guys much better than I do, but I don't see how Massey can just let things lie. Either they're serious about stopping us, or they aren't. Massey's obviously decided that he needs to show who's boss in the federation. Our plans are a heaven-sent opportunity to play the hard man. Premier, he's banking on your support crumbling at home so he can beat you back into line. Once he's been successful, the other premiers will think twice about giving him grief, even Quebec's."

"Victor, I'm not sure we've seen the end of this, but let's let it play through," Richardson said. "If there's going to be a major blow-up, I want the folks in BC to see the feds provoke it. They can't do that if we just slink out of town. James, I suspect you're right about Massey. Of course, there may be no grand plan. Could be that he's just an asshole." Victor looked uncomfortable with the premier's language but listened attentively. "Either way, I want him to show his hand. Let's get the driver back and get on with it."

Minutes later, the small BC delegation walked into the National Conference Centre. The format was straightforward. The meeting would begin with public statements by all principals. Then participants would go behind closed doors for the rest of the day. The first closed session was a First Ministers–only lunch.

The BCers waited tensely to see whether the prime minister would talk about anything except the publicly announced focus for the meeting. Massey made no reference to any subject other than pension reform, however, and Premier Richardson relaxed a bit. After the set-piece speeches had been delivered, James and Victor saw her off to lunch and called their offices in Victoria to see whether there were any new fires to fight.

As James was listening to an update from his EA, Georgina Ho, he noticed that some federal officials were circulating with paper through the crowd of grazing reporters. A stack had been dropped off on a press table near the doors. He wandered over, picked up the handout . . . and froze.

The paper was a three-page demolition of the BC resource auction plan. The federal briefing note was full of quotes from economists and legal authorities across Canada calling into question the public policy basis for the BC proposal and attacking it as a clear intrusion on federal authority. As he was scanning the detailed critique, he felt a tap on the shoulder. He turned to see one of the more prominent Press Gallery types, a short aggressive woman he had noticed lurking around the room.

"Hi, we haven't met," she rasped. "I'm Suzy Hampshire. Welcome to Ottawa. So what's with you and Premier Richardson? You two go way back, right?"

"Hello, Ms. Hampshire. I've known the premier for a long time, yes. We went to school together. But actually, until last year, we hadn't seen each other for ages," James replied cautiously, trying to make out where this was going.

"Good, then you're in a great position to comment on some stories we're hearing from federal sources. According to them, she had quite a spritely youth. Lots of sex, drugs, and rock and roll. Ring any bells?"

James's eyes narrowed. "You can't believe that I'd comment on anything that I haven't seen, especially something as scurrilous as that."

"Scurrilous!" Hampshire laughed. "Good word. I haven't heard that one for a while. Look, no offence, I just thought you might be able to give me a handle on the premier's time at university. The feds seem to think it's germane."

"Even if I knew what you or they were talking about, I wouldn't help you," James began, only to be cut off by a commotion at the back of the foyer. He turned to see the premier, red-faced and obviously angry, marching towards the group of mikes set up in the middle of the floor. He reached for his phone to call the driver, since this looked clearly like a sudden departure.

Standing before the microphones, she spoke to a growing gaggle of reporters.

"I just want to take a moment on my way out the door to make a quick statement. I recognize that I am a relative newcomer to politics and to the way business is conducted between the provinces and the federal government. That being said, I entered public life with a number of deeply felt views about how we should represent the people who vote us into office. And chief among these is that, to the extent possible, we should say in public what we say behind closed doors. There is no place, in my view, for two-faced politics, the politics of the hidden agenda, the politics of personal vilification." The premier took a deep breath.

"This was to have been my first meeting with the prime minister and my provincial and territorial counterparts from across the country. I came here looking forward to participating in a serious collective effort to develop a national approach in a critical area, the question of how to ensure that older Canadians are able to live out their lives in dignity and reasonable comfort."

The premier's voice rose. "Instead, I have been subjected to an entirely unwarranted attack on an unrelated aspect of my government's policies, an attack which the prime minis-

ter chose to make in a private session and in such a disrespect-
ful manner that I have been left with no option but to leave
this meeting well before its scheduled end. I do so with regret,
but I would like to take this opportunity to point out that this
incident is not about me personally or even about my role as
premier of British Columbia. It is about the clear unwillingness of the prime minister of Canada to respect the will of the
people of our province. The prime minister's behaviour today
calls into question his capability as a national leader and certainly his willingness to represent the people of this country
as a whole, not just the narrow political interests of his administration. Thank you. I will not be taking questions."

And with that, Premier Richardson stepped from behind the mike and swept through the Conference Centre's
doors into a howling gale. James had managed to contact
the driver, but it took the better part of five extremely cold
minutes before the car arrived and the premier could escape
the baying mob of reporters. He and Victor tried to shelter
her as best they could from the mikes and cameras, but as
James did so, he was aware that the visuals were not good. The
premier looked besieged and buffeted, by the weather and by
the press. All the viewers could see was a premier fleeing her
first big national meeting, unable to hold her own in the big
leagues. So much for her election pledge to give British Columbia a greater national voice.

II. THE BIG ONE

CHAPTER 9

June 2, Vancouver

A few days later, the mood in the cabinet chamber in Vancouver was somber. James was curious to see how Anne would characterize what by most accounts had been a disaster for her. She began by giving a straightforward account of the brief time she had spent at the lunch in Ottawa.

The prime minister had kicked off the session by making a series of gratuitous remarks about the need for government leaders to respect each other's roles and to recognize the constitutional division of powers. Staring directly at Premier Richardson, he talked about the need for leaders to act in a responsible way and to respect the overriding importance of maintaining national unity.

When Massey went on to make condescending references to "recent arrivals in politics," Richardson decided to fight back. While the other leaders watched in fascinated horror, Massey and Richardson went toe to toe.

Richardson leaned forward to respond to Massey. "I may indeed be relatively new to political life," she said, "but at least I know enough to respect the decision of the electorate."

The prime minister turned an alarming shade of crimson. "I have no doubt that the unfortunate BC electorate will soon have the opportunity to make a judgment on their earlier choice," he shot back.

"I'm not sure why anyone should trust the prime minister's judgment about the views of Western Canadians, since he and his party have been systematically ignoring their needs since their accession to power," the premier stated firmly. Richardson was angry but composed.

The PM's patience snapped. "I require no lessons on promoting accord in the federation from a hysteric with a questionable past," he shouted.

At that point, other government leaders intervened to try to calm the situation. In the ensuing confusion, the premier gathered her papers and suggested that there was little point in her remaining. The prime minister made no effort to stop her. Richardson then left the room and made her parting statement to an astonished press corps.

Richardson told her story now in a subdued tone. She knew she owed her colleagues an explanation. Although the BC press had been understanding in the immediate aftermath, the national media had been much more judgmental. Prime Minister Massey was far from a sympathetic figure, but the general view was that a rookie premier had been outmanoeuvred. She would need to up her game if she intended to make an impact on the national stage.

"I still believe that the resource auction is the way to go," said Richardson. "I'm prepared to defend it to British Columbians and to other Canadians as well, for that matter. I also think we were set up in Ottawa. I probably didn't help matters by the way I reacted. So I will understand if you believe that we need to re-think where we're headed. Let me just say that I remain convinced that backing off at this stage is the worst thing we could do. But I will understand if some of you have other views. I think we should talk this through right now."

Everyone in the room turned to look at de Groote, who did not look unhappy but paused to sip from the water glass in front of him before responding. But just as he put the glass down, the table bucked, the room tilted, and a terrifying roar blew the walls away.

CHAPTER 10

9:35 AM, June 2, Vancouver

James looked up at Vancouver Harbour from his seat behind the premier. The sky was suddenly full of noisy birds. Masses of seagulls shot by the windows, heading out to sea. A huge flock of pigeons swept into the air from the grain cars on the neighbouring railroad tracks and wheeled in a panicked cloud.

James felt his chest contract and the air crackle around him. A massive force threw him out of his chair and lodged him painfully up against a column. The room began collapsing in slow motion. He had no idea what was happening – all he knew was fear.

The floor-to-ceiling windows fronting the water to his right shattered. The floor tilted towards the exploding glass. Chairs, tables and people slid past James on their way out through a gaping hole in the wall. He fought to brace himself against the flow.

Deep rumbling and roaring assaulted his hearing and shook his core. People bellowed and screamed in fear. The noise was all-consuming. Unable to stand, he lay paralyzed in a moving tide of wreckage, his heart beating, his hands uselessly covering his ears. He saw the premier across the room, clawing at the table as she slithered sideways towards the void, and knew he should try to reach her. She spotted him and screamed his name.

Just as she was about to topple over the side of what was left of the wall, James finally shed his inertia. Vaulting across the room, he landed across her back. His flailing legs found some purchase against a window frame and managed to slow their downward drift. Two shrieking bodies hurtled over their heads out of the room into the water. Then furniture and bodies clogged up the hole. For a moment the horrid slide stopped and James was able to wrench Anne back into the room.

The quake had lasted only a few minutes. But even in his disoriented state, James knew nothing would ever be the same again.

CHAPTER 11

June 2, Vancouver

T he quake rumbled across the Lower Mainland. The Big One had finally arrived, the "full-rip nine" everyone had feared. A rupture in the fault a hundred miles out in the Pacific had generated a subduction-zone earthquake measuring more than 9.0 on the Richter Scale.

In the initial shock, the largest buildings in downtown Vancouver swayed to impossible angles. Windows shattered; glass and cladding scattered across the streets below. Horrified office workers fled from outside walls, staggering and crawling towards stairwells. Amazingly, the high-rises mostly withstood the stress and stayed upright. People trapped in the large hotels and office buildings fought to get outside, driven by primal panic. Bodies piled up on the stairs in the emergency exits.

Older brick buildings were soon shaken to rubble, burying cars and passersby. Many streets were blocked, especially in the Downtown Eastside. There, the Woodwards "W" on top of a ten-storey building waved as if buffeted by a huge wind and then toppled sideways into the street, squashing a car and turning the driver into raw meat. Bewildered street people were buried in the lanes of the decaying neighbourhood as old walls collapsed in on them and the shopping carts holding their few belongings.

The comfortable good folks of Point Grey were also afflicted. Staggering out of a stuccoed house on tree-lined Twelfth Avenue halfway up the hill, the stunned homeowner heard a hissing noise and saw the road in front of her fall away. Panicked, she called out, "Chloe, Jane!" and turned to run to her two small children. Out of the fissure licked a ribbon of flame as the natural gas line ignited. The last thing she saw as the fireball enveloped her and the house was a tidy hallway and two frightened little girls holding hands. Soon the entire neighbourhood was alight.

The venerable Lions Gate suspension bridge at the entrance to Vancouver Harbour whipped itself to destruction. The bridge-deck convulsed; the cables supporting it parted. Cars bounced off into the waters below. A bicyclist caught in the middle of the chaos fell heavily. He tried to crawl to safety, but a loose cable split him neatly in two and swept what was left into the frothing Narrows below. CBC radio's morning show had lost a host.

On the near shore, large trees collapsed across the causeway leading to the bridge, crushing cars and triggering a succession of accidents. On the far shore, landslides slashed down through the tony British Properties, piling up houses and grinding them to rubble. The Cleveland Dam ruptured, sending a wall of water cascading down the Capilano River through West Vancouver past the up-market Park Royal shopping centre. The whole North Shore was quickly cut off from the rest of the city, as access routes to the Ironworkers' Memorial Second Narrows Bridge were blocked as well.

Farther south, in the Fraser River delta, the soil under Richmond turned into brown soup, causing building after building to tilt crazily and collapse. On Sea Island, great fissures opened up in the runways at YVR. A Boeing 747 in the process of landing dug a nose-wheel into a suddenly appearing trench. It cartwheeled down the runway, exploding in a cloud of jet fuel. Trying desperately to keep their seats in a wildly shaking control tower, air-traffic controllers shouted warnings to incoming aircraft to stay away.

The initial quake lasted fewer than five minutes, but to people on the ground, the shaking seemed to go on forever. Any coherent thought was impossible. All was fear. Office-workers and shoppers staggered out of buildings only to be caught in showers of glass from windows above. Cars jammed on their brakes, and accidents spread through the city streets. The Georgia Viaduct pancaked, carrying cars and people into the valley below.

In neighbourhood after neighbourhood, natural gas lines ruptured. Fires exploded across town. Fire crews struggled to respond but, in several stations, jammed doors trapped the engines inside. The crews that got out made slow progress through wreckage-strewn streets. First responders were hard-pressed to move through the smoking ruins.

Most Vancouverites were left to fend for themselves. Many simply sat on curbs, stunned by the devastation surrounding them, cringing with every aftershock.

CHAPTER 12

June 2, Vancouver Island

Severe shaking hit Vancouver Island as well. In Victoria, older brick buildings crumbled. Lower Yates Street and the 150-year-old Chinatown beside it were reduced to rubble. The elaborate multi-coloured entrance to Chinatown – the Gates of Harmonious Interest – pitched forward through the roof of a car entering Fisgard Street. Market Square and Bastion Square collapsed in on themselves, burying tourists and locals alike. The graceful pink Victorian Customs House toppled into a harbour that had ominously started to empty of water, leaving float-planes and harbour ferries stranded on the mud.

Rattenbury's dome on the Parliament Buildings began to torque beneath Captain Vancouver. All seven feet of him toppled over, sliding down to shatter on the granite stairs more than 120 feet below. The breezeways at both ends of the Buildings collapsed. Staff from the Legislature and the Premier's Office rushed out of the few remaining exits. Somehow the dome remained in place, twisted but not collapsed.

Sitting in the library of his home overlooking the Straits of Juan de Fuca, Alastair Reid had felt the first impact of the quake. After the initial shock, the old man relaxed a bit. Perhaps the worst was over. Then, over one shoulder, he heard an unusual rending noise. Wheeling around, he looked up to see one of his enormous bookcases coming away from the wall and collapsing towards him. Unable to roll away, he threw up an arm as the avalanche of books and heavy shelving smashed down onto his wheelchair. Through the pain, his last, semi-coherent thought included an ironic appreciation for the instruments of his death.

Farther up Vancouver Island, the major damage arrived fifteen minutes after the shaking stopped. The crowd of people enjoying the sun on Parksville's long, flat Rathtrevor Beach suddenly noticed that the water was draining away. First one and then another group started to run back off the beach, up towards the Island Highway. Once they reached the main road, they ran straight into a traffic jam of major proportions made worse by the collapse of several storefronts and the fires that had broken out. Still in shock from the initial shaking, a mob of people and cars moved slowly inland, driven by the spectre of the wall of water they feared might soon be headed their way.

Across the Island in Port Alberni, the residents knew from bitter experience exactly what was likely to hit them. In 1964, the tsunami generated by the massive Anchorage quake smashed up the Alberni Canal, driving huge waves inland along a twenty-mile funnel. The resulting massive damage gave the people of the town a significant incentive to become the best prepared community on the coast. At least this time, as opposed to fifty years earlier, the tsunami would reach them in daylight. Even before the emergency sirens sounded, the low-lying parts of town emptied out, as people rushed for higher ground.

Just outside Tofino on the Island's West Coast, the premier's daughter Katherine Richardson and her partner Robert Williams were visiting some of Robert's cousins at the small First Nations community of Esowista. The shaking hurled people to the ground and triggered panic. Everyone in the room knew how exposed the island's outer shore was to a tsunami. As soon as the first quake ended, the push was on to leave the coast.

Katherine and Robert ran to his pickup, which was filled almost at once. A convoy of assorted vehicles set off at speed towards Radar Hill, some ten minutes away. As they reached the parking lot and piled out, they looked back down towards the beach and saw the long grey line of the huge waves advancing steadily.

CHAPTER 13

June 2, Vancouver

B ack in Vancouver, the water level in the harbour receded. Around the other side of Stanley Park, English Bay became a vast sandbank. Within minutes the flow reversed, and the water hunched up the beach, shouldering its way over retaining walls, lawns and curbs. The black tide surged strongly up Denman Street, carrying cars and wreckage along, shattering store windows as it went. People in second- and third-floor windows watched in terror as the water flowed by. In the older structures, the waves licked away at walls and smashed any storefronts that had survived the earthquake. In many cases, the buildings slumped forward into what had begun as a street and now resembled a river. Minutes later, the waves first calmed and then sucked back towards the beach, carrying a mass of debris with them. Terrified cats and dogs and their owners struggled against the current. All were swept out to sea.

At the same time, the muddy battlegrounds of Richmond and Delta, full of wrecked houses and survivors wandering aimlessly, were submerged as the tsunami hit with relentless force. Nothing much stood in the way of the incoming water. Those who hadn't made it to the second floors of buildings were engulfed.

At the airport, runways disappeared, aircraft were torn

away from their gates, and water smashed through windows into the ground floor of the terminal. The control tower presided, castle-like, over a spreading lake. The controllers soon lost power and could no longer warn aircraft away. The occasional plane approached what had once been an airport, but they soon swung away, headed mostly for Abbotsford and the last usable runway in the region. The pillars supporting the SkyTrain line into the airport were undermined and, one by one, heeled over and collapsed, pulling trains with them. People watched in horror as the train-sets toppled and burned like huge children's toys.

The Fraser River Delta had vanished beneath the waves.

CHAPTER 14

June 2, Vancouver

For five interminable minutes, the cabinet chamber had pitched and rolled. The air was full of papers, plaster dust and chunks of the ceiling. All the chairs, tables and floor lamps were piled in among the people on the low side of the room. Dislodged light fixtures swung crazily overhead.

Finally the shaking stopped, but everyone held their breath, waiting for the next shock.

James pulled himself off the premier and dragged her back up towards the centre of the room. He stood up uncertainly and looked around. The far wall was now a gaping hole through which he could see the harbour and the North Shore mountains. Those who had managed to avoid falling out were stirring, trying to crawl up the sloping floor to safety. James knew that he had avoided death by inches. He recognized that what was happening was real, but he felt detached – as if watching a movie.

The premier scrambled to her feet. She and James embraced, holding on for a long minute, trying to draw strength from each other. As they pulled apart, James stroked the side of Anne's face, and she smiled reassuringly. Then they both turned and reached down with others to pull ministers and officials up the slope and through the door into the inner office.

The two of them checked to make sure that no one was left behind in the wrecked boardroom. They became aware that the harbour below them was filling rapidly with wave after wave of debris-laden water, which washed over the piers and rushed across the railway tracks. For a moment they watched fascinated, and then they turned to the task of helping survivors.

"Are you okay?" James asked. He was surprised to realize that, apart from Anne's original cry for help, he and Anne had not actually spoken to each other since the quake had hit, fifteen minutes earlier. "A little winded and scratched up, but otherwise fine," she responded, swiping the hair out of her eyes. "You're not getting any lighter in your old age," she added wryly, "but thanks for keeping me out of the harbour. That's a nasty cut on your arm, by the way."

James looked down. He realized that he was bleeding on what was left of the carpet. "There should be a first-aid kit around here somewhere. I'll go find it. You try to sort out who needs help and who can give it. I bet there are a bunch of people here with medical training. We'll need to take care of ourselves for a while. Emergency services may not reach us any time soon."

Over the next hour or so, they worked together to give immediate first aid to the injured and to organize the evacuation of the entire floor housing the Premier's Office. By the time they all gathered outside on the pavement three storeys below, the grim toll was coming into focus.

Two ministers had been killed outright, crushed under a pillar. Several officials had simply disappeared, presumably having fallen into the harbour. A number of individuals had had to be carried out of the building, suffering from broken bones and major gashes. The rest of the group had a collection of injuries but were able to walk out into the smoke-filled sunshine. Everyone was in shock, some shivering silently with vacant faces, others better able to conceal their residual fear.

Except for his cut arm, James was unhurt physically, but

he was badly shaken. At first, he welcomed the opportunity to stay busy. He dreaded the time when he would have to look up and take in the suffering and destruction surrounding him. A number of aftershocks had rumbled through the city. Every time one hit, he had to grind his teeth to keep from crying out. He knew he should be demonstrating calm and self-discipline, but all he wanted to do was find a safe place to curl up into a ball and go to sleep. He was exhausted. He could barely lift his arms. His injury ached. Staying upright took a major effort, so he sat down abruptly on the curb.

James drifted back to the way in which he and Anne had picked up the threads of a desultory relationship. The fact that they were working together at all was in itself odd. Over the years, he had kept an occasional surreptitious eye on her career, but he had never expected to meet her again. His clients were mainly in the US, while Anne worked around the Asia Pacific and then in Canada at UBC.

After a relatively short term with the American intelligence community, James had been hired to do similar work in the private sector for an organization called the Destiny Foundation. That period of his life was not one that he was comfortable thinking about, even in passing. He had been young and ambitious. The pay had been good.

He had even discovered in the head of the foundation a mentor, a person whose judgment he respected and from whom he learned a great deal. As it turned out, however, his own judgment in terms of associates was revealed to be seriously flawed. The foundation had an agenda that included a willingness to ignore the law when necessary. This inclination towards illegality culminated in a bloody episode in Mexico that had haunted him for years.

More through good luck than good judgment, or so he thought at the time, James was given a second chance when he was hired by an Oregon-based family firm that was developing a stable of high-tech companies in what became the Silicon Forest. James served as a political fixer as required. In addition, his contract was sufficiently flexible that he was able to work for a succession of Democratic candidates across the US. It turned out that he had a real knack for providing practical political advice. His reputation grew. The Mexican affair faded into the darker recesses of his consciousness. After a while, even the nightmares stopped.

In the early 2000s, the Oregon group had been bought out by a conglomerate based in Washington, D.C. The purchasing firm styled itself as a global science and technology leader. It had international revenues in the $15- to $20-billion range. That company (or more precisely, its billionaire owners) had in turn also made use of his political advice. One of their more recent acquisitions was a promising bio-science start-up originating at UBC.

By then Anne had moved from developing a high-profile Asian Studies Institute at UBC to the presidency of the university. When she subsequently started to contemplate the leap into politics, James's corporate associates had ensured that she hire her old friend from graduate school as a key campaign aide.

James remembered the occasion of their reunion. Anne had swept into the posh Vancouver restaurant overlooking the harbour, her tall good looks turning heads and triggering a buzz of conversation. James rose to shake her hand. He found himself completely unable to speak. He took in the deep blue eyes, the carefully coiffed hair, the stylish suit, the wave of familiar perfume, and he just blanked. Anne was clearly pleased at the reaction. She let him off the hook by starting the conversation herself. After a moment, James regained his composure, and the lunch went well. Anne decided to make use of James's services. Neither of them talked about past lives.

James helped with the leadership bid. He then coordinated her party's polling for the general election. Working together had seemed remarkably easy after the initial awkwardness. James appreciated Anne's high energy level and intelligence, just as Anne valued James' political experience and practical advice. When they were both in town, they often jogged side by side first thing in the morning. Issues that had seemed problematic at the beginning of the runs often seemed simpler by the time they returned.

Eventually, however, fuelled by long days in a succession of pressure-filled hotel rooms over the course of the campaign, the sexual tension had built. In the excitement of the election victory, that tension had been released, delightfully and at length, in the small hours. The years had melted away.

James awoke from a drugged sleep late the next morning. Anne had disappeared, leaving behind the enchanting ghost of her scent.

Until Ottawa, Anne and James had never spoken about that election night celebration. There was no regret on either side, but there was a tacit agreement that there would be no sequel either. Now those good intentions appeared to have evaporated, at least for the moment.

James looked across at Anne moving purposefully from group to group of stunned survivors, offering sympathy and support. People responded to her touch, listened carefully to her suggestions. James watched the premier as she began the slow process of bringing order out of chaos. In that moment of admiration, he knew that here was a commitment he would not be prepared to slide away from. However their episodic romance turned out, in a fundamental sense, James was hers to command.

CHAPTER 15

June 2, Vancouver

Survivors staggered out of the building and joined the group from the Premier's Office and the crowd from the Pan Pacific Hotel next door. Most of them were trying without success to use their mobiles. The networks were down. The feeling of isolation only jacked up the general anxiety level. Everyone had a family member or friend they desperately wanted to call. This included Anne, whose frustration with her inability to make her phone work was peaking. Her daughter Katherine's safety was her overriding concern.

As for James, apart from the premier, he was close to few people. He worried about his new friend Alastair Reid, however. He had no idea what conditions in Victoria were like. Surviving an earthquake in a wheelchair would take some doing. But Alastair was a tough root of a man, and James clung to the conviction that the old guy would not go down without a fight. With the phone system crashed, though, contacting Alastair would have to wait.

The more immediate concern was Matt Russell and his family, who lived right here in Vancouver. James had met Matt early in his tenure in the Premier's Office. The premier had introduced the two of them, making a point of mentioning beforehand that Matt was one of the few wise people she had ever met. In time, James came to accept this judgment. He also gained a friend.

Matt served as an adviser to the oldest Japanese trading company, or *soga shosha,* in BC. He had an interesting background. His father was a transplanted Scottish engineer who had married a Japanese-Canadian girl in the early 1950s. Matt's mother had grown up in an internment camp in Slocan City, one of 23,000 Japanese-Canadians relocated by the government at the beginning of the Second World War. She emerged from the wartime experience in a fragile state. Her recurrent melancholia had shadowed Matt's growing up.

Despite the fact Matt spoke no Japanese, he radiated a bicultural aura. James had never known a person more besotted with paper, for example. A room in his house was lined with shelving full of various sorts of hand-made paper, mostly from Japan. Matt's friends regularly received marvellous creations crafted on an appropriately seasonal basis. Even more special, Matt sometimes felt moved to send friends samples of origami for no apparent reason at all. James treasured these random gifts.

Matt's day job with the trading company brought him into contact with all the key members of the Vancouver business community. Over the years, he had acquired the reputation of being a good person to talk to if an important political decision was pending. His tenure stretched back into the 1960s, and he had watched as the province's economy morphed slowly away from traditional dependence on rocks and logs. Matt was a strong believer in BC's Asian vocation. That said, his mother's experience in the Slocan Valley was never forgotten.

Matt and his family lived in an older wooden Arts and Crafts house on Waterloo Street below Fourth Avenue in one of the leafier parts of Kitsilano. His wife's warmth and good cheer served to even out Matt's tendency to see the worst in the world. His two teenaged daughters took no prisoners over the dinner table, and he adored them unreservedly in return. Every month or two, James would have dinner with the Russells and leave full of delicious food, calmer than when he arrived.

One evening after the dishes had been cleared away, Matt had talked about the province James had come back to.

"What you've got to remember," he said, "is that the province's strengths lie with its people and its resources. For years we've been eroding the links between the two. Before logging and mining became so mechanized, we had a kind of instinctive tie with the land. Kids don't take jobs in the woods any more. All anyone cares about is teaching them to code. We're emptying out the heart of the province and pouring it into the cities." Matt looked morose.

"As for this province's people, I've told you before – BC has a black soul. Difficult though it is to remember, given how diverse Vancouver's streets look now, racial prejudice is buried deep in our history. Beginning with the systematic attempts to eradicate First Peoples, the transplanted Europeans who settled here went to a lot of trouble to use the law to marginalize later Chinese, East Indian and Japanese immigrants, basically anyone of colour. You can't assume that our recent success at integrating non-whites will continue unchecked either. Wait until we hit really bad economic times – then we'll see."

Engaging though Matt was, James found him overly gloomy about the future and something of a throwback. He had none of the crisp detachment of James's other history-minded friend, Alastair. Nonetheless, Matt had a dense network of contacts across the province, and his sense of the Interior was a useful antidote to the world as described by the *Vancouver Sun*.

In the wake of the premier's speech announcing the resource auction, James turned to Matt for an assessment. Matt had been expecting James' call, but he didn't look encouraging as they settled over coffee in Matt's minimalist office full of varnished wood and a small collection of restrained woodblock prints.

"Do you have any idea what chaos your auction scheme is likely to cause?" he began. "You can't just take an established set of commercial and regulatory relationships between business and government and throw them out the window. I assume you didn't bother to talk to anyone in the business community before you set off your little bomb."

"It's great to see you too, Matt," James said as he stirred the coffee in his cup. "How's the family?" Seeing real concern on his friend's face, he dropped the flippant tone. "I didn't expect you to be a great supporter of our approach, but don't you think you're exaggerating the impact a bit?"

"No," replied Matt. "If anything, I'm understating the problem. You and your premier don't realize how fragile the links are that hold the economy together. Once you destroy basic confidence, people stop investing, and whole sectors go dead. You weren't here then but, in the 1990s, the NDP had the reputation of not liking the mining industry, and the guys simply stopped exploring or expanding existing operations. And that lasted for as long as that government was in power. It's one thing for a new government to take a while finding where it wants to go. It's entirely another for it to alienate the business community as a whole."

Matt was clearly upset. James was torn between taking him on and trying to calm him down. He decided to go the emollient route.

"I know that your company has reason to be wary, Matt, but you should know that a number of prominent local firms have indicated to the premier that they have no real problem with her proposal. They might not be able to come out publicly and say so, but they like the condition that the successful bidder would have to fully involve BC companies. There's a sense out there that this could be a significant opportunity. They agree that something needed to be done to jump-start the economy."

Russell remained unconvinced. "Some locals might think that this offers them something, but I doubt that you'll see the big international players coming on board. If there's one thing they hate, it's having the rules changed in the middle of the game – and this is a big deal that might encourage resource-dependent jurisdictions in other parts of the world. You have to remember that nowadays, everything is connected to everything else. BC has always been an international price-taker. If anything, the province's economy is even more locked into the global system than before. Once you develop the reputation for unpredictability, look out! Investment will dry up, and you'll find pressure to back down coming from all sorts of places. If you keep on with this, the feds, for one, are going to do everything they can to defeat the government. What they've done so far is just the start."

There was silence as Matt fiddled with his coffee. James had never seen him so troubled.

"It gives me no pleasure to speak to you this directly," Matt went on. "You know I have the utmost respect for the premier. I know she understands how BC fits into the larger Asian context. But it is precisely because I respect her so highly that I owe her and you my honest opinion. I think this policy she is embarking on is a disaster. It is going to shatter the pattern, and you have no idea what will replace it. This is a dangerous world. There are folks out there who will be more than happy to take advantage of any weakness you display or any chaos you generate. I hope I'm wrong, but my advice is that you think long and hard before you proceed further."

"If the premier didn't value your advice, I wouldn't be here. You know that," James said. "I promise that I will lay out your concerns in detail when I see her. I know she will take them seriously. In the meantime, however, can I ask you to help me set up a number of meetings in Tokyo, so we can touch base with our Japanese friends directly? We want to be sensible about this. You should know that at the premier's request, we'll be taking discreet soundings around the Pacific to see how her speech has been received. The premier wants this done quietly and without involving the bureaucrats, at least at this stage. I'll be starting in Japan and moving on from there."

With a sigh, Matt agreed to pave the way as best he could. "You realize that major players in Japan will see opportunities where I see danger. MITI, the Keidanren, some of the other *sogo shosha* might well see this as a way of gaining more reliable access to natural resources. If nothing else, the Japanese government will want to ensure that the Chinese, among others, don't steal a march on them. I just don't see much good coming out of this for British Columbia, that's all," he finished sadly. "Just because I work for a foreign firm doesn't make me any less a local."

James knew that Matt had taken a chance being this open with him. He was grateful, even if the message was difficult to hear.

Several days later, during an early morning jog, James debriefed Anne. She was disappointed, but her friend's reaction was not unexpected.

"Matt's right," she said. "It would have been safer to keep plodding along. Certainly I would have had a much better chance of getting re-elected. But I think that fundamentally he's wrong to suppose that we could wait for things to turn around. I'm still convinced that we need to shake the economy up and make people try something new. I suppose I should be pleased that he believes that we're making significant change. I'd just feel more reassured if he didn't think we were headed in entirely the wrong direction."

James emerged with a start from his reverie about Matt. In the face of all this destruction and pain, worrying about abstract government policy seemed entirely pointless. People were what mattered, people like Matt and his family.

Even in his current shocked state, James felt a wry recognition that this was an unusual thought for him – unusual but not completely unwelcome.

CHAPTER 16

June 2, Vancouver

Despite having made it to the dubious safety of the sidewalk, James felt himself starting to lose control again. His arm hurt, and every few minutes he would start to shake. He knew he should be doing something constructive, but he simply could not think of what to do next. His experience in government and politics had not prepared him for the demands of a crisis of this magnitude.

The water in the harbour had calmed down, but the surface was a mass of wreckage. Many of the docks were ripped out. Several boats had been pulled away from their moorings. Others ended up thrown ashore, lying at crazy angles. Huge container cranes had toppled as the shaking had undermined them. They lay half in, half out of the water like broken children's toys. The piles of containers they serviced were scattered along the shore or floated awash in the harbour.

The air was full of smoke and the reek from the shattered sewage system. A disturbing smell of natural gas reminded everyone that a random spark could set off a major fire. Except for one or two police officers who had been nearby when the earthquake struck, there were few first responders in evidence. Sirens could be heard, but so far no ambulances or fire trucks had made their way to the waterfront.

The modern buildings nearby and along Coal Harbour

seemed to have weathered the quake reasonably well. People were pouring out of emergency exits. The growing crowd milled about, filling a road blocked off by several traffic accidents.

Someone grabbed James's arm, and he turned to find himself looking into Anne's calm blue eyes.

"James, I need you to start pulling things together. I've got to contact the rest of the government and the rescue services. I need to know just how bad things are and what's being done. None of our cell-phones seem to work. I know, because I've been trying to get hold of Katherine non-stop. We can't get through on 911. My first priority is to reach the Emergency Management folks. I think we have a satellite phone upstairs in the office. Let's get hold of it and see if that works any better."

Given a specific task to undertake, James felt the world begin to settle down. "Georgina came over from Victoria with me this morning, and I saw her on our way out," he said. "She actually had the presence of mind to grab a hard hat and organize the evacuation. If anyone knows about that phone, she will. I'll track her down, and we'll focus on establishing communications."

Georgina Ho was James's impeccably groomed executive assistant and doorkeeper. Her instructions concerning access to her boss were straightforward. The premier and most cabinet ministers could be admitted to his office on request or put through on the phone. Everyone else needed an appointment or left a message. Often that appointment unaccountably took weeks to arrange. Phone calls rarely got returned. James was, after all, a very busy man.

Georgina did not actually approve of James. She found him disturbingly unsystematic and messy. Her frustration was increased by his steadfast refusal to allow her to bring order to his office or his schedule. She became especially testy when James wandered away without telling her where he was going. Nevertheless, Georgina respected James's role as the premier's closest confidant and was adamant in her refusal to allow unwanted visitors or calls.

Georgina also possessed one of the most sophisticated intelligence networks in the government. Her informants often occupied quite junior positions across the bureaucracy but, collectively, they had uncanny access to gossip, much of which turned out to be true. At the centre of this web sat Georgina, judiciously sorting through the mass of information and extracting the nuggets that she occasionally proffered to James. Her boss was not naive enough to think that she passed on all she knew, but he was grateful for the few tidbits she provided. As a relatively recent arrival, he could use all the inside information he could get. Clearly, however, Georgina felt it would take several more years' seasoning before she would consider him an adequate senior official. In the meantime, she would do her best to ensure that his blunders were neither too serious nor too frequent.

"Anything else you want done right away?" James asked.

"No, you concentrate on that," Anne responded, as she turned to walk away, "and I'll try to pull together a group to restore some order around here. There are lots of badly hurt people. We need to make them as comfortable as we can before medical help arrives." Left unsaid was the worry they shared that the size of the disaster might mean no help at all for hours, or even days.

In the meantime, there was plenty to do. Activity seemed to make the situation more bearable. Just before he went off in search of the ever-efficient Georgina, however, James had a disturbing thought. He caught up to the premier.

"Anne, isn't Katherine up on the west coast of the island?"

"Yes, she is. I tried to call her, but the phone service is gone. I'm sure she'll let me know where she is once things get back to normal..." Anne's voice faltered; her eyes filled. For a moment she looked remarkably vulnerable. Then she squared her shoulders. The grieving mother was gone.

"Get me back in touch with the damn government, James! We'll deal with the personal stuff later." And with that, she strode away into the middle of the crowd, dispensing comfort and issuing orders as she went.

CHAPTER 17

June 2, Vancouver

I t turned out that not only did the estimable Georgina know about the satellite phone, but also she had brought it with her as she left the building. Within moments, James was connected with Vancouver's Emergency Operations Centre. Georgina had actually been briefed on – and remembered how to use – the relatively new E-Comm 911 system, which allowed for all the police, fire and ambulance services in the Lower Mainland to maintain communication in a crisis. They in turn were able to patch in the Provincial Emergency Coordination Centre in Victoria. Confronted with Georgina's astringent competence, James's feelings of isolation started to seep away.

Once the various parts of the BC Government were stitched together again, it was possible for decisions to be made and resources marshalled. Police and fire fighters were starting to reach the group milling around in the road outside the Premier's Office. The premier herself was able to turn over rescue efforts to them. She then called together a small group of the surviving ministers in the largely undamaged bar of the Fairmont Hotel across the street.

It was a battered, shocked collection of politicians and senior aides who turned to Richardson for reassurance and a plan of action. What they got was a crisp succession of orders.

"Georgina – I want you to find the least damaged office building downtown so that we can set up a temporary headquarters. We need to be operational by the end of today. Willem – once that office is in place, I want you to coordinate the rescue efforts throughout the Lower Mainland on behalf of the provincial government. I'm going to be moving around the various sites and talking to people, but I want you to make sure things happen. We mustn't get bogged down over jurisdictional issues. I'll start things off by talking to the mayor and the prime minister but, after that, it'll be up to you to drive the machine – okay? Take as many people with you as you need."

De Groote nodded and set off after Georgina Ho, who had already left the room and was rounding up staff and several ministers.

Richardson turned to the elegant but somewhat rumpled attorney general, Indira Dhaliwal. "We need our legal ducks in a row, starting with declaring a formal State of Emergency. Work with Willem, and make sure we have all the legal authorities we need. Also, as minister responsible for Emergency Management generally, you should be back in Victoria as soon as possible to lead the effort from there."

"I was able to use Georgina's sat-phone to talk to the office in Victoria and the Canadian Forces at Joint Task Force Pacific," Dhaliwal responded. "The army can lay on a helicopter within the next hour, and I was going to use that to get back to the island. Incidentally, they also have some ground transport you can use to get around the city, Premier. I'll ask them to get it here as soon as they can."

"Great," said the premier. "I'll feel a lot better when we're connected and mobile. By the way, James, track down that sat-phone and contact PMO. I want to talk to the prime minister personally as soon as it can be arranged. We've had issues in the past, but I assume Massey will be a bit more helpful now that we're hip-deep in rubble. If he's not, he can write off any seats in BC for a while."

With that, the group broke up and went to work. James could feel the level of panic recede. It was not as though the situation were actually improving. In fact, as fires broke out across the city and as the full dimensions of the disaster were revealed, things were getting worse. The premier's ability to take charge had helped to kick-start the core group in government, however. At least there were now the beginnings of a more organized rescue effort.

As James waited to be patched through to the PMO switchboard, he thought of a number of "personal" items he would want to take care of.

First, he wanted to know whether he still had a functioning float-home in Victoria. This vessel was a two-storey modern version of a traditional houseboat. It sat close to the end of one of the jetties that made up Fisherman's Wharf. From the outside, it looked square and unprepossessing, but James loved the well-planned interior, with its cunning collection of cupboard space and its array of small, up-to-date appliances. Although for a man his size the rooms were a bit tight, the limited space wrapped him in comfort as soon as he walked in the door.

His home was only partially sheltered from the chop that often built across the harbour. In bad weather, the wind rattled the name-plate beside the door. A previous tenant had christened the float-home *Shangri-la*, and the name had stuck, largely because subsequent Wharfies found it too much trouble to re-paint the sign. Every time the wind blew, however, James reminded himself that he needed to screw the thing down to stop the noise.

And then there was the cat. Shortly after he moved in, James had returned from work one evening to find a dark grey presence on the window ledge beside the front door. The cat stared at him calmly through unusual orange eyes. He made no effort to jump down when James came over to scroffle him behind the ears. He also seemed generally unimpressed. James opened the door, and the cat slipped down and darted in ahead of him. He headed straight for the bed and began washing himself in a proprietary fashion.

James now had a roommate. Although somewhat scruffy to begin with, the cat soon groomed himself to perfection. Since he clearly expected to remain *in situ*, James felt obliged to make room. And since continuing to call the creature "cat" seemed impolite, he settled on Einstein, a name that reflected the feline's general air of omniscience. Most evenings James and Einstein reviewed the day's events and reflected together on the state of the world. Fortunately a woman in the next float-home took a fancy to Einstein as well, so during James' many absences he could rely on her to keep the cat fed and watered.

James may have harboured concerns about the fate of his home, but he had no doubt Einstein would survive perfectly well. A mere category 9 earthquake was hardly enough to trouble him. Still, he wouldn't mind receiving confirmation to that effect.

For that matter, he was worried about that cat-sitting neighbour as well. She was a well-preserved, blue-haired woman in her forties called Jenny Lynd, who was a much more characteristic representative of bohemian Wharf life than he was. She had lived in the floating colony for more than ten years. She earned a mysterious, if comfortable, living as a freelance software engineer. Her rustic float-home was crowned with an array of antennas which kept her in touch with clients around the world, although her main links seemed to be with Cupertino.

Soon after Einstein's arrival, Jenny and James had fallen into the occasional habit of late-night assignations which began with tea and edibles and ended in bed. James found Jenny's unbridled cynicism a relief after the restrained stuffiness of many of his government colleagues. He objected to Jenny's habit of referring to him as "Jimmy Dean", but she was a warm episodic presence – and besides, she reduced Einstein to purring mush on contact. Finding out if she and the cat were safe was critical.

Second, and perhaps more importantly, for Anne's sake he desperately wanted to know how Katherine Richardson was. During Anne's rise to public prominence, her private life had remained an intriguing mystery, although there were un-confirmed rumours of links to an extremely rich, extremely handsome businessman who lived in Singapore. Apart from that, her evident devotion to her daughter provided the only clue to the premier's personal priorities. She travelled a lot, and Katherine usually accompanied her. This young woman was an appealing figure in her own right, someone who had grown up just to one side of the spotlight. She had developed the faux sophistication of a young person who had seen too many airports at an early age. The older she got, the more committed she had become to a variety of "green" causes. In Katherine's eyes, the fact that her mother questioned the util-ity and/or practicality of most of those causes added to their lustre.

After a recent meeting James had been given a glimpse into the sometimes tense relations between mother and her twenty-something daughter. Anne had been obviously pre-occupied, and James had stayed behind to find out what was bothering her. Anne wandered up and down the Cab-inet Chambers, and finally responded only when James asked directly whether there was something else he should know about.

Anne hesitated, stopped pacing, and came back to the table.

"It's Katherine. We had a huge fight last night after the resource auction speech was broadcast. You know she's see-ing Robert Williams these days. He's a First Nations guy from Tofino. Seems nice enough, but he's really quiet around me. I don't think he approves. Between the two of them, they've de-cided that all I care about is raising money for old people and leaving the province a smoking ruin. In the last few months, she's been working with that green group, the Environmental

Defence Force. I checked their website. They look fairly radical. Katherine's smart, but I worry about them using her."

She ran her hands through her hair. "Anyhow, once she'd seen the speech, she really unloaded on me. She thinks I've given up whatever ethics I ever had in the interest of generating money. She doesn't believe we'll enforce environmental regulations once we've given the resource access rights away. She's convinced we're prepared to ignore aboriginal rights and title altogether. I made the mistake of getting into an argument with her. By the time we finished, she was packing her bags and leaving the house. We both lost our tempers. I feel terrible."

She slumped back in her chair. "Apart from that and having every news outlet in the province attacking me as naive and incompetent, everything's fine."

James looked at her sympathetically. "I can't give you any child-rearing advice. I'm hardly qualified. Painful though it may be to recognize, though, Katherine's not a kid anymore. There's a limit to how much influence you're going to have."

Registering her unimpressed expression, James moved on quickly to other business. The premier was equally relieved to change the subject, but James was left with no doubt that Katherine's welfare was her overriding concern.

Finally, as he now took a moment to reflect – what about his place in Depoe Bay in Oregon? If the tsunamis were as big as they looked, he might have lost not one but two homes in the past couple of hours.

Before he returned to Canada, the one constant in his itinerant, if well paid, way of life as a political consultant in the US was a small cottage on the Oregon coast, on a bluff just outside Depoe Bay. Happenstance had led to ownership of this white clapboard retreat not far from "the world's smallest harbour." After every assignment, this was where James ended up, safely isolated until the next call promising an intriguing problem and a useful paycheck. Now, for all he knew, he could be the owner of a small pile of sticks with a great view. The prospect of losing the Depoe Bay cottage knotted his stomach. While he knew that others faced much worse in the wake of the earthquake, that realization did nothing to reduce the sense of loss.

James had always prided himself on "travelling light." This meant keeping his physical possessions to a minimum (although acquiring the latest electronic gadget was apparently an exception to this rule) and being prepared to move to a job on a moment's notice. It also meant limiting his emotional attachments. Faced with the quake's devastation and the immediate example of Anne's bravery and wholeheartedness, the benefits of cultivating this level of detachment were beginning to feel questionable.

And in fact, what was new in his life since his return to BC was precisely the fact that his world was being steadily populated by people he cared about. There was Anne, of course, although the exact nature of that attachment remained obscure. But there were also Alastair, Jenny, Matt, Georgina. Einstein was a bonus. The list was growing; maybe he was too.

CHAPTER 18

June 2, Esowista/Tofino

K atherine Richardson sat with her arms around her knees, rocking back and forth, staring at the slowly receding waters below. Most of the convoy of trucks and cars that raced up Radar Hill had made it safely to the top ahead of the waves, but she remembered with a shudder the three or four vehicles she had seen overtaken by the flood and sucked back down the slope. The pickups toppled slowly sideways, engines racing as tires vainly attempted to gain purchase in the mud. She watched helplessly as the passengers in the trucks disappeared, screaming.

She had never seen people die before. She felt numb.

Looking farther down towards where the beach had once been, she saw a pockmarked plain with the stumps of trees sticking out at random. What she could not see was any trace of houses or sheds or garages. It was as if a giant hand had simply wiped the area clean, leaving behind a curiously uniform brown mud-flat. She tried not to think about how many might be entombed there. Perhaps some were still alive. Even if they were, she was incapable of movement. All she knew was that somehow she had survived.

Then, with a start, she remembered her mother. If the earthquake and the tsunami had hit here, they must have threatened Vancouver. She reached for her cell-phone. All she got was a busy signal. Five minutes later, she gave up in disgust and rising concern. She looked around for Robert. He was in the middle of an intense conversation with a group of folks from Esowista. As she walked up, it was clear that they were making plans to go down the hill and start a rescue operation.

"I've got to find out what happened to my mother," Katherine said to Robert. "This damn phone won't work."

Robert swung around. "Katherine, she'll be fine. There'll be lots of people to look after her. She's the premier of the province, for God's sake. I'm more worried about the people down there." He paused, looking bleakly down the hill to the mud below. "Look, we're going down now, to see what we can do. At this stage, one person more or less won't make a difference. What we really need is equipment and medical help. Why don't you take the truck and try to get back to Tofino. You can tell the Emergency Measures officials about the situation here. Maybe they can get something to us. They should be able to track down your mom as well." He tossed her the keys and hurried away after the group, which had already set off down the slope.

Katherine felt dismissed and a bit hard-done-by but, as she drove back towards town, she knew that Robert had many friends and relatives in Esowista. She could hardly blame him for worrying about them first. She herself had a desperate need to hear her mother's voice, to be reassured that she was all right.

Driving back to Tofino took longer that she expected. Large sections of the road were washed out or covered in fallen trees. Only the four-wheel drive on the truck made it possible for her to keep going.

Several hours later, she arrived to discover a community damaged and full of activity. The low-lying sections of Tofino had been badly affected by the tsunami. The streets in the rest of town were jammed with traffic, and recovery efforts had begun. Katherine headed to the fire hall to pass on the information about Esowista. A harassed fireman responded that they would do what they could, but pointed out that there were villages all up and down the coast that had simply disappeared.

"Your friends may have to wait a while, before we can get heavy equipment out there. You made it, so the road must be passable. I'll add Esowista to the list." He told her curtly to go to city hall if she wanted information about her mother. With that, he turned back to a satellite phone.

Katherine moved on, feeling increasingly like a spare part. The shock of the tsunami was wearing off now. She decided to see if she could find a way of making herself useful instead of just wandering around. She dropped by city hall and signed up as a volunteer. She also asked whether she could borrow a sat-phone to call her mother. To her surprise, a moment or two later she found herself talking to James in Vancouver.

"Katherine, thank God you're okay! Your mother will be thrilled. You aren't hurt, are you? Where are you?"

"No, I'm fine. I'm in Tofino. How's my mother? How much damage is there?"

"Your mom's fine, but things are pretty bad here. The harbour's a mess. We've lost a lot of older buildings. It sounds as though YVR's a write-off and Richmond's a mud-hole. We don't have any casualty figures yet, but I can't believe they'll be small. Katherine, this is worse than I ever thought it might be. Look, I can't stay on the line. Your mother is in major save-the-world mode, and the telephone traffic is overwhelming. I'm just trying to coordinate things a bit for her. But don't worry, I'll let her know right away that you're all right. You should be able to talk in a few hours. Got to go. Take care."

Then James was gone, and Katherine was left staring at the phone.

CHAPTER 19

June 3, Vancouver

While Katherine was joining the relief effort in To-fino, her mother was taking charge in Vancouver. The premier commandeered a Canadian Forces vehicle and set off to the temporary BC government offices being established nearby.

She had already talked briefly to a rather subdued prime minister to emphasize the seriousness of the disaster and to plead her case for full federal cooperation. Massey made all the right noises, but Richardson rang off with low expectations. At least at first, the people of the coast would have to dig themselves out from under the rubble. Federal help would take time to arrive, if only because of the destruction at YVR.

Looking around the temporary offices, the premier was reassured that de Groote and the other ministers were pulling things together organizationally. They didn't need her there looking over their shoulders. She assigned James to keep her up to date on key information and requests for decision. James had taken over custody of the premier's cell-phone as the networks started slowly to come back to life.

Anne decided to join Angus McCarthy, the young Vancouver mayor, as close to the front lines as she could get. Her sense was that people needed to know that their political leaders were working hard to get them what they needed.

Besides, anything was better than just sitting around. She wanted to see for herself what was going on out there.

* * *

Watching the premier, James realized his old friend had finally found her feet as a politician. He had never seen her so focused yet so calm and certain about what she must do.

Over the next few days, that impression was confirmed. Premier Richardson seemed to be everywhere at once. One moment she was helping to hand out food and blankets to dazed survivors in the Downtown Eastside, the next she was talking to devastated Chinese-Canadian elders in the huge pile of rubble that used to be Richmond. Wherever she went, people responded to her obvious concern and willingness to do the simplest things to provide comfort. She was to say later that she had never realized the power of a hug, had never touched so many people as she did after the quake, not even during an election campaign.

She travelled tirelessly, first throughout the Lower Mainland and then up and down the coast. Wherever damage was greatest, she was there, galvanizing rescuers, comforting victims, putting a human face on government. Survivors knew there was a limit to what she could do personally, but they also needed to know that someone in power understood what they were up against and had their backs.

In the immediate aftermath of the earthquake, and especially as the media came back online, she transformed herself from a fledgling politician into an inspirational leader. Her endurance was legendary. The woman seemed never to need sleep.

Her patience with supply bottlenecks and jurisdictional bickering was non-existent. In the first few days after the quake, she could occasionally be seen making clear to senior municipal, provincial, military and federal officials her disappointment in their collective accomplishments. After these episodes, the recovery effort settled down. A highly effective integrated team emerged, with the premier as its undisputed leader.

Eventually the national media took notice, especially after a lengthy CNN report that profiled the premier and praised her willingness to work with mayors and governors in Washington State and Oregon. The damage in those two states was less severe than in BC, but the entire Pacific Northwest faced daunting challenges. Premier Richardson was disinclined to allow the international border to limit cooperation where it was needed.

The implicit comparison between the responses of the two federal governments tended to flatter Washington, D.C. The US president had swiftly declared the Northwest a national disaster area. He had no desire to have a Katrina episode on his watch. Personnel, equipment and supplies quickly rolled into the region. The president's staff saw the CNN report too. One day in the middle of a discussion of how to get Vancouver Airport operational again, the premier was handed a telephone. She found herself talking to President Curry.

"Madame Premier," he began, "I just want you to know how impressed I am at the work you're doing and how grateful I am for your collaboration with my friends, Governor Sloane and Governor Mitchell. They've told me about your taking on this great recovery task together, and I'm going to tell you what I've already told them: if there is anything at all I can do to make your life easier, just let me know."

To her chagrin, she made a less-than-coherent response, but President Curry boomed along, ignoring her hesitation. "I'm planning to be out in the Pacific Northwest next week. I'd consider it an honour to meet you while I'm in the neighbourhood. Nothing elaborate, but I'd be pleased if you could make time for me. My staff can be in touch to make arrangements that work for you."

"Thank you for calling, Mr President," she finally got

out. "I'd be delighted to meet you. Perhaps we can meet jointly with the two governors, as well."

With that suggestion, the stage was set for an event that gave the premier an even higher public profile.

The full White House press corps came with President Curry to Seattle. He met with the premier and the governors of Washington State and Oregon, and then separately for a half hour with Premier Richardson. Press coverage in the United States was major. This was reflected across the border. From Ottawa came nothing but a sulky silence – plus a not-for-attribution comment from an unnamed PMO official complaining about the president's lack of attention to protocol. It seemed that the president's private meeting with the premier was not regarded as especially proper.

CHAPTER 20

June 6, Vancouver

F ederal noses were put even farther out of joint as a result of some exchanges James had with some of his friends. Matt was the first to turn up. James had been working in the premier's temporary headquarters, when Matt walked in the door.

"I thought I'd make sure that the wheels of government were still turning over," Matt said. "I hope everyone in your office made it through."

James came over and gave Matt a hug. "Well, not all of us. We've had some losses. Two ministers were killed outright when the quake hit and several people in the Cabinet room disappeared. Even now, we have no idea where they are. It's so sad. The rest of us had bumps and bruises, nothing too bad." James gulped as the sights and sounds of the shattered Cabinet Chamber swept over him once more. Matt laid a hand on his arm.

"How about your family, Matt? And your house?"

"We were very fortunate," Matt responded. "Nobody got hurt, and the house is intact. Which is more than many people can say. There are a ton of folks we haven't been able to contact at all. It's really bad in some neighbourhoods. The Fraser Valley delta is a wilderness. I'm really worried that many people just got swept out to sea." Matt's eyes filled, and then he went on quickly.

"I've been thinking. You know I have good contacts in Japanese industry. Japan is always having one disaster or another, and they have a highly developed heavy rescue capability. Do you think your officials would be interested in some help?"

James expressed gratitude and referred Matt to the Emergency Management officials. Within days, small teams of Japanese engineers were landing at Abbotsford Airport and hurrying to the worst-hit spots on the Lower Mainland.

✳ ✳ ✳

A second friend, Johnny Chen, checked in as soon as cell-phone service was restored. James remembered the last time Johnny had called, shortly after he had begun working for the premier. It was late in the afternoon when he picked up a call that had been rerouted to his Vancouver office and heard a familiar voice.

"Just when I thought I could trust you to work as a political hack for hire, how is it that I find you now operating like some kind of bureaucrat? I hope the hours are short and the money's good."

Johnny clipped accent had brought back a hot, humid Wednesday night at Hong Kong's Happy Valley racetrack. Johnny seemed to know everyone at the track, which was surrounded by high-rise buildings but redolent of colonial times. James remembered the beginning of the evening, and even recollected the occasional winner, but the rest of the night was a pleasant blur, with Johnny's sardonic smile the one constant.

"Hi, Johnny. I'm not sure you should talk about working for a living. I don't recall ever seeing you toiling away. How on earth are you? I haven't seen you for, what, two years? And where are you? Here in Vancouver?"

"Got it in one, old son. Not only am I here, but I'm on the

brink of starvation. Any chance of cadging a meal?"

After a short exchange of insults, the two settled on an obscure restaurant in the heart of old Chinatown and rang off. As James strolled eastwards after work along Cordova Street to dinner, he reflected on the coincidence that Johnny would turn up again shortly after the premier's resource auction speech.

James had first met Johnny in the course of the political campaign he was managing for a Democratic Senatorial candidate in California in the 1990s. At the time, James had been having a great deal of trouble penetrating the Chinese community in San Francisco. Seemingly out of nowhere, the extraordinary figure of Johnny Chen had materialized to make his life easier.

Although he was not a tall man, Johnny stood out in a crowd. Always impeccably dressed in the latest colourful Jermyn Street garb, he would float through a ballroom full of earnest, dark-suited Chinese-American business folk dispensing gossip and good cheer in slightly British-accented English that was likely to explode into several different Chinese dialects at a moment's notice, depending on whom he was talking to. Travelling in his wake, James soon found himself making more contacts in an evening than a previous year of hard graft had generated. Evidently if Johnny knew you, then you were worth knowing. More importantly, once Johnny's introductions had been made, a steady stream of campaign contributions began flowing in from key Chinese communities throughout the state.

James was unclear about what Johnny did for a living, apart from attending fund-raisers, charity balls and political meetings. At least one of the man's business cards suggested that he was a correspondent for the Xinhua News Agency. Certainly he travelled a lot, seemingly based for the most part in San Francisco and Singapore, with frequent side trips to Hong Kong. In fact, wherever there was a significant overseas Chinese community, Johnny Chen had friends and relations.

James's CIA contacts raised an eyebrow when he mentioned Johnny's name but did not try to discourage relations with the dapper newsman. They did, however, appreciate the occasional debrief after one of James's episodic encounters with him. James drew his own conclusions and assumed that Johnny reported back to someone in China in addition to his editor at Xinhua. None of which stopped Johnny from being an engaging character and a great source of information, both scurrilous and mundane.

James joined Johnny at a back table in an undistinguished restaurant. Marvellous smells filled the air. He was unsurprised to find Johnny being treated by staff like a long-lost cousin. He fully expected an excellent meal.

"So to what do I owe this honour? Would it be unjust to suggest that you're more interested in the premier's speech than the state of my health?" James began, after the obligatory formal handshake.

Johnny smiled. "My dear fellow, how could you think that I would be at all interested in you, when your estimable boss has just given such an interesting address? You would hardly be worth the price of Sam's excellent dinner if you weren't able to fill me in on what she's up to. I'm sure that my readers would be fascinated to know."

As a succession of plates hit the table, James elaborated on the government's plans. As James spoke, Johnny's attention deepened. After the account James gave, Johnny had two simple questions. First, would existing rights-holders be adversely affected? And second, was the premier serious about managing the auction through the controversy that would inevitably surround it? Johnny's usual bonhomie was gone. He ignored the food covering the table between them, as he waited for James's answers.

James paused before responding. He knew that this would be a critical exchange in the process of convincing the Chinese government to take the auction idea seriously.

"The thing you need to know about the premier is that

she's absolutely clear about why she is in politics," he began. "She wants to make a significant difference, and she wants to make it in real time. Her view is that the BC electorate is understandably cynical about politics as usual, but desperate for some hope. She thinks she can work with people to provide the ideas that hope can be built around. I've watched her close up. She's not your average politician. For one thing, she's a real gambler – that should appeal to some of your Hong Kong friends. For another, she's impatient. She understands the Asian long view of history, but she wants to give it a nudge, not wait for it to quietly arrive. Finally, she's prepared to fail. She doesn't need the aggravation; she had lots of options before she went for the leadership."

"I saw that last part first hand," Johnny said. "She was the star turn at a reception I attended in Singapore several years ago. It was obvious that most of the major Asian firms would have been happy to make use of her services one way or another. I remember being curious about what her next step would be. Being president of UBC was obviously not the end of the road for her."

"Neither will being premier of British Columbia," said James. "I've worked with lots of politicians over the years, and Anne Richardson has something different. Look, I can't guarantee that this resource auction idea of hers will pan out. Frankly, the odds are probably against her. What I can tell you is that she is totally committed to making a success of this and will see it through to the end. If your readers are interested in whether the premier is serious, you can assure them she is."

Johnny looked across the table for a moment and then nodded. "As I recall, you were good at picking winners in Happy Valley. Let's hope your skills have not eroded over the years."

And with that, the meal continued in the warm aromatic fug of a traditional Chinatown kitchen. James brought Johnny up to date on his limited personal life. Johnny expressed interest in Jenny with the bright blue hair. The evening ended up at a series of bars across the East End, each more questionable than the last. Everywhere Johnny was greeted with open arms.

After Johnny had dropped him back at his hotel, and before collapsing into bed, James thought about the exchange in the restaurant. He concluded that he had no idea whether he'd made a sale. At least there was interest there, although probably more from the Ministry of State Security than from the followers of dispatches from Xinhua.

The next day over morning coffee in her office, James mentioned the conversation to Anne. She was amused by the approach and tried to recall the occasion in Singapore Johnny had mentioned.

"All I remember is a very rich crowd populated with a raft of people much better dressed than I was. They were friendly enough, but I had the feeling that if someone really important had walked into the room, I would have been left talking to the canapés. Johnny was certainly there. He was charming. In fact, I ran into him once or twice more after that, always with an interesting group and always charming. I assume he doesn't support himself by writing tidbits for the news agency."

"Funnily enough," said James, "the question of how Johnny earns a living has never come up. All I know is he sure wears fine clothes."

"I think the approach from Johnny is good news," the premier said firmly. "At least the Chinese have noticed the speech, even if they have some doubts about me, and even though they're having troubles of their own right now. What about touching base with our Japanese friends here in town? They aren't going to want to leave the running to 'elder brother,' especially with the tensions over those islands ramping up."

Now calling from Singapore in the middle of the night, two days after the earthquake, Johnny was all business. He asked about ways that the Chinese communities around the Rim might be helpful. He was especially concerned about the terrible damage in Richmond. By the end of the call, Johnny had undertaken to set up a major relief campaign aimed at the Chinese community but broad enough to be inclusive. Food, clothing and workers would arrive within weeks, much coming from ships moored offshore.

James was touched by the quick responses from Matt and Johnny. Of course, the help they promised for the province was important but, on a personal level, their obvious concern confirmed friendships which he valued more than ever.

* * *

Most importantly, James had managed to contact his neighbour Jenny by e-mail. Jenny assured him that Einstein was in fine form and that their houseboats and the Fisherman's Wharf community as a whole had weathered the tsunami with just a few nicks and scratches. She had also undertaken to track down Alastair Reid.

There, the news turned out to be much less reassuring. Jenny reported that Alastair had been discovered in his beloved library, crushed under a large bookcase and a pile of quarto volumes. It was unclear whether he would pull through.

The news hit James hard. He had not known Alastair for that long, but the wizened, plainspoken little man had worked his way into his heart. He desperately wanted to see Alastair for himself. The flinty old guy might regard this level of concern with amusement, but James didn't care.

He might not agree with all of Alastair's advice, but he had no trouble asking for it. Reid filled a need James knew he had for an elder he could trust. Sometimes that search for validation had led him astray, but that was surely not the case with Alastair. It seemed unfair that this relationship might be snatched away from him so soon.

As he thought about the old whistle-punk, he found himself tearing up. James knew that he had been extremely fortunate to survive the disaster, but that seemed not to matter much. Alastair's brush with death and the widespread anguish James had encountered as he trailed the premier from one disaster site to another were chipping away at his spirit. His emotions were raw. He was finding it difficult to focus on work, but it was only work that kept him from collapsing. Sleep was hard to come by, and his Mexican nightmares were recurring.

He would have to take himself in hand – though he had no idea how to do that.

III. FOREIGN COMPLICATIONS

CHAPTER 21

June 16, Victoria

When Premier Richardson walked into the first formal cabinet meeting in Victoria some two weeks after the earthquake and tsunami, the mood was decidedly, if somewhat irrationally, upbeat. She received a standing ovation from her colleagues. Large parts of the province might be in ruins, but the premier was riding high.

Anne had averaged about three hours sleep a night in the weeks since the quake, but her blue eyes sparkled, and her back was straight. She wore a simple, pearl-grey tailored pantsuit and little makeup. James thought she looked tired but triumphant. The sun slanting through the windows of the Cabinet Chamber lit her up.

The meeting settled, and the premier began with a request for reports from de Groote and Dhaliwal. The two ministers were able to assure the group that the rescue stage was complete, for better or worse, and that the recovery phase was well underway. The list of casualties was still being finalized, but the toll was sobering – more than three hundred dead and several thousand injured. In economic terms, the costs of rebuilding would run into the billions.

Both ministers highlighted the good work of officials under trying circumstances, and commented on the willingness of all concerned to set aside formal jurisdictional mandates and collaborate effectively. As an afterthought, Dhaliwal noted that while the local Canadian Forces and federal departmental officials had pitched in, the support from Ottawa had not been overwhelming.

"You couldn't say that the feds have refused to act," Dhaliwal summarized. "It's just that there doesn't seem to be much in the way of urgency or enthusiasm. I guess Vancouver is a long way from the Rideau."

"Thank you, Willem and Indira," the premier responded. "Your leadership has been notable and praiseworthy. In fact, I want to thank everyone in this room for all your hard work and dedication. I know that many of you have faced personal challenges as a result of the disaster, and we've all lost colleagues. Yet I know you have all kept at it despite everything. I'm grateful, and I know that the people of the province are grateful as well." She paused, swallowed, and then went on briskly.

"I think that Indira's point about the federal government is a really important one. I want to talk to you about what I think follows from it." She looked across the room at her Attorney General.

"I think Indira is absolutely right about the prime minister's lukewarm reaction to our problems. If there was ever a chance for the feds to step up and prove their commitment to the people of BC, this was it. As far as I'm concerned, they've dropped the ball. I know they've sent money and expressed concern but if a significant chunk of Quebec City or Hamilton had been devastated, I guarantee you the response would have been a good deal more whole-hearted and consequential. I think the lesson we draw from this performance is a simple one. We have to be able to take care of ourselves.

"In a way, I don't blame Prime Minister Massey for his attitude. BC is a long way away, and his party has few seats here. But we're still part of Canada, and I expected better. Certainly, I never expected the amount of quibbling we've heard about the assistance our Japanese and Chinese friends have been providing. Just for once, I'd like to hear something more out of Ottawa than whining over protocol. More to the point, I am convinced, based on the conversations I've been having with British Columbians since the disaster, that most people on this side of the Rockies share this view of Ottawa's behaviour. They may not be saying much at this stage, but I could feel an undercurrent of resentment out there."

The room became very quiet as she paused for a sip of water.

"I realize that some of you had serious reservations about the resource auction plan we put in place before the quake hit. But in light of the circumstances we find ourselves in, I am more convinced than ever that we need to take control of our own future. I believe that the auction will be a significant step in that process. Now, some would argue that the main priority for this government should be the recovery effort, to the exclusion of anything else. But I believe that this is precisely the time when we should be clear and firm about how we see the way ahead. We can't simply focus on fixing a few roads and clearing away the rubble. We have to give British Columbians hope, and we have to explain to them how we plan to move forward. I think this means following through with the resource auction and making it a central aspect of recovery.

"Simply stated, if we are to put the province back on its feet in a reasonable period of time, we need money and we need it now. The auction gives us a realistic shot at generating this injection of funding on our own terms. If we decide to wait for significant federal reconstruction funding, we could wait for a very long time. I just don't think the prime minister is prepared to contemplate the level of unconditional assistance we need in the timeframe we need it in."

The premier looked around the table. She saw little disagreement. Staring directly at de Groote, she went on. "I would like us to confirm that we will be proceeding with the resource auction, as discussed earlier. Can I just ask if anyone seriously objects to this course of action?"

De Groote cleared his throat. "Premier, I think I can speak for all of us when I say that now is not the time to hesitate. Now is the time to press ahead. There is nothing about the resource auction that will stop the recovery effort, and the eventual influx of funds will give us a real shot in the arm. Let's get on with it!"

There was a rumble of assent around the room. The meeting moved on to detailed consideration of next steps.

CHAPTER 22

June 16, Victoria

Late that afternoon, James stopped by the Premier's Office to catch up. Immediately after the quake, he had tried to manage the flow of information and calls to the premier, while she was out on the street dealing first-hand with the impact of the disaster. Press interest had spiked with the premier's meeting with the US president.

As soon as he could, however, he had passed most of this work to Allan Jacobson's press office crew and made his way back to Victoria. His first stop was the hospital where Alastair lay, pale and shrunken. James walked into the room as quietly as he could, but Alastair's eyes opened at once. The old man managed to produce the ghost of a smile.

"They found you under a pile of books. Typical."

Alastair licked his lips. "It wasn't entirely my fault. The room was shaking at the time. How's your vessel?"

"I haven't seen it yet, but apparently most of the docks are intact, so I may have lost some crockery, but that's all. I talked to my neighbour, and Einstein is just fine as well."

"Good." Alastair paused. He was obviously pleased to see James, but talking was an effort. "I haven't been following the news, but Vancouver's pretty smashed up, is that right?"

"Yes, but everyone's working hard. It's amazing how people help each other when they have to. And you'd be proud of your premier. She's been a rock."

"I'm not surprised. Anne's a quality person. Is Katherine okay?"

"I talked to her myself, and she's okay too. Stuck in Tofino, but she should be back soon. She and her mother seem to be speaking again."

Alastair nodded and lay back on his pillow. "I should be out of here soon, if they'd only stop fussing. I'm not about to be taken down by a bunch of books."

"What you need is some rest. Anne's got everything in hand out there, so you can relax. We can do without your advice for a week or two."

Alastair mumbled indistinctly and closed his eyes. It seemed to James that his friend was a little calmer than when he came in. But for the first time since he'd known him, Alastair looked frail. James reached over and took his hand. It was dry and delicate. He felt an answering squeeze, and then Alastair's breathing evened out and he was asleep.

James sat beside the bed for about an hour. Nurses came and went as a shift changed. The people visiting patients in the other three beds talked quietly. He found himself nodding off. Eventually he decided to investigate the state of the *Shangri-la*. Alastair was sleeping peacefully, and there was nothing more he could do for the moment. At least the old man was alive, and it looked as though he'd pull through. As he walked out into the sunshine he could feel the knots in his stomach relax a bit.

Twenty minutes later the cab dropped James off at Fisherman's Wharf. His float-home was battered but essentially intact. He walked down the dock to be greeted en route by a large grey cat, who escorted him to his front door. Einstein allowed himself to be patted but only came in after a proffer of treats. It was clear that Einstein held James personally responsible for the earthquake and the attendant dislocation. His routines had been disturbed, and the cat was unamused.

Despite the impacts on the older buildings in town, Victoria was much less seriously affected than Vancouver and its suburbs, so it was a relief to be able to get back to a city that enjoyed a semblance of normalcy. His major objective now was to get some sleep. Before he let go, though, he went down the jetty to thank Jenny for keeping track of Alastair.

"No problem", she responded, "he's a cool old guy. He wasn't awake much when I looked in on him. I'm not sure exactly why, but I think he liked my hair – ask him about it when you see him again." Jenny opened the door wider and smiled invitingly.

James grinned in return, but declined the implicit invitation. "If I don't get some sleep soon, I'm going to keel over. I'll catch up with you later. Thanks again for checking on Alastair."

That evening, he settled into his pillows and listened to the familiar lap of waves against the hull. Then, to his relief, James felt Einstein hop up onto the bed and curl into his back. He would have to work hard to get back in the cat's good books, but the process of forgiveness was underway. Reassured, James drifted off to a steady chorus of purrs.

✻ ✻ ✻

Two days later James was back in Vancouver walking into the government's temporary offices. He'd checked in on Alastair several times before leaving Victoria, and he was progressing well, judging by the growing exasperation of his nurses.

Anne looked up as James came in and shut the door behind him. "James, I was terribly sorry to hear about Alastair Reid. I know you two had been spending time together. He is an old grump, but he's awfully hard not to love." She stopped, clearly not knowing what else to say.

James tried to answer, but not much came out. He bowed his head. Anne came round the desk and took his hand. They stood together for a moment.

Anne finally broke the silence. "I think the time has come for you to hit the road. Before the world came apart, we had talked about your visiting some of our international friends. Now that cabinet is fully onside, we need to get you out there. I hope you won't mind that it involves a lot of flying."

James moved away and cleared his throat. "Premier, all I ask is that you not send me back to Terrace. I don't think the staff would understand if I left your office in tears."

The premier smiled as James sank into a chair. "Not to worry. This time you're hitting the flesh-pots – Tokyo, Beijing, Seoul, New Delhi, and Washington, D.C. You'll have a wonderful time. Besides, I've never heard of anyone actually dying from jet-lag. You'll be fine."

James slumped deeper. "I assume I will be wearing my salesman's outfit and trying to convince our overseas friends of the necessity to rent out our resource base for a while."

"The message I want you to hammer home now," the premier said, "is that we're open for business. This disaster has brought out the best in British Columbians. I need you to emphasize that we plan to use reconstruction as an economic springboard. Whoever wins the auction will be in prime position to take full advantage. I've sent some back-channel messages to my friends in Tokyo and Beijing. You should get a good hearing there. As for Washington, I want to make sure that we pursue the opening with the president. It's time to renew your contacts in or near the White House staff."

"As it happens, one of my former bosses in an unnamed American intelligence agency has ended up working for the National Security Advisor. I'm pretty sure I can buy him lunch, although that probably means that from here on, we all have our phones tapped."

"That's not a problem. Ever since the Ottawa trip I've assumed that CSIS is listening in anyway. Besides, I never say anything interesting on the phone anyway. Do you?"

"Not anymore," said James, as he got up and headed for

the door. "I'll make sure that Georgina gets you my itinerary, once it's set up. By the way, if anyone here notices my absence, you might want to suggest that I'm off in Oregon checking on my house there. There's no need to make this trip seem too dramatic. And if word leaks back about my meetings from Tokyo or wherever, the most straightforward response would be to say that I'm simply reassuring our friends abroad that BC is recovering well. That even has the merit of being true."

As he was about to leave, James turned. "Can I just say that I think that your work over the last few weeks has been amazing. I'm proud to be on your staff." He paused. "And I'm even prouder to be your friend."

For a moment, the two stared at each other. The colour rose in Anne's face. "Get out of here," she said softly. "I'll keep watch on Alastair while you're gone. And bring me a souvenir from someplace interesting."

James closed the door quietly behind him. Anne gazed into space for a moment and then returned to her reading.

CHAPTER 23

June 30, Victoria

J oe sat on a bench beside Victoria's harbour and contemplated the view. Behind him were the Parliament Buildings, surrounded by scaffolding, topped by a lopsided dome that gave it an almost jaunty air. The ruined breezeways at either end of the main block had been cleared away, and workers were moving in and out of the side entrances as the efforts to restore the building gathered pace. The main entrance overlooking the harbour was still blocked by the remains of Captain Vancouver's statue, fallen from its perch at the dome's pinnacle.

The harbour itself was full of activity. The recent tsunami had forcibly rearranged the wharfs and damaged some boats, but the worst of the wreckage had been towed away. Now new facilities were being constructed. At the head of the harbour the stately Empress Hotel was ruffled but mostly undamaged. A steady stream of Asian tourists was already filling the lobby, undeterred by the earthquake's impact.

The man known as Joe was following instructions and getting to know something about British Columbia. In practice, this meant wandering around Victoria and Vancouver and talking to people, while watching the local TV news in the evening.

Joe had his own way of gathering information. He

started by dropping in on a couple of Legion branches. As a vet himself, he had no trouble making connections over a beer. It wasn't long before animated conversations ensued about the state of the world in general and the shortcomings of the BC government in particular. Through contacts at the Legion he got to know one or two security guards at the Leg.

In the course of his travels he chatted with policemen, courthouse sheriffs, waitresses, store-clerks, bus drivers and cabbies. Joe wasn't looking for specific information; he just wanted to develop a feel for the town, based on the opinions of people he respected. He knew he could read political columnists and academics for background, and he did some of that. But he placed more credence in the views of the working men and women he ran into – plain-spoken, honest folk who weren't afraid to say what they thought.

Joe drifted around the harbour towards Fisherman's Wharf. Even in the early afternoon crowds lined up in front of the fish-and-chips shop, the ice-cream stand and the other tourist attractions. The little harbour ferries growled into the dockside every fifteen minutes or so and decanted another load of sightseers. He walked over to the working area of the docks where the fishing boats were moored. He watched the fishermen unloading their slick silver catch. Little damage seemed to have been done to the boats, and the business of the fishery had apparently returned to normal.

On his way back he turned off down one of the piers lined with float-homes. He stopped at the sign optimistically announcing *Shangri-la*. The place was deserted but lived in, judging by the collection of household detritus on the deck. A large grey tomcat stared at him from the safety of a window ledge on the second storey.

Joe looked over the float-home carefully. He liked to think that he could tell something about a person by examining where he lived. In this case, there was little to distinguish this houseboat from its idiosyncratic neighbours. He noticed a curtain twitch on a window next door. A moment later a woman with bright blue hair emerged.

"If you're looking for Jimmy Dean, he should be back in a week or two. Can I give him a message?"

"I was just looking at this float-home. I've always wanted to live in one. Any chance one of these might be available?"

The woman replied that there wasn't much turnover, but he could ask at the wharfinger's office. She seemed disinclined to continue the conversation, so Joe thanked her and strolled back along the pier. He glanced back and saw her watching him. At least one of James Franklin's neighbours was concerned about his privacy.

It didn't matter. If need be, he'd be back.

CHAPTER 24

July 18, Vancouver

Several weeks later, James walked into the area where the Premier's Office had once looked out over Vancouver harbour. He picked his way through workmen and around building supplies and headed towards the desk where Georgina presided. He had not seen Georgina since the earthquake, when she had played a critical role in the evacuation of the Premier's Office. Now she was back in Vancouver again, just in time to greet James. Her organized desk radiated calm, while the reconstruction went on around her.

"The premier is expecting you," she said. "I'm helping out while some people take time off. I'll be back in Victoria next week."

"And here I thought you came over specially for my return," James responded brightly.

Georgina shook her head in mock displeasure and waved him in.

James stepped into Anne's office, which at this point had a door, a desk and walls, and not much more.

Anne came around the desk and gave James a big hug. James felt her body move against his. He could smell the jasmine in her hair, the same perfume that he had first encountered so many years ago.

"I don't think I ever thanked you properly for keeping

me from falling out that window," she murmured into his shoulder. "One moment you were saving my life, and the next, you jetted out of here. I know I'm the one who sent you out there, but I missed you."

"I doubt that, Anne. You were too busy putting the province back together," he said unsteadily. He brushed a strand of auburn hair away from her face and looked into those blue eyes, losing all sense of their surroundings. All he cared about was holding her and breathing in her scent. It was Ottawa all over again.

And then, with a sigh, Anne stepped away. The moment passed.

"So, what have you brought me? I'm expecting presents."

"Premier, you know I was travelling light. If I had had room, of course, I would have loaded up. As it is, all I have for you is this." James handed over a small, exquisitely wrapped package.

Inside, she discovered a plain fan with sturdy metal ribs.

"It's a *gunsen*," James said, "a type of Japanese war-fan, often carried both by *samurai* and their female counterparts, the *kunoichi*. It looks decorative and harmless enough, but properly wielded, it will deflect a sword thrust. Under the circumstances, it seemed like an appropriate keepsake."

The premier beamed her thanks. "What a great gift! I'll carry it into my next meeting with the PM. He'll never know what hit him. Now, how did the trip go? Is there still a market out there for our resources?"

"Absolutely, Premier. I'd say that, overall, the interest in our auction is pretty high. The question I kept running into, though, was whether we were still serious, given the damage caused by the earthquake. I used the springboard line we talked about before I left. That seemed to satisfy people. In fact, you can expect a number of letters offering various kinds of reconstruction assistance. Whether or not you decide to accept the help, I think our Asian friends rather liked the idea of providing aid to a North American country. As you know, China and Japan have already provided some emergency help. It might be worth accepting some of their longer-term offers, if only to get up Ottawa's nose."

"We'll have to be a bit careful about that, even if the prospect of raising the PM's blood-pressure is tantalizing," Anne responded. "Did you run into any trouble from the Canadian posts as you went along?"

"Not really," James said. "As you know, I wasn't meeting directly much with government officials. For the most part I was talking to well-connected intermediaries. I'd be surprised if the embassies didn't know I was in town, however. Their own sources are good enough, and their connections with the Americans and the Brits could be called upon, once they knew I was in the region. In any event, nobody tried to get meetings cancelled, although I think our working assumption should be that the feds know exactly what was said. Which is fine. We want them to know we are moving ahead. This is just a more elegant way of keeping them in the loop than sending them a letter."

James perched on one of the two plain chairs in the partially renovated room. The premier leaned back against the front of her desk. Apparently more interested in him than usual, she looked a touch predatory, in a desirable way. With some difficulty, James kept his mind on business.

"You'll get a written account of all the meetings I had, Premier, but I can give you the highlights now. In Tokyo, I followed Matt's advice and met with one of the Keidanren committee chairs. He was very pleased we were not backing down and suggested that we might get a joint bid from a collection of key trading companies. The one thing that emerged from our conversation was the major concern they have that the Chinese might get in ahead of them. I tried to assure him that the fix was not in, and that all the bids would be judged on their merits. He was politely dubious about that, but my take from the meeting was that we can expect a very strong Japanese bid.

"As we were finishing up, he mentioned that Japan had had a lot of experience with natural disasters, and that the Japanese government was likely to make a generous offer of technical assistance in addition. He knew about the engineers Matt had arranged to come over early, of course. I told him that we were well able to take care of ourselves, but that no doubt British Columbians would greatly appreciate the Japanese willingness to help out."

"That was very polite of him," said Anne. "The Japanese are always nothing if not polite."

James nodded. "My next stop was Hong Kong," he went on. "Our friend Johnny Chen was actually there at the airport to greet me. He had arranged for me to meet a key official in the Chinese Foreign Ministry who just happened to be passing through Hong Kong. Oddly enough, this guy also turned out to be one of Johnny's cousins. You'll recall that Johnny has one of the largest extended families in the world. You've probably met some of them at one time or another."

"I probably have," said the premier. "Johnny has a lot of cousins, especially in Hong Kong."

"The cousin and I had a remarkably frank talk," James continued. "Notwithstanding all the problems the Chinese are having with the Uighurs and the recent uprising in Hebei around air pollution, the cousin went to great lengths to emphasize that the government and the Party had everything under control. When I suggested that the longstanding regional stresses were starting to reappear across China, he was adamant that the problems were manageable. He emphasized that the Chinese would never allow what had happened in the former Soviet Union to happen to them. The bottom line, he claimed, was that the current economic slowdown was just temporary, whatever the Western press might say."

"It's remarkable," said Anne, "how similar we pols sound all over the world. Remind me never to use the words 'problem' and 'manageable' in the same sentence."

The premier didn't seem all that focused this afternoon, James thought. She looked him in the eyes, and then glanced down at his mouth. James's chest tightened.

"Yes, well, I responded that BC had already suffered from major reductions in Chinese imports. We were wondering whether China was still likely to enter the bidding, given their own economic problems. He pointed out that the Chinese way was to think in terms of decades, not quarterly reports. The Chinese interest in the BC resource auction had to be seen in that longer-term context. The need for raw materials at a predictable price was not going away, as far as China is concerned. We could expect a very serious bid centred on a coalition of state-owned enterprises. He warned, however, that they would be watching closely to ensure that the bidding process was run fairly."

"I bet they will," said Anne. "Surely he can't doubt our sincerity. After all, we're Canadians."

"Well," said James, "he did want to be reassured that the BC government could actually deliver on what it promised. Fairly clearly, he thinks the Canadian government is crazy if they let us act the way we are, but I think he was willing to believe that we were credible partners for them. By the way, he was also curious about what sort of a reaction we'd had from the Americans. I told him we had had some nibbles, but nothing formal. I suspect that, at the end of the day, he was more concerned about what the US might do than he was about our feds. He can obviously recognize impotence when he sees it."

"He's probably right," Anne said. "Still, the Chinese seem to be on board so far. And you went to Seoul as well."

"Yes, but the meetings there were less satisfactory. I met a couple of academics who supposedly had tight connections with the Blue House, but you wouldn't know it. I really couldn't tell what we might expect. I suppose that some of the *chaebol* might pull together a bid, but I wouldn't bet on it. I'm not certain they have the financial heft or the scale required. On top of which, their northern neighbours keep testing missiles, and that's understandably occupying a large part of their attention. We'll see. The Koreans certainly hate the idea of being left behind by their large neighbours."

"My next port of call was New Delhi. I must say that the city struck me as remarkably rundown. On top of which, the air is close to unbreathable. Despite this, the people I met were impressive, especially a small group of multi-million-aires who made a point of coming up from Bangalore to meet me. I can't say that I expect a coherent bid from the Indians, but you never know. There's lots of brain power there, and some of them are outrageously rich. They have the additional major advantage of having significant connections here in BC already. Anyway, my last stop was back across the Pacific to DC."

"At this point, you must have been starting to totter," Anne said without much sympathy. "Still, at least in Washington you were going to see familiar faces."

"Actually, I only saw one familiar face – John Schmitt's. I told you that this was a guy I used to work with when I briefly went over to the dark side. He was my first boss. We kept in touch over the years as he climbed the ladder of spookdom. He's ended up in the White House, in the office of the National Security Advisor. I'm not sure whether to be thrilled or appalled that he's there. He's a reasonably strange dude, but very smart. Maybe that's why I have concerns. Anyway, he returned my telephone call a couple of weeks ago when I was planning the trip, and agreed to have lunch. So, after flying from one end of the Pacific to the other, I found myself sitting in a small Georgetown restaurant across from one of the president's key advisers."

"One day we'll have to discuss those parts of your misspent youth that I never knew about," Anne said. "I always wondered where you disappeared off to so suddenly after New Haven."

There was silence, as James looked uncomfortable. Anne made no move to let him off the hook.

"Perhaps we could talk about that over a drink at some point," said James in what he hoped was an unencouraging way. The pause extended.

"For the moment," he said finally, picking up the story, "you should know that Schmitt's main concern is maintaining stability in this part of the world. I told him that BC's interest was precisely the same, but that we had major financial needs that the earthquake had only made worse. We talked a bit about the practicalities surrounding the resource auction. Schmitt claimed not to know which major US corporations might be interested. I did assure him that the contest would be a fair one, however, and that seemed to go down well. Clearly, you made a good impression on the president. Schmitt implied that the administration might be inclined to cut us some slack, if we needed it. I don't know what that might mean in concrete terms, but it can't be bad."

Anne was pleased. "President Curry was certainly charming – maybe a bit hearty for my taste. Whether that ever turns into actual help, who knows?"

"At the end of the day," said James, "the American interest lies in maintaining a prosperous, united Canada. That will trump personal relationships or pressures from the Canadian regions for more autonomy. The US would have to have a very good reason to contemplate anything other than the traditional state-to-state arrangement they have with Canada now. That being said, I don't get the impression that Washington will act to stop us from pursuing the auction route. Just don't expect any cheerleading."

"Okay," said Anne, "so if I had to review for my colleagues the results of your travels, it would be something like this. For the moment there are no show-stoppers out there. In fact, in a couple of cases, such as Japan and China, there is major interest. The key questions most potential bidders had were – first, is BC serious about carrying through with the resource auction, and second, will the process be transparent and fair?"

James agreed with her summing-up. Shortly afterwards he headed out in search of somewhere to lie down. He had very little idea what time-zone he was in.

His confusion was worsened by the unexpected display of affection from Anne. He had thought they had tacitly agreed that the joyous carnality on election night would never happen again. And then there was that wonderful night in Ottawa. Now he wasn't so sure what Anne's intentions were. Perhaps she wasn't so sure either, which made the whole situation that much more awkward. On top of which, in the wake of the earthquake and concern about Jenny, Matt's family and the injuries to Alastair, he found it difficult to assess exactly what he felt about anything. His emotions were seemingly frozen but, just under the surface, he felt shuddering instability. It was as though he were standing on the edge of a high cliff, unbalanced and uncertain.

As he walked by Georgina, she passed him a note with just two words on it: *Call JJ.*

"The woman I talked to about this was very insistent that this message reach you as soon as possible," she said. "It took me five minutes to convince her that I couldn't just interrupt a meeting with the premier to pass on a two-word note. She sounded very American."

Georgina looked up accusingly. "Is this one of your friends from a past life? She didn't seem to know very much about how we do business. How did she know you were here, anyway?"

James stared at the note. The return number had a Texas area code – 210 – the code for San Antonio. He even recognized the rest of the number. It belonged to the Destiny Foundation. It was not a number he had thought he would ever see again.

"Georgina," he said abruptly. "Is there an office nearby I can use to return this call? I think it's fairly urgent."

Moments later, James dialled the number and asked for Alison.

"Howdy, stranger," came the husky voice, "it's been a

while."

James resisted the urge to hang up immediately, and replied, "Yes, it has, Alison, although perhaps not long enough. There better be a good reason for you and JJ calling me. We haven't spoken in years, and that was fine by me." His voice echoed around the bare office.

"Oh, come on, James, is that any way to talk to an old friend? As I recall, you weren't always this standoffish."

"I don't have time for social chit-chat, so what is it you both want?"

Alison Collette's voice hardened. "It's quite simple, James. We want you to get your ass down here. We need to speak to you about your new playmates. Unlikely though it may seem to you, our interests are converging again. We need to talk. JJ will expect you in his office tomorrow afternoon. And don't even think about ignoring our kind invitation. Not unless you want to see the inside of a Mexican jail. I understand they can be quite nasty. See you tomorrow, darling." And she rang off before James could respond.

James walked back to Georgina's desk. "Could you tell the premier that if it's okay with her, I'm going to take a couple of days off. I want to check on my cottage in Oregon. If she needs me, she can reach me on my cell."

Georgina expressed silent disapproval, but James knew the message would be passed on.

Two hours later, he was on a flight to Los Angeles, connecting to San Antonio.

CHAPTER 25

July 19, San Antonio

As he walked into the offices of the Destiny Foundation, James remembered his surprise the first time he had seen them. He had expected more ostentation. The foundation's site was spectacular enough, taking up the top floor of the classic 1920s building that contained the Emily Morgan Hotel overlooking Alamo Plaza. The appointments were simple, however – spartan, even. The furniture was plain southwest – lots of wood, leather and colourful fabrics with Native American or Hispanic patterns. The walls were aggressively beige and the area rugs restrained. The crisp air conditioning made wearing a jacket sensible. The tinted windows kept the hard Texas sun at bay. The overall impression spoke of money and power without the flash. There wasn't a dying Indian in sight, but around the walls there were several Remingtons, which looked suspiciously genuine and featured US cavalrymen at various stages of taming the West.

After a brief wait in front of a well-dressed blonde receptionist whose desk was graced with a framed picture of herself in Dallas Cowboys cheerleader regalia, James was ushered into a rectangular boardroom, one long side of which faced onto the Alamo. He had seen the view before, so he ignored it and strode to the far end of a fine long table, where two people sat – Jonathan Johnson, the chairman of the Destiny Foundation, and Alison Collette, the CEO.

"So what is this about, JJ?" James demanded. "I was hoping that I would never find myself in this room again."

"Welcome back to San Antonio, Mr. Franklin," responded Johnson.

Johnson was not a big man, but he radiated the coiled energy of the Special Forces colonel he had once been. Johnson had been renowned in the army for a fanatical level of fitness. He had taken that commitment to strength and endurance into retirement. He was now in his early seventies. His grey hair was cut short, but his eyes were clear and his waistline trim. Neither he nor Collette rose to shake James's hand.

James sat down opposite the two and waited. Johnson's face was set. Collette watched with mild amusement.

Johnson began, speaking formally in an accent tinged with the hill-country southern twang of Appalachia. James remembered how impressed he had been as a young man with the worldly common sense that voice had conveyed.

"Mr. Franklin, when you left us, many years ago now, I was disappointed. I thought that we had established a level of mutual trust and that you shared our longer-term aspirations and objectives. I know that the last task you undertook for us did not turn out all that well."

"That is an understatement," James interjected angrily. "I barely got out of Mexico alive, no thanks to the foundation."

Johnson leaned forward and locked eyes with James. "Mr. Franklin, I do not think it would be useful at this stage to rehearse old grievances. Whatever you think you know about that operation, I can assure you that it was not the foundation that caused it to end negatively – for you and for us, I might remind you. What I would like you to do now is to sit still and listen. Some of what I am about to say, you will already know, but I want you to understand the broader context within which we believe that the time has come for you to work with us again. Are you prepared to pay attention?"

When James gave a curt nod, Johnson sat back and

started what sounded like a prepared speech. After the first few minutes, James had the eerie feeling that JJ was addressing a wider audience, unseen but real. He decided not to interrupt the flow. One thing he knew about the foundation for sure was that it was both powerful and dangerous. He needed to understand why it had chosen to come back into his life.

He remembered the first time JJ had explained the Destiny Foundation's antecedents. He had suggested that its purposes could be inferred from its name and from the location of its headquarters in San Antonio. The name itself derived from the concept of "manifest destiny" developed in the 1840s by a prominent American journalist, John L. O'Sullivan. At the time, O'Sullivan was keen to add Texas and Oregon to the United States as it expanded westwards. Nowadays, the foundation believed that manifest destiny more properly applied to ensuring that American power was maintained on a global basis. And as for the Alamo itself, what JJ liked to call "this monument to American courage and sacrifice," it symbolized the foundation's determination to take any measures necessary to guarantee that the United States fulfills its destiny. Moreover, it was prepared to take significant risks to reach its objectives. Not for nothing had JJ caused the words of William Travis, the Alamo's commander – "One crowded hour of glorious life is worth an age without a name" – to be emblazoned prominently on one wall of his office.

JJ launched into his presentation. "The foundation's long-term view is that the global geo-political game has irrevocably changed since the fall of the Berlin Wall, mostly to the detriment of the United States. Just as after the Second World War, the US stood virtually alone in the early 1990s as the predominant power. But unlike on that earlier occasion, we proved completely incapable of devising a coherent plan for making best use of that fortunate circumstance. For a variety of reasons, some of them in our control, and others beyond it, the US is clearly no longer the global hegemon – at least in economic terms. It will remain for the foreseeable future, however, one the two main economic superpowers. The other is China. The second-level powers are of course Japan and the EU, but neither has the weight or, more importantly, the determination to apply that weight, of the big two."

JJ stretched a leg under the table. James knew that Johnson was in almost constant pain from wounds in that leg from a Vietcong *pungi* trap. Johnson's ability to ignore that pain had added to his mystique, as far as the young James was concerned. Somewhere, deep down, James still mourned the loss of an exemplar, a person he could pattern his life after.

"At the same time," JJ went on, "militarily, the United States remains unmatched. Simply put, given the shifting balance of international economic power, the American comparative advantage lies with its military power. The key question is whether America's leaders are prepared to make full use of that advantage, or whether they will stand by as we are revealed to the world as an impotent giant. Our view, and the lesson of history, is that the credible threat or direct application of military strength is critical if it is not to become a diminishing asset."

JJ paused to make sure James was paying full attention. "At the intersection of these economic and military considerations lies what we regard as the key to the geo-political game – access to natural resources. Given the finite nature of those resources, both renewable and non-renewable, we are talking about a zero-sum exercise. Whichever country gains access to a given resource by definition excludes all other nation states from most of its benefits. As an island nation, the Japanese are painfully aware of this characteristic. They fought the Second World War because they felt that their access to resources was threatened. And the Chinese, although they benefit from a huge land-mass, have for decades been amassing access to resources all over the world to ensure that they can keep their population fed and their industries supplied.

"What this means for America, Mr. Franklin, is simple. At a bare minimum, we must establish total control over the resources of the continent we inhabit. This is the necessary pre-condition to keeping the United States as a viable player in the race for global pre-eminence. Without this firm strategic base, we are building on sand. And this in turn brings us to the government to which you have decided to offer your services.

"Mr Franklin, given your familiarity with our methods, you may not be surprised to hear that over the past few months we have kept close watch on your Premier Richardson's exploits. Like most observers, we did not expect her to win her first election. We have been even more struck by her subsequent policy directions. That resource auction idea of hers really caught our attention." And here, JJ smiled beneficently.

"You know, Mr. Franklin," JJ said nostalgically, "in the old days, if we had ever caught wind of a wild-ass socialist scheme like that auction, especially so close to home, we would have been on to our friends on the Hill and in the administration like a shot to ensure that the BC government had a limited shelf life. The demonstration effect alone would have made ending Richardson's political career worthwhile. But circumstances change, and we have to move with the times. We don't just send in the 82nd Airborne anymore. We adapt and overcome – preferably with as little bloodshed as possible. The last thing we want is a slew of YouTube clips demonstrating once again that the United States has only one way to deal with rogue governments."

JJ flexed his leg again, seemingly unaware of the tic. "No, we came to the conclusion that we kinda like your little auction. But only, of course, if the right country wins it. What your premier has done is to give us the opportunity to 'finish the job' as far as Canada is concerned. We should never have allowed the Brits to set up a bunch of puppet provinces north of the 49th in the first place. And now comes a great chance to rewrite history and start the process of gaining unfettered access to Canada's resources. This might mean breaking up a nice quiet little country, but you can't make an omelette without breaking a few eggs."

James bristled but kept silent.

"The fact is that our main target is the hydro-carbon base in Alberta, but we need to start somewhere. Once we have BC under our belt, we can move on from there. The foundation believes that the premier's resource auction represents a major target of opportunity. The timing will never be better. Your premier is a very attractive leader, the Canadian prime minister is an idiot, and in the wake of the earthquake, BC will never need the money more. If we can detach BC, then Alberta will realize where its best interests lie. Our friends in Quebec can be counted on to take full advantage and finally break free. At that point, the country will be reduced to its constituent pieces."

JJ adopted a reassuring tone. "Now, you don't need to worry about the United States actually taking over the various parts of what used to be Canada. We'd prefer a variant on the Puerto Rico solution, something along the lines of a series of associate states. We wouldn't want a bunch of Canadians inside our political system anyway. They'd unbalance American politics and, in any event, most of them would vote Democrat, and that would be unhelpful. The last thing this country needs is a bunch more Californias and New Yorks."

Johnson's mood shifted away from the pleasant prospect of re-fighting the War of 1812 with less effort and a more positive outcome. His attention returned to James, who had been listening to this recitation in growing disbelief.

"So, what do you want from me?" he asked, entirely uncertain that he wanted an answer.

"It's quite simple, Mr. Franklin," JJ intoned. "First, we want you to do your job and make sure that the resource auction takes place, just like your premier wants. When you go home, you can assure Ms. Richardson that a powerful consortium of US companies will be entering the auction with an extremely credible bid. By the way, those companies would be committed to working with their BC counterparts, so the chances for everyone concerned to make a lot of money are high."

"Second, after a fair and transparent process, we want you to arrange for the US bid to win. How you achieve that is entirely up to you, although we have some ideas we'd be happy to share with you."

JJ had finished his recitation. "I trust we have made ourselves clear."

James was at a loss for words. Johnson's speech reminded him forcibly of a scene from the movie *Dr. Strangelove*, with the unnerving exception that JJ was deadly serious and apparently had the means to enforce his will. The fact that Collette was by now smiling broadly, increased rather than decreased James's discomfort. How do you respond effectively to a crazy person?

"JJ, when we last had dealings," James began slowly, "I was a young man with little experience. You gave me an unforgettable introduction to a world I had no idea existed. Although things didn't work out at the time, I've always valued that crash course in *realpolitik*. But what you're asking me to do now is not realistic; it's unhinged. Even if I wanted to do what you asked – most of which I think is unethical and wrongheaded, by the way – there is no possibility that one person acting alone could achieve the results you want. I will have to decline your gracious offer to betray my boss and my country." James stood up and turned for the door.

Johnson waited until James was several steps away. His words lashed across the room.

"Just so that we are clear about the alternatives in play, Mr. Franklin, do you have any doubts about the ability of this organization to arrange for you to be delivered directly and promptly to Mexican authorities for processing?"

CHAPTER 26

July 20, Victoria

J ames stared out the window of his float-home. Normally the view across the harbour and the quiet rhythmic slosh of the waves against the hull would calm him down. But not now. He was trying to make sense of the past twenty-four hours. What had happened in San Antonio had shaken him badly.

He was not proud of his performance at the Destiny Foundation. In response to the demand that he cooperate with the foundation's scheme to rig the resource auction, he had not acted heroically. He had simply told JJ and Alison that he would have no difficulty working to ensure that a consortium of US companies could enter the bidding process. He also undertook to keep Alison informed as the bidding moved ahead. He remained silent about whether he was willing or even able to affect the outcome.

The threat to deliver him to Mexican authorities obviously remained in play, however, at least as far as JJ was concerned. James had half expected that one of JJ's large aides would stop him from leaving the premises but, in the end, nobody stood in his way. JJ contented himself with a single remark as James walked back across the large boardroom.

"You know, Mr. Franklin, despite what some people say about the efficiency of the Mexican legal system, it can be remarkably persistent if given the appropriate incentives. I understand that their file on Roland Barker is still open. Imagine that, after all these years."

James had not turned back, but he heard Alison's low chuckle as he left the room.

He had not thought about Roland for some time. Roland Barker was a young man James had recruited when he worked for the foundation in Mexico. That foundation contract had turned up just when James needed a job, in the months following his departure from a small, extremely secret offshoot of the Central Intelligence Agency.

Alison Collette had been one his main trainers at the agency, instructing him on techniques related to industrial espionage. They had also been lovers off and on. Their episodic, enthusiastic sexual encounters had suited them both at a time when the two of them were working under extreme pressure.

It was Alison who subsequently made the first approach from the foundation. She explained that she had grown tired of the bureaucracy and cant that pervaded the agency and its related organizations and had joined the Destiny Foundation. She described the foundation as a place where worthwhile things could be done without all the trappings and limitations of government. She had urged him to join her. James was at loose ends, the pay was tempting, and the lure of a return to a secret world was considerable. After remarkably little consideration, he signed on.

The foundation ran with a small staff. New employees were indoctrinated thoroughly before being sent out into the field. In James' case, this meant extensive contact with the foundation's founder, Lieutenant Colonel Jonathan Johnson (Retired). JJ was always willing to talk. James knew that JJ had a full agenda of meetings, but he set aside time every day to explain to the young recruit the foundation's history and to provide a detailed rationale for the organization's work. JJ's grasp of the practical mechanics of international relations was remarkable. He seemed to know all the main players in all the key countries. His ability to overcome his own physical limitations to carve out a stellar career in the army and later in civilian life was admirable.

Most weeks, James and JJ would have dinner together. James especially treasured these long, lazy meals, because the conversation ranged far beyond the work of the foundation. He found himself talking about his childhood, a subject he rarely brought up. Most of his recollections centred on playing alone. In return, JJ shared tales of his own upbringing as a poor boy in the hills of West Virginia. JJ managed to make growing up in grinding poverty sound amusing, but James could feel the hurt that lay behind the funny stories.

As the only child of a single mother himself, James identified with the older man's experiences. JJ possessed an endless stream of anecdotes, which he delivered with folksy Southern charm. Some of them had a point; most were just yarns. Within a month, James felt remarkably close to this contained but candid man who limped about the office dispensing encouragement and common sense.

All too soon, the training period came to an end. James' initial assignment was to work with a US-based security company and the Mexican federal police. This was how he met Roland Barker. One of his first decisions was to hire Roland to join him in Mexico City. Their office consisted of four rooms in a modest three-storey building on a leafy back street in the Colonia Cuauhtemoc, not far from the American Embassy.

The objective was to devise and deliver a public relations campaign for the company aimed at attracting business from corporations that had operations in both countries. Part of the campaign tried to demonstrate how well the company cooperated with Mexican authorities and how effective it could be in resolving security-related issues that American corporations might face in Mexico.

Ignorant of the Mexican scene, James had been quite prepared to take this on, because the direct involvement of the *federales* reassured him of the legitimacy of the US company's activities. In addition, Alison and JJ had painted a glowing picture of how this effort would benefit the broader US–Mexico relationship while avoiding the hang-ups caused by bureaucracies on both sides. Here was an example of practical bilateral diplomacy without engaging the striped-pants brigade.

At first, the contract had been fun. Ronald was a congenial colleague. Although they worked hard, they conducted a meticulous exploration of Mexican nightlife as well. Eighteen months into the exercise, however, James came to realize just how naive he had been. The public relations scheme was apparently providing cover for an elaborate drug-smuggling operation that generated a significant ongoing source of revenue both for the foundation itself and, on a much larger scale, for a branch of a major drug cartel. The federal police he worked with turned out to be corrupt. Their "security" activities in Mexico seemed to be thinly disguised attacks on rival cartels.

As James' doubts about his assignment multiplied, he had a series of unsatisfactory calls with the San Antonio headquarters. At first Alison had dismissed his suspicions out of hand. Then, as the evidence mounted, she suggested that James' information was of doubtful provenance. Finally, she undertook to check with the foundation's Washington contacts to seek confirmation one way or the other. In the meantime, she urged James not to worry and to keep on with his activities. After one particularly unhelpful exchange with Alison, James had taken Roland to lunch. They discussed career options if this operation didn't pan out.

Roland was largely unconcerned. He claimed to have had a wonderful year or so learning about Mexican politics and improving his Spanish. He ended up reassuring James in his usual sunny way.

"Look, if this gig doesn't pan out, I won't feel bad, and neither should you," Roland said. "I've added a great line to my resumé and had lots of fun doing it. You've taught me a lot. I'll always be grateful for the opportunities you've given me." The rest of the lunch passed in a good-humoured alcoholic haze.

The next morning, James came into his Mexico City office late, to find the door ajar and no lights on. Exasperated, he pushed his way in, took one look at Roland's office and threw up all over the floor. The chair contained a bloody torso, its legs awkwardly splayed out under the desk. A mass of flies slowly circled the slumped mess, most of what was left of Roland Barker. The air reeked of the metallic stench of blood.

He staggered back into his own office and stopped, transfixed by a carefully arranged scene. There, painstakingly centred on his computer keyboard, was his assistant's head. Roland's eyes were wide open. He looked both startled and disappointed.

Spiralling into a vortex of anguish and guilt, James collapsed.

Afterwards, he could never recall clearly how he made it to the airport. He remembered stopping briefly at his apartment to rip off clothes stinking of vomit and blood. He could recall standing under the shower to try to erase the smell. He remembered the strange looks he received from other travellers as he yelled, panic-stricken, at an airport ticket clerk, but much of his escape from Mexico was, mercifully, a blank.

The next day, he stormed into the conference room in San Antonio and confronted JJ and Alison. Johnson was calm in the face of James's noisy distress. He listened carefully, expressed sympathy about Roland, and dismissed any possibility of foundation involvement with a drug cartel.

"My friend, I can only imagine that you misunderstood what was going on," JJ said. "Mexico is an unusual place with its own way of doing things. I hadn't wanted to raise this with you before we met in person but, just the other day, we obtained unfortunate intel about young Roland. It turns out that he was consorting with some very shady characters. They seem to have decided that he had become a liability. I just want you to understand that, horrible though Roland's fate was, it had nothing whatsoever to do with the job you were doing or with the foundation. I'm sure that, after you've had time to think about it, you'll come to realize that this is the case." JJ paused.

"And in the meantime, I think we'll send another contractor in to finish off what you so ably began. I would suggest that you take some well-earned time off, at our expense, of course. You've been working extremely hard, and this last experience has obviously taken its toll."

James stared at the little man with the sincere face and the sharp eyes. He knew perfectly well that JJ was lying about Roland, but he also knew that, if he pursued the matter, the outcome could only be painful. The threat was all the more impressive for not having been explicitly stated. James should move on and forget what he had seen.

James was as angry as he had ever been, but he was also scared and ashamed. He walked out of the office, straight to the nearest bar. He woke up the next morning with a raging hangover and discovered a message on his phone telling him to contact a high-tech company based in Portland. They needed a person on retainer for dealing with any political and public relations issues that might come up. James took the job, which left plenty of time for developing the more specifically political practice that he went on to develop over the years.

Altogether, James mused grimly, this had been a satisfactory outcome – except for what happened to Roland, as collateral damage, of course, and the recurrent nightmares James had suffered, centred on that stinking, blood-soaked office.

Eventually the nightmares had subsided. Months would go by without his thinking about the young man whose death he had inadvertently caused. What never left him was an ingrained conviction of his own inadequacy when he encountered danger.

James knew that the foundation must have reached out to his new Oregon employer, but he had never heard from Alison or JJ again – until three days ago. And now he had seemingly done exactly the same thing he'd done twenty-five years before. He had succumbed to fear. He had refused to act in the face of evil. Even more galling, JJ had known exactly what would happen. James had taken the easy way out before. The clear expectation was that he would do so again. JJ's assessment of his character was entirely accurate.

The disorientation generated by the earthquake and its aftermath had been compounded. The sudden return to his life of the Destiny Foundation conjured up feelings of apprehension and powerlessness that he thought he had long outgrown. In addition, even before the trip to San Antonio, the nightmares had come back. Once more he was in that stinking, blood-soaked room, staring at a disembodied head, unable to move, terrified to remain. As each night approached, his tension increased. Sleep seemed more of a threat than a release.

Einstein jumped up into his lap and nudged his hand, demanding pats. James duly obliged, but not even the touch of the silky grey fur could offer much consolation.

IV. THE PEOPLE SPEAK

CHAPTER 27

July 22, Victoria

I n a foul mood, James reported back to the premier. As if out of spite, the sun streamed in through the windows of the Premier's Office in Victoria. Outside, the bagpiper on the corner played *Amazing Grace* for the fourth time in half an hour.

James recounted a fictional approach from a consortium of US companies. He suggested that, if they met all the criteria for participation in the resource auction, they should be included. The premier was pleased at this indication of American interest and concurred. She quickly moved on to tell James about the latest efforts by the federal government to discredit the province's recovery efforts in general and her in particular.

The criticism of BC's response to the earthquake was especially ironic, because the federal government's own involvement had been lukewarm so far. Ever since the closing of the Chilliwack army base and several other federal installations in BC, there were few tangible federal assets left to deploy. The expressed willingness to "send money" seemed cold-blooded in the circumstances. When a regional federal official suggested to the press that his government's actions were being sabotaged by BC officials' lack of cooperation and called into question the competence of those officials, the reaction across the province was swift and negative.

The attempt to blacken Anne Richardson's reputation was even more ill-considered in light of her performance in the immediate aftermath of the disaster. Her local standing was still high. Leaked references to a sprightly youth (sex, drugs, and rock and roll) and tendencies towards subsequent instability gained little traction. People liked Richardson, admired her recent commitment to earthquake victims, and regarded tales of her supposedly misspent teen-aged years with amused tolerance. The premier was not worried about any of this mud sticking, but she found federal behaviour aggravating in the extreme, at a time when much of southwestern BC still lay in ruins. Moreover, hundreds had died, and thousands of West Coasters remained homeless.

"These guys really piss me off," Anne grated. "I've been thinking about it, and I've concluded that Quebec has had the right idea all along. I am absolutely not going to back down in the face of this federal crap. But if I'm going to get into a serious fight with the feds, I want some leverage. What I need is the equivalent of a strike mandate. We've reached the point where I think it would make absolute sense to hold a referendum. The people need the chance to express their will directly. What do you think?"

"What exactly would the vote be about, Premier?" James asked doubtfully. "Are you seriously suggesting that, at a time when a fair amount of the province is still covered in rubble or water, the voters would appreciate having to pay millions of dollars for a vote? On what? Independence?"

"Okay, my reading is this," she said. "British Columbians resent the idea of Ottawa on the one hand telling us how to manage our own natural resources, and on the other not responding in a whole-hearted manner to the worst disaster this province has ever faced. And without making it personal, they don't much like it, either, when outsiders denigrate their premier, apparently for no good reason. I just think our folks are fed up. They need the opportunity to express that frustration. Without something as concrete as a vote, we can whine away at the feds until the cows come home, but they won't pay attention.

"What I want," she went on, "is something that will simultaneously make the feds sit up and take notice, and provide British Columbians with an outlet for some significant anger. I don't expect the pundits to think this is a good idea, but those are the same people who never thought we'd win the last election. I know what I hear when I'm on the street, James. I owe BCers the right to be heard."

"Have you talked to caucus or cabinet about this, Premier?" James asked, hoping the answer would be no.

"Actually, while you were away in the States, I did have a chance to touch base with my colleagues. You would perhaps be surprised at how many of them are sick of federal condescension and non-performance. One or two of them told me that they had doubts, but not many. Everybody is so focused on rebuilding the province that anything that stands in the way is seen as irrelevant at best and dangerous at worst. Rather than being seen as an expensive distraction, the view seems to be that this would be a valuable opportunity for British Columbians to come together." Anne looked a little smug.

"I assume that this growing consensus you found does not include First Nations or our friends in the environmental movement," James responded. "I can't imagine either of those groups would support a referendum, the net effect of which would be to justify the resource auction. The First Nations in particular would look to the federal crown to protect them against this attack on their interests. If you include any threat of separation in the referendum wording, they'll go nuts."

"We haven't worked out the precise wording yet," Anne replied, "but essentially it will assert the province's constitutionally protected capacity to manage its own resources. It will also state that in the face of unacceptable federal interference, we would reserve the right to renegotiate the terms of union with the rest of the country, up to and including the possibility of outright separation. I've asked the attorney general's lawyers to come up with something snappy but legally credible."

"I don't envy them that job," James observed. "But from what you say, you're less concerned about legalisms than you are about tapping into the emotional state of the province. I just hope you're right about where most of the voters are, because this could be a major disaster if you've misjudged the public mood."

James was tired enough that he was more straightforward than he might otherwise have been. He supposed that Anne might decide to dispense with his services. That didn't seem like such a terrible option.

Instead, she smiled and said, "I didn't think you'd be so thrilled with this idea, but I hope that won't stop you from continuing to help me. If we can get through the referendum period with the sort of outcome I think we'll get, we can finish up the auction process and move ahead from there. At that stage I wouldn't blame you for taking a hike. Between now and then, I need you."

Anne looked across the desk straight into his eyes, and James felt his professional detachment waver.

"Anne, you pay me to give my best advice, so here it is. I think that holding a referendum now, in effect threatening to secede if the feds don't stop attacking the resource auction and calling you names, is a terrible idea. We're all tired and stressed, and so are the people of the province. Whipping the electorate up into a frenzy on top of everything else would, in my view, be extremely unhelpful. The referendum campaign itself is bound to divide us, not unite us. If people like your daughter were already angry at the policies of this government, a referendum is quite likely to drive them over the edge.

"Angry, desperate people do regrettable things, which under any other circumstances they would never consider doing. And even if we get through the campaign in one piece, there are absolutely no guarantees. You could lose. And, frankly, if you do lose, I can see no choice but personal resignation and perhaps another election – which your party would have almost no chance of winning." James paused, bracing himself for Anne's reaction.

Her blue eyes glinted as she stood up. "You're right, James; I pay you for your best advice. I appreciate your giving me the straight goods. It is possible that cabinet may agree with you, but I doubt it. If we decide to move ahead with the referendum, however, I need to know I can count on you. You'll be delighted to know that I have yet another air-miles-related task for you. Come and see me tomorrow morning, and we'll talk about it."

* * *

That night, James came close to drafting a letter of resignation. Anne's latest scheme made little sense. He found it hard to believe that British Columbians really wanted to go to the polls again. After a desultory dinner, he wandered around downtown Victoria streets, some of which were clogged with rubble. There were few people about, and those who were out looked grey and discouraged.

Despite the evidence from recent visits suggesting the old man was holding his own, the serious injuries to his friend Alastair left James empty and heartsick. He assumed that most of those affected by the earthquake felt even worse. At least he still had a house in Victoria. All he wanted to do was fall into bed and pull the covers over his head.

Only his loyalty to Anne Richardson kept him from quitting. He couldn't just leave her to fight her referendum campaign alone, no matter how dumb the idea was.

#

The next day, James and Anne met on Government Street for an early morning run. James was morose, but Anne was jubilant.

"I think I may be getting the hang of this politics stuff," she said as they jogged towards the sea. "Cabinet has completely bought into the referendum idea."

"Even de Groote?" asked James.

"Even him," she responded. "He didn't say much during the discussion, but he was very supportive by the end of the meeting. The one person with doubts was the attorney. I suspect that was because she knows that crafting the referendum question is going to be difficult, and it will be her folks leading on that. Incidentally, we're going to save some money by tying the referendum vote in with the municipal elections at the end of October. So, the plan is to announce the vote in the next few days, with the wording coming out a week or so after that."

James's shoulders sagged, but Anne moved on crisply, picking up the pace.

"In the meantime, I want you to go and have a chat on my behalf with the Quebec premier's principal secretary. I've already spoken briefly with Premier Ferland on the phone. I've told him he can expect a visit. He was very gracious and offered to send help for the reconstruction. You know, I never had a chance to meet him the last time we were all in Ottawa, but I gather that he is supposed to be quite sensible – for a separatist. Can you get to Montreal in the next few days? The Premier's Office there says that the principal secretary will be in town on some other business, so you can have a quiet word. This is not a meeting I want advertised."

James worked at keeping up. For some reason, the more enthusiastic Anne became, the faster she ran. "Right, Premier. What is the message you want sent, keeping in mind that it is not likely to stay secret very long."

"I simply want them to understand directly from us what our situation here is and how we expect the next few months to roll out. If Premier Ferland feels that he can make supportive noises, that would be great too. After all, we have quite a bit in common with Quebec's longstanding desire to maintain full control over its natural resources."

From Anne's shoulder, James snorted in exasperation. The inmates seemed to have taken over the institution. "You realize, of course, that Quebec might regard this as a perfect opportunity to raise the temperature themselves. Do you really want to be seen as a close ally of a government that is intent on breaking up the country?"

"Well, I wouldn't mind all that much if the feds find themselves with battles on several fronts at once. Hard though it is to imagine, they may end up looking even more hopeless than they are now. My sense of Massey is that, if you keep pushing him and pushing him, he's bound to say something stupid in the end. Let's ramp up the pressure and see what we get."

James shrugged in resignation and mock enthusiasm. He settled into a longer stride. "After all, we have a referendum to win!" he muttered to himself.

CHAPTER 28

July 23, Montreal

A lbert Dupuis, the principal secretary to the premier of Quebec, turned out to be an entirely civilized fellow, about the same age as James. At Dupuis' suggestion, the two met for dinner at a small, exquisite restaurant in Old Montreal instead of sitting stiffly in a government boardroom.

Very little of the dinner was devoted to the matters at hand. Dupuis was interested in James' experiences in American politics. James found the former academic's analysis of the long Quebec struggle for cultural survival on an Anglophone continent fascinating. Both men loved good food and wine as much as they did politics so, after an initial wariness, the evening went pleasantly. Dupuis knew the staff well, and the service was impeccable. Their table was well placed for privacy, just to one side of a crackling fire that banished the chill of an unseasonably cool summer's evening.

Over coffee and *digestifs*, Dupuis finally broached the reason for the meeting. "This has been an enjoyable evening, *mon cher* James, and I now know a lot more about American politics than I did before, but I take it that your premier had a reason for allowing you to stretch your expense account in this fashion."

James swirled his cognac for a moment before replying.

"Albert, it's really pretty simple. Premier Richardson wanted you and your boss to know first-hand from us what's going on. I'm sure that from the perspective of Quebec City, the past few months in BC must have looked like the usual West Coast chaos. Certainly, the earthquake was not something we planned for but, for the rest of it, we have a fairly clear sense of where we want to go."

James could feel Dupuis taking mental notes. "The original motivation for the premier's approach to managing our natural resources was twofold. First, we wanted to make more coherent use of the revenue that our resource base would throw off. We just can't plan for the sort of social programs we think are necessary if that revenue stream isn't more predictable. We're also not sure that we are getting top dollar for resources that in most cases are non-renewable. And second, in order to accomplish our objectives, we need unquestioned control over the disposition of those resources under our jurisdiction. Otherwise, why would any potential bidder be prepared to make significant investments over the long term?

"In particular," James continued, "we cannot afford to have the federal government second-guessing our decisions and threatening to reverse them. The recent disaster makes the case even more compelling. We have an obvious requirement to generate money as quickly as possible so that we can get on with the enormous task of reconstruction. In our view, reconstruction and the resource auction go hand in hand."

After several reflective sips of his brandy, James went on. "The premier has not been impressed by the scale of federal assistance so far. All through the piece, the feds have kept up a steady drumbeat of criticism of the BC government's performance. Most of that criticism has come from the proverbial anonymous 'informed sources.' It has included some especially nasty personal rumour-mongering. Premier Richardson regards this kind of gratuitous sniping as par for the course from this federal administration, but it has not gone down well among the public at large. People have seen the premier at work since the quake. The respect she is held in has climbed. She may have been an unknown quantity when she was elected, but her actions have prompted a run-up of personal popularity. BCers don't much like outsiders telling them what to think, anyway. That should sound familiar, Albert."

"Oh yes, Quebeckers aren't too keen about that either," Dupuis rejoined. "And for that matter, most of them, whatever their political persuasion, would want their province to maintain the ability to manage their resources as they see fit. Interestingly, I don't think it would ever occur to even the most wooden-headed federal government to try to take Quebec on in this area. It's recognized as an extremely neuralgic point."

"Which is precisely why," James said, "the premier and her colleagues have decided that they need the sort of leverage that Quebec governments have tried to generate from time to time. The premier believes that her government must have available the sort of support that only a direct vote of the people can give her. That is why cabinet has decided to schedule a referendum on the issue at the same time as the municipal elections late in October. The government wants the equivalent of a strike mandate in collective bargaining terms – something to be used if needed, but not an absolute certainty."

Dupuis looked at James with wry amusement. "This all sounds a bit familiar, but you do realize that our attempts to generate what you call a 'strike mandate' haven't worked out all that well in the past? Are you sure you can actually win this vote?"

James responded with more confidence than he felt. "I'm sure we can. The timing is right, and we are blessed with a prime minister with a big mouth and a tiny mind. It should turn out just fine. After a positive vote, we can get on with the job. The feds would be hard-pressed to challenge us directly at that point – unless they want to turn separatist talk into separatist action."

"Well, thank you for coming all this way to give us a heads-up. I'm sure that the premier will be interested in this initiative. Please convey to Madame Richardson our thanks and our best wishes for the next few months. They should be very active."

Dupuis paused, and then went on quietly. "You know, I'm sure you have considered carefully the consequences of the course of action you are embarked upon. But as someone who has lived through a series of elections and referenda fought on matters of fundamental principle, perhaps you will accept a well-meant warning. When people are asked to choose a future that is fundamentally different from the status quo, they often become fearful, and they sometimes become angry.

"Your premier is unleashing forces, the impact of which is difficult to predict in advance. Old friends will stop talking, families will split, individuals and companies may abandon the province. This sort of social stress is not something one would want to go through unless one were very certain that the objective was worthwhile." Dupuis added sadly, "You know, my sister and I still rarely see each other since the last referendum. Only at funerals, it seems."

* * *

On the flight home, James thought about Dupuis' last comments. He liked the dapper principal secretary, although he had no doubt that the separatists would use the turmoil in the West to their own advantage if they could. Under those circumstances, any public support they gave BC would only serve as ammunition to a vengeful federal government. Still, he could understand the premier's desire to reach out to another provincial government that had undergone a similar experience, albeit for vastly different historical reasons.

Dupuis' warning stuck in his mind. James hoped Anne

understood what she was leading them all into.

CHAPTER 29

July 26, Victoria

When the premier rose in the House a couple of days later to announce a referendum for the beginning of October, she looked anything but uncertain. Standing at her place in the high-ceilinged chamber wearing a bright yellow tailored suit, Anne radiated calm assurance as she waited for the members to settle. For such an important announcement, the premier's address was remarkably brief.

She summarized the difficult situation the province found itself in after the earthquake and praised the people of British Columbia for their resilience and courage. She then moved on indict the feds.

"In these circumstances, we had a right to expect the wholehearted support of the federal government. Regrettably, in stark contrast to the outpouring of encouragement and assistance we have received from ordinary Canadians from coast to coast to coast, federal authorities have chosen to second guess the local relief efforts and place a succession of bureaucratic obstacles in the way of those working to rebuild the province.

"BCers will find this feeble response sad, but they will not be surprised. This is, after all, the same federal government that recently called into question the right of the people of this province to manage their precious natural resource base and coupled their unconstitutional opposition to the provincial government's recently announced plans in this regard with an unprecedented series of scurrilous personal attacks on the leaders of this province."

Anne looked around the chamber, gathering her audience.

"Well, I'd like to point out to the prime minister that, unlike him, I have spent the past few weeks travelling across this province, marvelling at the courage of our citizens and struck by their commitment to shaping a vibrant, sustainable future for themselves and their children. What they do not want or need is a federal government standing in their way.

"Accordingly, my government has decided that the people of this province deserve the opportunity to express their views in the most direct way possible. Mr Speaker, on October 2, we will hold a referendum on whether to proceed with the resource management plans that we announced prior to the recent disaster. The objective of this vote is to give the government a clear mandate to move ahead free of federal interference. In the event of what we are confident will be a renewed mandate, this government intends to make this innovative approach a key aspect of its massive recovery effort.

"I know from personal experience that British Columbians are determined to come back from the terrible blow that struck them on June 2. The referendum I am announcing today is an important step in that long journey. I have absolutely no doubt that this vote will demonstrate conclusively that we are united in our dedication to a prosperous and sustainable recovery. Thank you, Mr Speaker."

With that, the premier sat down to applause from the government benches and jeers from across the aisle. The opposition attacked the referendum as an egregious waste of money at a time when the government should be focused on practical rebuilding activities. They went on to catalogue the dangers related to the resource auction itself, describing it as a recipe for economic chaos, a sell-out of valuable resources to foreigners, an invitation to environmental destruction, and a betrayal of the rights of the province's First Nations.

The premier responded that the vote would be held in conjunction with the scheduled municipal elections and would entail few additional costs. She denied that the auction would result in a loss of sovereignty, claiming that the scheme in itself represented a significant exercise of jurisdiction. She pointed to the assistance that Chinese and Japanese crews were currently bringing to Vancouver as an example of the benefits of international cooperation, which would be enhanced rather than reduced by the auction process.

She emphasized the immediate injection of revenue that would result from the auction. She maintained that the successful bidders would have to meet all existing provincial environmental standards. Finally, she argued that any group developing a resource in the province would have to deal directly with First Nations. The auction would not change the underlying constitutional requirement to consult and accommodate.

Local press reaction to the premier's announcement was relatively restrained. The auction itself was now old news. The premier's recent performance under pressure insulated her to a degree. The national media were less positive. They repeatedly questioned Richardson's judgment and emphasized her lack of government experience. Columnists close to the PMO rehearsed stories about the premier's allegedly chequered past.

Not that the rest of the country noticed, but the French-language press in Quebec was considerably more sympathetic. The idea of maintaining control of natural resource development in the face of federal interference was unexceptional from a Quebec perspective. The personal stories about the premier were more admiring than condemnatory.

❋ ❋ ❋

The next day, James sat in his office in Victoria watching the reaction to the premier's speech roll in. The federal government made its objections clear, a minister at a time. The Finance minister characterized the province's economic policies as naive and ill-informed. The minister of Foreign Affairs harrumphed about the province encouraging foreign disaster relief teams to assist the recovery efforts, calling this approach a gross abdication of Canadian sovereignty. The minister of Environment claimed that the province was giving up on any meaningful commitment to environmental protection. The minister of Aboriginal Affairs expressed sorrow and indignation at the provincial government's evident lack of respect for the rights and title of First Nations.

And after the Quebec government issued an extremely mild statement supporting a sister province's right to manage its own resources, the prime minister answered a planted question in Question Period with a brief but cutting comment on the apparent willingness of the BC premier to sacrifice national unity on the altar of financial expediency.

More troubling and local was the anger of green and First Nations groups. The mainline organizations contented themselves with threats of lawsuits and passive resistance, but anger from splinter groups and individual young people was splattering across social media.

The postings on the main websites were becoming increasingly violent. *#DeathtotheReferendum* trended on Twitter, spinning off a succession of related hashtags devoted to proposals for direct action and lists of potential targets. James noticed with mounting concern that many of the West Coast activists who had been involved in attacks on seniors were gravitating to the online protests against the referendum.

Even before the official start of the referendum campaign after Labour Day, the political temperature in the province was rising fast. James had little to do with logistical preparations for the vote, which were taken care of by Elections BC. He helped a bit with developing materials that the government planned to put out in connection with the referendum, but for the most part he spent August managing routine tasks and visiting Alastair Reid.

* * *

Alastair's recovery was encouraging. He was now out of hospital and rusticating in an up-market care home while waiting for repairs to his apartment to be completed. James dropped by most days for a chat. Alastair's strength was clearly improving, and this made for longer conversations. Unfortunately, it also meant that, as his tolerance for what he regarded as "fuss" rapidly diminished, the patience of his caregivers was sorely tested.

One afternoon over tea, James started to talk about the relationship he had with Anne. He had not planned to raise the subject, and certainly not with the crusty Alastair. He had gone for a run with Anne earlier in the day, however, and his feelings about her were top of mind.

"She's one of the most interesting people I've ever met," he said. "Certainly she's the smartest boss I've had. What's fascinating is to watch her grow. In some ways the quake has set her free. She always had a bit of an academic distance from her political work. I had the sense that she tended to treat the issues I'd bring to her as kind of abstract – a puzzle to be solved. But her work with people after the disaster has grounded her, given her a way to connect more directly. And the folks in the neighbourhoods feel that difference and really respond. It's remarkable to see."

Alastair put down his cup. "We're not talking about Anne's technical capacities here, are we?" he said quietly. James looked uncomfortable. "I admit that working with Anne recently has seemed a little less straightforward – perhaps for both of us, and certainly for me."

"So is this the point at which you finally admit you have

feelings for the premier, and more importantly, do something about that?"

"Actually, Anne knows that I have serious reservations about her referendum idea, but she asked me to stay on until that's done with, and I've said I would. But that conversation wasn't personal, it was professional."

Alastair burst out laughing. "If it makes the two of you feel better to dance around how you both feel about each other, then be my guest." He cut off James' objections: "I should tell you, though that, as an unbiased observer who holds you both in high regard, that's just nonsense. Maybe the middle of a referendum campaign isn't the right time to deal with the fact you love each other, but at some point the elephant in the room will trample you both. Best of luck!"

James forcibly moved the conversation onto less delicate ground but later that evening, as he stroked Einstein's ears, he thought about Alastair's words. If it was true that he was not very good at relationships, the same could be said of Anne. Whether James stayed on with the premier or not, they would eventually have to confront their rekindled emotional attachment. True to form, however, James decided to deal with this later rather than sooner.

CHAPTER 30

August 22, Victoria

Towards the end of August, James received a call from one of his friends who worked in an obscure offshoot of the National Security Agency.

"James," came the familiar gravelly voice, "I assume you're still doing the gig with the cute premier. Is that right?"

James decided not to make an issue of that particular characterization of his employer and replied that he was still on the job.

"Well, the way the international situation has been evolving recently, we've stepped up our monitoring of comm traffic involving home-grown, radical groups in North America. Makes for boring listening, for the most part, but some of the brothers and sisters in your part of the world have been very busy lately. We've noticed that chatter among your local activists has really taken off."

"Given what's been going on here, I'm not surprised," replied James. "Is it just a question of volume?"

"No, if all that was happening was a higher level of the standard paranoia, I wouldn't have bothered you. It's what they're talking about and how they're doing it that caught our attention. People want to stop the referendum in its tracks. And they're getting quite specific. They're exchanging recipes for home-made explosives. They're debating the priority that should be given to attacking the most vulnerable targets. They're transmitting what they claim are floor-plans for public facilities like power stations."

"Where is all this taking place?" asked James. "I assume most of the traffic is not on the usual websites."

"That's right. Almost all of this is on the darknet; most of it is encrypted. These bozos are smart enough to be dangerous. Speaking of which, we've run across a very tight group that's seriously taking a run at hacking BC Hydro's software. If they were ever to succeed, that would present a major problem on our side of the line as well. That power generation system is integrated right down the coast. I've been authorized to tell you that D.C. is now officially concerned. They'll be contacting their Canadian counterparts later today about all this."

James thanked his contact and walked downstairs to see the premier in her office on the ground floor of the West Annex. He wasn't too specific about the source of his information, but he passed on enough to prompt Anne to call together a small group of ministers in the Cabinet Chamber later that afternoon. As it happened, she was receiving similar briefing from the RCMP.

Doing nothing didn't seem like an option. After some discussion, however, the group agreed that publicly drawing attention to the activities (or at least the rhetoric) of fringe groups would only serve to enhance their importance artificially and perhaps broaden their support.

Instead, ministers were detailed to talk quietly with the First Nations leadership and a representative selection of environmental "elders." The hope was that these leaders would reach out to their supporters and try to convince them to remain inside the law. Most of the people approached in this way were as concerned as the government about the radicalization of their movements. They undertook to put out the word but expressed doubt about whether their warning would dissipate the waves of online anger.

* * *

In the opening weeks of the referendum campaign, the range of opposition tactics from the No side broadened. A coalition of First Nations organizations in the province made an expedited appeal to the courts challenging the referendum itself on the grounds that aboriginal rights and title were imperilled. The case failed, and the campaign ground on. First Nations and environmental groups turned to large demonstrations across the province as a means of mobilizing the No forces.

James attended one of these mass rallies, in Prince George. The crowd that day was a mix. It included lots of young, counter-culture people, with a significant sprinkling of native kids. Joining them, though, were many "grown-ups." It was noon on a sunny, brisk weekday. Office workers on their lunch-break and moms with strollers wandered around the square. A local country band warmed up the crowd. People listened good-naturedly to speeches attacking the government. There was little animus and much ribbing of local politicians.

Then, to one side of the square, James became aware of a line of black-masked figures. One or two held signs, but most were content to stand menacingly. People nearby looked at the group with apprehension. The few policemen in the vicinity walked over but, as suddenly as they had appeared, the silent, masked protesters faded away.

James gave little thought to the incident until a few days later, when a similar group attended a rally in Williams Lake. This time, the black-clad protesters did more than stand still. They started throwing eggs and vegetables, most of which, admittedly, landed well short of the stage. In Prince Rupert, the black gang showed up again. This time, they launched what was to become their signature protest – bright, green paint. A government minister was showered with it as he approached the stage.

Green paint became a symbol of the forces battling the resource auction and supporting the No side. Yes-side speakers were regularly hit by green paint balls. Paint-ball guns became the weapon of choice. Across the province, the front doors of government offices were given an emerald coating. Sometimes there was no message left behind, but soon the letters *EDF* started to appear. Then one evening, a small government office in Chase burned to the ground. The slogan *EDF Rules* was left on the side wall in fluorescent green paint.

At this point, the premier's anxiety spiked. Her daughter Katherine was an avowed member of the Environmental Defence Force. That group had been prominent in protests against the resource auction from the beginning. Anne found it hard to believe that her daughter would be directly involved in violence, but she worried nonetheless. She'd seen Katherine briefly in Vancouver after the earthquake, but then the referendum had been announced, and she'd dropped out of sight.

Early in the campaign, the attorney general had come to her with pictures of Katherine and Robert in the crowd at a rowdy demonstration full of EDF placards. At that point, the EDF's activities had been confined to rallies and a very active website, nothing more.

This time, the premier walked into James' small office and shut the door. James dumped some papers off his one chair and waited for her to sit and explain her unusual visit. He couldn't recall another occasion when she had intruded on his cramped space. He caught a glimpse of Georgina's outraged face in the hall as the door swung shut.

"I'm really worried about Katherine. You've seen the reports on the EDF? That fire in Chase? I haven't heard a word from my daughter since we announced the referendum. Have any of your spook friends caught sight of her?

James was at something of a loss to reassure her. He didn't know Katherine very well. His private view, based on fleeting glances as Anne's daughter rushed by to embrace a succession of worthy causes, was that she was an especially headstrong young woman. From time to time, Anne had regaled him with tales of Katherine's obduracy. From clambering up trees to falling off horses, young Richardson seemed to specialize in activities involving risk, especially if her mother happened to be in the vicinity. These stories tended to confirm his relief that he had no children of his own to worry about. Nevertheless, he had no wish to worsen Anne's anxiety.

"Katherine may have strong views, but she strikes me as being a sensible person," said James, deliberately downplaying his actual opinion. "From what you've told me, she's got a clear sense of right and wrong. She's also got the best role model in the world." This part James was convinced of. "She's not going to do anything stupid."

"I'm not so much worried about what she might do. I'm more concerned about the company she's keeping. When you're that age, it's hard to hold back."

"Remember, anyone can splash a bunch of initials across a wall. I'm not convinced that the EDF is actually all that dangerous as a group. The reports I've seen suggest they're dedicated and they're angry, but not violent."

And indeed, after the arson in Chase, the EDF had posted a clear message on its website disavowing any involvement. The post suggested that obvious attempts were being made to discredit the organization and the entire No side.

The premier remained troubled. "I just wish I could hear her voice. Even when she was in college, we'd talk every couple of days or so. It's been weeks."

James tried to calm Anne. "Remember how quickly Katherine got in touch after the earthquake. This has got to be a case of no news is good news. Once the referendum is over, you'll hear from her. Incidentally, I made sure that a press person I know got a message through to Katherine reminding her of my personal cell-phone number as well. Katherine didn't follow up, but I'm fairly sure that the message reached her. She knows she's got lots of people to call if there's a problem."

The premier looked dubious but allowed the conversation to turn to the speeches she was making around the province.

In the days after this conversation, James made sure that he talked to her regularly when she was out of town. It was easy for Anne to become isolated. The premier had almost as few good friends as James did. Being separated from her daughter was making her crazy.

CHAPTER 31

September 14, Kelowna

The premier wasn't the only politician out and about, of course. Two weeks into the campaign, to universal amazement, the prime minister showed up for a No rally in Kelowna. In front of what he assumed was a friendly crowd, Prime Minister Massey categorically refused to accept the outcome of the referendum vote in advance. He called the exercise illegal and provocative. He went on to stress the impracticality of calling an expensive referendum, when most BCers were focused on recovering from the province's worst-ever natural disaster. He attacked the premier's judgment and lack of experience, apparently not noticing that the more personal he became, the quieter the crowd became.

In one last flourish, Massey said with a smile, "Oh well, I guess we shouldn't be surprised that the premier doesn't understand the meaning of 'no.' I gather that in her youth, 'no' was not a word she employed very often." At which point, open booing broke out.

As the PM made his way off the stage, a rain of eggs and vegetables descended on his head. A reporter's microphone picked up his last remarks – "Those fucking crazy BCers!"

Prime Minister Massey did not return to BC prior to the vote. Commentators speculated on how low in single digits his party's seat-count would be in the province at the next federal election. The feds became a non-factor in the referendum.

CHAPTER 32

September, Victoria

A s the weeks passed, James carefully followed the ebb and flow of public opinion. The whole process was decidedly surreal, because it unfolded against a backdrop of massive earthquake-generated destruction, at least down on the coast. Power and water still hadn't been restored to parts of the Lower Mainland. Thousands of people were eking out an existence in a variety of public shelters, encumbered with children and pets, and with few prospects of returning to their homes any time soon. In fact, the clearance of debris was nowhere near finished, and reconstruction on any meaningful scale would take years.

James wondered whether the actual arrival of the "big one" would have any immediate psychological impact. Would the self-confidence of Vancouverites in particular be shaken? Would they simply turn inward and ignore anything unrelated to digging out from the rubble?

Generally, support for the resource auction was lowest in rural constituencies. This reflected a sense that the federal government should retain the authority to override provincial actions and a distrust of the quiche-eaters in Victoria and Vancouver. The coastal, largely urban, vote was going disproportionately to the Yes side, however, apparently seeing the revenue potential from the auction as helpful in the context of major reconstruction efforts. The weight of city votes seemed likely to carry the day.

The youth vote trended towards the No side. Katherine Richardson was at the centre of an extremely effective social media campaign fostering the notion that the auction amounted to selling out the province's future. First Nations were unanimous in their condemnation of the government's approach. Their dignified focus on aboriginal rights carried considerable weight, even with the people committed to voting Yes. The wild card was the occasional act of vandalism or arson. Every week or so, there was an especially violent act on the part of protesters. A paint attack would empty a stage, or a power pole would be bombed. In reaction, the polls would swing around, and the referendum was no longer headed for trouble. After several events-driven swings back and forth, James was hard-pressed to judge what the outcome would be on the day. One thing was certain. The longer the campaign went on, the higher the tension in the province became and the greater the impression that events were spiralling out of control.

* * *

The one form of respite James had during the campaign was visiting Alastair. After the frightening week during which Alastair seemed close to death, the little man had rallied strongly. Any time James could spare from his job and, later, the campaign, he spent at Alastair's side. Within days, the two friends were talking politics again.

"I just want to make sure that I understand the full brilliance of the strategy that you and the premier have cooked up," Alastair said one morning in September after his breakfast had been cleared away. He was feeling much perkier now that he had moved back into his fine old apartment with its marvellous view.

"First, more or less out of thin air, you devise a radical plan to divest the government of most of its ability to manage the economy. Then, you send the premier to Ottawa so she can be publicly humiliated, thereby cleverly generating sympathy from BC voters. Then, you organize a major earthquake so that the premier's standing will be heightened even more, albeit at the expense of most of the housing stock on the Lower Mainland. And finally, you decide to give the by-now-totally-entranced, if under-housed, electorate the opportunity to give the premier what amounts to a blank cheque in the event that she feels moved to lead BC out of the federation. Does that about sum it up?"

"This must mean you're feeling better, is that right?" replied James. "I take it you believe that our current situation doesn't reflect all that well on the government – or me, for that matter?"

"No, not really," said Alastair. "Over the years, I've come to believe that dull government is bad government. So, with entertainment value as the main criterion, your premier's performance is right up there with the greats of BC politics like Bill Vander Zalm. Certainly, she follows in the grand tradition of instability established by your Finance minister's ancestor, Amor de Cosmos."

James couldn't summon up a pithy reply. He contented himself with handing Alastair a sippy-cup of water. As he gave it back, Alastair asked, "Have you heard anything about Willem de Groote lately?"

When James said he had not, Alastair looked grave and gave him some background.

De Groote was a member of a Dutch family that came to the Lower Fraser Valley as part of a major immigration in the early 1950s. They were fleeing a country devastated by war and offering few opportunities for young, ambitious farmers. After several years working on nearby spreads, his mother and father bought their own farm close to Chilliwack. They sent their five children to local church-run schools. They attended the Abbotsford Christian Reform Church. Work never ended on a dairy farm, and the children all participated as they grew older.

The eldest son, Willem expected that he would eventually inherit the herd and the land. As a sideline, in his twenties he started to help his siblings and other members of the Dutch community to find properties elsewhere in the Valley. By the time he was thirty-five, his flourishing realty company was out-earning the farm. Population pressure from the neighbouring big city of Vancouver intensified, and the value of land in the Valley increased, even with the restrictions imposed by the Agricultural Land Reserve.

With the home farm run day-to-day by his younger brother, and the realty interests in the hands of a competent manager, Willem found himself at the age of forty with more money than he could use and spare time on his hands. Local politics seemed like a natural option. After several terms as a local councillor, election as an MLA followed easily. His steady work in opposition over the years made him a logical front-runner when the party leadership became available.

De Groote's home-life was less settled. According to custom, in his mid-twenties he married a local girl, Anneke Bakker. As de Groote progressively immersed himself in politics, Anneke became increasingly unhappy. Finally, after one photo-op and one missed meal too many, she left home, taking their young son Mikki with her. De Groote was incensed at what he viewed as a betrayal and spent the next decade pursuing Anneke through the courts. Eventually, he acquiesced grudgingly to minimal child support and settled down to a life entirely devoted to pursuing his own inclinations. Rumour had it that those included leather and restraints.

"So you see," Alastair concluded, "this is a methodical, determined fellow. I assume he feels that your friend became premier through sheer luck, and I have no doubt that he's waiting quietly for the opportunity to take over. If you haven't been already, you should keep an eye on him. In addition to being stubborn, de Groote is ruthless."

James thanked him for the warning, and made a mental note to touch base with Anne about her colleague. He had always felt a bit uncomfortable around the bulky dairy farmer. The conversation moved on to political gossip of a less ominous kind. The one piece of information James did not share, though, was his run-in with the Destiny Foundation. Alastair wasn't ready for that revelation. And James felt sick at the thought of trying to explain his own reaction to JJ's threats. He could imagine all too clearly Alastair's contempt for his behaviour.

CHAPTER 33

October, Victoria

By the time E-day arrived in October, people just wanted the process over with, no one more than James himself. His initial doubts about the advisability of going this route had been confirmed. The province was badly split. Even if the premier won, it seemed unlikely that she would receive a clear-cut mandate. The level of bitterness, especially among young people, was escalating. Pro- and anti- meetings were becoming tenser, with skirmishing around the edges more common. The tone of the campaign rhetoric was getting harsher.

On top of which, just getting to the polls was going to be difficult, given the damage on the Coast to local roads. There, not all bus routes were back in service and many roads remained blocked. Elections BC had to work hard even to find usable sites for the ballot boxes.

James had spent a good deal of time maintaining links with the potential resource auction bidders, trying to calm them down. He would provide encouraging snippets of information designed to demonstrate that the province remained a stable place to invest. He also had a couple of conversations with Albert Dupuis, who politely refrained from reminding James about his warnings over dinner.

Matt Russell was a regular caller. He was in a state of

accelerating distress. "Do you and the premier realize what you've done?" he demanded towards the end of the campaign. "I hardly recognize the people of this province any more. You've managed to turn law-abiding citizens into a mob."

The main reason for Matt's reaction sat rocking in front of the television set, anguished by the scenes of violence on the news every night. Matt's elderly mother shrank back into herself as events unfolded, recognizing the power of the anger and resentment sweeping her home. Her son knew that she was convinced it was only a matter of time before they came for her again. Matt could do nothing to console her.

Two days before the vote, the courthouse in New Westminster was torched. The building was destroyed. Two people lay incinerated in the wreckage. James knew from his police contacts that the arson had been a professional job. Not for the first time, he wondered where the radical wing of the No campaign was getting its funds and logistical support.

The deaths in New Westminster had a major impact. It was as if the entire province caught its breath, stunned at the degree to which politics seemed to be drifting over the edge to disorder. The growing level of anger on social media was palpable, as was a sense of dread. Events seemed to have careened out of control.

It was too late for James' pollsters to get into the field, but his feeling was that with this one last act, the government's opponents had ensured a Yes win.

CHAPTER 34

October 3, Victoria

B ack in his float-home in Victoria, James settled in, glass in hand, cat in his lap, to watch the returns. The premier was in Vancouver. She planned to attend what she assumed would be a major victory rally. James hoped she would not have to use the short, dignified recognition of the electorate's will that he had drafted for her use in the event that the referendum lost.

Within half an hour of the coverage, it was clear that the premier could dispense with that speech. The numbers were definitive, if not overwhelming. Yes – 56.7%; No – 43.3%. The regional breakdown, with its strong urban bias in favour, was a little worrying, but there was no gainsaying the outcome. The premier's latest gamble had paid off.

The talking heads droned on about the meaning of the referendum result. They noted some downsides for the government, but generally gave the premier credit for iron nerve and a stubborn willingness to engage the voting public. They pointed out that an earlier extensive consultation process that the government had launched around the province had been a fiasco. They agreed, however, that her victory in this vote amounted to a re-boot for her administration. The cameras cut away to a simple podium with a set of microphones.

James and the premier had had a brief but spirited

discussion about the backdrop for this occasion. James had wanted a bit of ceremony. She had insisted that people didn't want to see stage management; they wanted to hear a brief comment from her and then see a return to normalcy.

True to her word, she'd ensured that the stage was plain in the extreme when she came forward to speak to the crowd in the room and the province as a whole about the outcome of the vote. She emerged simply dressed, but in a bright red, well-cut suit. No fancy backdrop was needed. The premier provided all the glitter that was necessary. Her smile was restrained, nonetheless, and she quieted the crowd after only a few moments of cheering.

"After the past several weeks," the premier began, "I am sure that the last thing most of you want is yet another political speech. So I won't give you one. I simply want to take this opportunity to say how proud I am that the people of the province have made a clear decision for our future in such difficult conditions." The crowd broke into applause.

The premier barely waited for the clapping to subside. "I know that it has been only a few years since I was given a mandate to move the province forward. I also recognize that just recently we have faced together the earthquake and tsunami that have ravaged much of the coast. Since that disaster, I have travelled around talking to the brave people who are quite literally re-building the province from the ground up. They refuse to be cast down by personal tragedies and remain determined to work together to reconstruct their houses, their neighbourhoods, their towns and their lives." Applause built in support.

"It was while I was meeting these inspiring BCers that I realized how important it was for us to unite around a common goal – building a new British Columbia. I also realized that we needed to re-confirm our commitment to managing our resources so that we could generate the significant flow of revenue needed to allow us reach our objectives in a reasonable period of time."

The premier paused as if considering what to say next. James admired her skillful, almost invisible, use of the teleprompter.

"As most of you know," she went on, "we have not found it easy to gain cooperation from our friends in Ottawa for this task we have set ourselves. This was the fundamental reason that we called for a referendum, the outcome of which would make it crystal clear that we British Columbians stand together. I believe that the results tonight confirm that we are a resolute province and that we will stand for no outside interference as we move forward." Applause filled the room.

"For that support from the voters of BC, I am both humbled and grateful," she added, prompting another ovation.

"Before I close," she said after waiting for quiet, "I want to take a moment to address those beyond our borders who may be puzzled or perhaps concerned by the outcome of this vote. I want them all to know, even the federal officials and politicians who have seen fit to challenge our plans, that we bear no grudges, and we have no desire to leave the country that we all call home.

"We are clear about our objectives, however, and we look forward to working with all Canadians to achieve a more prosperous British Columbia, a more humane British Columbia, a British Columbia that is sustainable in every sense of the word. Thank you, and good night."

The room erupted, and the premier moved towards the steps at the side of the stage, waving as she went. She started down the stairs. The cameras followed her as she embraced supporters.

Suddenly, there was a flash and a roar. The camera was momentarily jerked away and then tried to re-focus, but everything was engulfed in smoke. Shouts and screams drowned out the attempts of shocked commentators to describe the scene.

James leapt out of his chair, scattering Einstein. He searched the screen desperately for some sign of Anne. All he could see was a mass of bodies on the floor amid a welter of blood and a wreckage of torn banners and shattered chairs.

Grabbing his jacket and his phone, he ran from the room. He had no idea what had happened to Anne, but he was determined to find out for himself.

V. NEW REGIME

CHAPTER 35

October 3, Vancouver

J ames sat fuming in the cab heading for Vancouver General Hospital. He had only barely made the last airport-to-airport flight to Vancouver. The lounge had been full of people, often total strangers, talking in shocked terms about the assassination attempt. For himself, he was still having a hard time believing what he had seen on television. It was one thing for some idiots to burn empty buildings down, but bombs? And where was RCMP security?

James had not been party to the regular security up-dates the premier received, but he doubted that this attack came with no forewarning at all. His experience with other candidates or government leaders was that there was a steady stream of threats into their offices, all of which had to be checked and some of which turned out to be more than drunken ravings. James assumed that the Department of the Attorney General and the Police Services Branch were running hard to catch up, but that was hardly enough.

James fought his way through the various police officers patrolling the hospital halls and finally reached the premier's room. Outside he found Georgina, shaken in a way he'd not seen before. He put his arms around her and held on, as she began to sob. He desperately wanted to know how Anne was, but Georgina was unreachable for the moment.

"Oh, James," she said brokenly, "it was so horrible. I was waiting outside the hall to take her back to the office. There was a huge explosion. It blew the doors right off and flattened me. By the time I could stand up again and look into the meeting room, it was full of smoke and flames. There was nothing I could do. She was lying under a pile of bodies. There was blood everywhere. Everyone was shouting and screaming."

She shook and wept as James stroked her hair. "Georgina, there's nothing you *could* have done. Are you sure you weren't hit or injured yourself?"

"No, I'm fine. I just can't get the screaming and the smell out of my head. I thought I'd seen it all with the earthquake, but this was so much worse."

"We'll get through it," he replied. He took her gently by the shoulders and tried to get her to focus. "Have you heard how Anne is? What are the doctors saying?"

Georgina pulled herself together and wiped her eyes. "There's been a bunch of people in and out of her room. They haven't said a word to me. The attorney's in there with her at the moment. Perhaps she knows something."

Letting a somewhat embarrassed Georgina go, James turned towards the premier's room, just as Indira Dhaliwal emerged, wearing her sadness like an elegant shawl.

James grabbed the minister's arm. "What's happening? What are they doing for her?"

"Hello, James, the premier will be glad you're here. She's unconscious right now, and they'll be taking her into theatre shortly. They need to alleviate the pressure on her brain." Dhaliwal reached out to touch his arm. "They're doing all they can. They tell me that most of her wounds are superficial. It's the brain injury they're worried about. They'll be attending to that shortly. Do you have a number where we can reach her daughter? She should be told what's going on."

"I'd be amazed if Katherine hadn't heard what happened," replied James. "It's all over the media. In fact, I'm surprised that I haven't had a call from her already. She has my number, as well as her mother's, of course. Has Anne been unconscious the whole time?"

"No, she woke up on the way to the hospital. She's been in and out ever since. Look, I have to talk to my staff about all this. You'll be staying, won't you?"

"Absolutely. You go off to do what you have to. Perhaps you could work with Georgina to manage the press."

Georgina looked relieved to have been given a specific task and walked away down the corridor with the attorney general.

In the hospital room, James saw Anne in the bed, a nurse fiddling with her IV. Anne's eyes fluttered open. He sat down beside her and reached out for her hand. Anne tried to concentrate, smiling weakly when she saw James sitting there. She spoke haltingly through parched lips.

"You're looking a bit shocky, James. I wish the room would stop moving around. Who else was hurt?"

"I just got here. I don't know much, but I'll find out. You should just take it easy. Would you like a sip of water?"

Anne nodded, and James helped her wet her lips. She swallowed, paused and then grabbed James's hand again.

"Listen, I think they're going to send me for tests or something, and I want to tell you something first. Something I should probably have told you a long time ago." She swallowed again, and went on, fighting her way through dizziness and pain. "You left New Haven in a hurry back in grad school. We didn't have much of a chance to say goodbye."

"I've always felt badly about that. I was in a situation where I had to disappear. I was told I couldn't let anyone know where I was going. I'm really sorry." James had no idea where this was leading.

"I'm not telling you this to get an apology out of you. You did what you had to do. The one thing you didn't know, though, was that . . . I was pregnant."

James stared at her. He struggled to make sense of what she was saying. *Katherine?* "Why on earth didn't you tell me before now? I mean, I would have helped if I had known."

Anne shook her head slightly. "I doubt that you could have done much. After all, you were off saving the western world. At least, that's what I assumed." Her eyes narrowed. "I was really angry, but I was damned if I was going to whine to you. I was perfectly capable of taking care of myself – and Katherine."

Anne visibly tried to gather her strength. "After a while, Katherine and I had a good life together. There didn't seem to be any reason to disrupt it. When we met again last year, re-opening old wounds made no sense at all. But now, if anything happens to me, I need to know that you'll take care of things. She's a big girl now, but it never does any harm to have some-one looking out for you." Anne's head sank back into the pil-low. She could barely keep her eyes open.

James sat back, stunned. He had never once suspected that he was Katherine's father. Katherine was just his boss's slightly annoying daughter. He had paid more attention to her activities during the referendum campaign only because of her involvement with the environmental protest move-ment. But even after the earthquake, he had not seen much of her. When they met, Katherine regarded him with amused tolerance. From her perspective, he was a middle-aged guy her mother used to know – probably too well. He was a gov-ernment drone of little interest to her, except insofar as he seemed to give her mother questionable advice. James had not made any effort to get any closer to her.

He could tell that Anne was slipping away again. He squeezed her hand hard. "Don't even think about it. You'll be fine in a week or two, and you can take care of Katherine your-self. In the meantime, I'll keep an eye out. I'll make sure she knows where you are."

Anne gave James one last grateful look and then closed her eyes. Medical staff bustled into the room, and James found himself shunted aside, as the team rolled her away towards the operating room. He was left staring at the space Anne had just vacated. Suddenly he had a reason to concern himself with someone other than himself. He wasn't sure he liked the novel sensation. He *was* sure he wasn't about to tell Katherine that he was her father. He did not think that would be well received. Up to now, Katherine had hardly noticed his presence. When she had, she seemed unimpressed. So, no weepy father–daughter reunion, then.

But he couldn't help thinking about the young woman who he now knew to be his daughter. Katherine was lovely, energetic, smart and determined. She had many of Anne's most estimable traits. James was hard-pressed to find bits of him in her make-up. It felt odd to even be trying to discern his personality in someone else.

He traced back what he knew of Katherine's background. From a successful school career through the blossoming of environmental activism, the brief survey confirmed that a man could be proud of having her as a daughter. He brought himself up short. He had had absolutely nothing to do with her upbringing. He was in no position to take any credit for this vibrant, interesting girl.

What he needed to do now was stop this pointless daydreaming and do something practical to fulfil his promise to Anne. He needed to find Katherine and let her know what was going on. As he stepped out into the corridor, his cell-phone buzzed. Katherine was on the line, anxious and upset.

"James, I just saw the TV news. What the hell is happening? How is Mom?"

James knew he should try to sound reassuring, but he struggled to find the words. And the thought came to him: *This is my daughter I'm talking to!* "I'm outside her hospital room. We're at the General. Your mom is pretty banged up, but they're working on her. Where are you? Can you get to Vancouver soon?"

"I'm calling from Whistler. We've been in the Interior," she added vaguely. "Can you help me get down there in a hurry?"

"I'll call Helijet and see if they can get you on the next flight in. What's your cell number?"

There was a short silence. Then Katherine said, "I'm calling on a land-line. I'll call you back in half an hour to check about the flight. Are you sure Mom's okay?"

After he had been as comforting as he could be, he rang off, wondering why Katherine had been so unwilling to give him her number.

* * *

Katherine arrived in the late afternoon, by which time Anne was back in her room resting after successful surgery. James was sitting by the bed, Anne sleeping, when Katherine walked in. James motioned Katherine out into the hall.

Once they were out of Anne's earshot, he said, "I glad you're here. I told your mom you were on your way. The surgery went fine. According to the doctors, what she really needs now is bed-rest."

Katherine looked tired and edgy. She thanked James tersely for staying with her mother and went back in. A moment or two later, James could hear Anne wake up. He walked away, comfortable that the premier was in good hands. With Anne likely on the mend, he felt a real need to get plugged back into the government. He also wanted to stop thinking for a moment about what his new parental responsibilities might be. Somehow, Katherine looked different now that he knew who she was.

CHAPTER 36

October 3, Vancouver

S tanding in the chilly, wind-swept entrance to the hospital, he first called Georgina.

"To begin with," he said, "you should know that the premier's out of surgery. She seems to be out of danger. It will take some time, and you can never tell with head injuries but, by all accounts, she'll be fine. What else is going on? I've been completely out of touch all day."

A relieved Georgina started a debrief.

"We knew you were with the premier, so I told everyone to back off until we knew how she was. Cabinet met a few hours ago. I gather there was a bit of a fight over what to do. It looked as though the premier would be out of the line for a while, but there was no firm information. Some ministers were apparently keen to wait for as long as it took to find out the premier's condition before doing anything. Others, led by de Groote incidentally, insisted that the work of the government had to go on. They claimed that it was imperative to select an interim leader as soon as possible.

"De Groote got his way and, after running the decision through caucus, ended up appointed interim premier. I'm told that there was no formal vote. He was seen by everyone as the logical person to take on the job. So, we now have a new premier, and I'm not sure where that leaves you – or me, for that matter."

"Well, if there's one person who doesn't have to worry about being unemployed, it's you. If people thought you were available, you'd be snapped up."

"I'm not at all sure that I want to be snapped up by anyone," Georgina responded crisply. "It's been hard enough to train you over the past few months. I have no desire to start again anytime soon."

James refused to rise to the bait. "It's probably a bit early for either of us to start re-touching the c.v. Whatever happens, happens. We've got more pressing things to worry about. Which reminds me, have you heard how many people were injured or killed? The hospital officials wouldn't tell me and, the last I saw, three people had been confirmed dead and lots of people injured. Do we know anything more?"

Georgina's professional manner slipped a bit as she passed on the latest information on casualties. A campaign worker and two members of the public had been killed outright. As many as a dozen others, most of them supporters there to celebrate the referendum victory, had various sorts of injuries. Some of these were quite seriously wounded, but no one else was expected to die. No senior officials or ministers had been hurt. Apparently, they had stayed back on the stage, as the premier made her way down through the enthusiastic crowd.

The TV news reported that the bomb had been planted under steps leading off the stage. Footage showed it exploding just after the premier reached the bottom. The police were refusing to say anything specific at this early stage in the investigation. There were no reports that any organization had taken credit for the action.

Georgina continued. "My friends in the Cabinet Office over here told me that most of the ministers were really shaken up, especially those who were at the rally. One thing I did hear was that Minister de Groote – Premier de Groote, I guess we have to call him now – was pretty calm about it.

He wasn't even at the rally. He was in his constituency office in the Valley. He's due to speak on TV this evening. I never thought I'd see the day that man actually sat in the big chair." Georgina stopped abruptly, seemingly shocked that such a personal reflection on a cabinet minister had popped out. She was normally discreet to a fault.

"Old Willem certainly has an instinct for self-preservation," observed James. "He's probably right, though, about filling the leadership vacuum. Somebody has to be in charge right now."

"Well," replied Georgina, "he reportedly looked quite unperturbed considering that a significant number of his cabinet colleagues just missed being blown up. You know, one of my friends said that, right after the meeting that made him premier, he locked himself in the office for half an hour or so, with strict orders – no one in or out, and no calls. Then one of the ministers walked in on him and almost got his head bitten off. De Groote was as angry as anybody has ever seen him. The minister bailed pretty quickly. Just as the door was closing, my friend swears that she heard de Groote say something like, "Relax, Jay, leave Franklin to me." She knew we worked together and thought I'd like to know.

"What do you make of it?" asked Georgina. "Who's Jay, and what's he or she got to do with you?"

James froze. Jay? Could Georgina's contact have misheard? Was de Groote talking to *JJ*? The possibility that someone else in the BC government had some connection with the Destiny Foundation had never occurred to him. Nor had he expected ever to be of direct concern to Willem de Groote. They had been in meetings together, of course, but James couldn't recall an extended conversation between just the two of them.

James's advice had been given directly to the premier. His involvement in cabinet meetings had been limited to occasional summaries of survey data. He knew that de Groote had been around for a long time and had a considerable network across government. Alastair had given him a bit of background and warned him about the man's ambition. James hadn't supposed that de Groote cared much about *him*, though, one way or the other.

Georgina waited quietly for him to respond.

"I haven't the slightest idea," he finally managed. I've never heard of a 'Jay,' and anyway, maybe your friend misheard my name. It could have been anyone. De Groote and I are hardly good pals."

Georgina was clearly unconvinced. "Whatever you say, boss. I was just curious. Anything else I can do for you?"

James was about to reply when he was tapped on the shoulder by a person who could only be a plain-clothed policeman. "Sorry, Georgina, gotta go. I'll call you later. Thanks for the information."

He rang off, turning to face the large, impassive individual who had interrupted the call. Soon afterwards, James found himself in the small featureless hospital room that the police had taken over as their temporary command centre.

The interview began in a routine way, with a Sergeant Hoskins asking the questions. He arrayed his notepad, cellphone and pencils precisely in front of him. His strong, stubby fingers fluttered fussily over the tools of his trade. In addition to being tall, husky and very pale, Hoskins managed to give the impression that whatever James said was unlikely to be believed.

"Where were you at the time of the bombing, Mr. Franklin?"

"I was at home, alone, on a houseboat in Victoria Harbour. I'm sure the Air Canada people would be happy to confirm that I flew over to Vancouver immediately after the explosion. What are the latest casualty figures?"

"I'm not in a position to share information from an ongoing investigation, Mr. Franklin."

James became testy. "I want to be in a position to let Premier Richardson know how things stand. If you can't give me any useful information, who can?"

Hoskins referred James to the VPD public affairs office. He then asked, "Mr, Franklin, have you ever heard of or met an individual named Charles Forrester?"

James thought for a moment and said no.

Hoskins asked whether James had ever gone to a bar in New Westminster called the Fisherman's Rest.

James replied that he had only been in New Westminster once or twice with the premier and could not recall a bar of that name.

"Was one of those occasions in the days before the recent referendum?" Hoskins enquired.

"It might have been," said James. He had no idea where this was heading, but he assumed it was bad news for him. He felt increasingly nervous and hated himself for it.

"Would it surprise you to know that we have a credit card receipt with your name on it from the Fisherman's Rest? The date of that receipt was shortly before a major fire in New Westminster claimed the lives of two government employees," Hoskins went on.

"It's entirely possible that at some point during the premier's visit to New Westminster we stopped for a bite to eat at a restaurant or bar. I can't say that I recall the name if we did. And anyway, are you seriously suggesting that I had something to do with that terrible fire?" James heard his voice rising. He knew that getting angry was a bad idea, but he found the deadpan interrogation annoying and irrelevant. He was anxious to get back to Anne's bed-side. This large detective was wasting his time.

Hoskins looked steadily across at James. "We're just doing our job, Mr. Franklin. We need to put together a picture of the circumstances that led up to the bombing, that's all. Anything you can do to help us in that regard would be most appreciated."

"So you think there's a connection between the fire in New Westminster and the bombing? And you think I'm involved? Given my job, isn't that a bit far-fetched?"

Hoskins tidied up the papers in front of him and stood up. "We're not ruling anything out at this stage, Mr. Franklin. We're just going where the evidence takes us. Thank you for your cooperation. I have no doubt that we'll be in touch again."

And with that, James was ushered out of the room.

CHAPTER 37

October 3, Vancouver

James' first port of call after this disquieting interview was the premier's hospital room. Katherine was there, holding her sleeping mother's hand. James stared at this new person in his life. Not wanting to wake Anne, and uncertain whether he could behave sensibly around her daughter, James contented himself with waving to Katherine and going over to the nursing station for an update. The nurse asked if he was a family member. When told he was on the premier's staff, she smiled and refused to say a thing. Faced for the second time in an hour with apparent official indifference, he stamped off down the hall.

By the time he reached his rental car outside, James was calmer and sadder. He knew perfectly well that the police were following procedure – as was the nurse, for that matter. Still, he felt useless and out of sorts. On the plus side, now that Anne seemed to be out of immediate danger, he was not as panicked as he had been immediately after the explosion.

The issue of his sudden paternity was another matter. Over the years he had not missed the experience of fatherhood. He had not even noticed much loss over the lack of a family life in general. After his mother died while he was away at college, he had felt sadness. He had hated sorting out the practicalities surrounding her death. Though he kept expecting a wave of grief to overwhelm him at some point, it had never come. Occasionally he would wonder, was he abnormal, a kind of emotional cripple? Then life would go on, and he would realize that he hadn't thought about his mother for weeks.

As for romantic attachments, James acknowledged that that aspect of his life had generally been a wasteland. He had been happy to sacrifice meaningful connections to the demands of his work. He might suffer from occasional loneliness as a result, but he knew he had no one but himself to blame for that condition.

So far as he could tell, Katherine didn't much like him. There was certainly no mysterious bond between the two of them. He couldn't see any physical resemblance. Now that Anne was apparently healing, he supposed that her revelation no longer mattered as much. He might have taken responsibility if Anne had died but, under the circumstances, he felt no special obligation—beyond avoiding the sort of self-indulgent confession that would end badly, and needlessly complicate all three of their lives.

Still, despite this self-serving analysis, James couldn't help feeling that it would be difficult to pretend that Anne's request had never happened. For better or worse, because he cared for Anne, he had come to care for Katherine. The prospect left him uncomfortable and disoriented. In addition, he and Anne seemed to have reached a new stage in their own relationship. He knew that neither of them felt the need for the usual trappings of coupledom, but lately they had moved to an unaccustomed level of intimacy. He was surprised at how much he welcomed the closeness. Even more surprised that he felt he would have to work to deserve it.

More broadly, the whole situation the government found itself in, and the role he had played in generating it, gave him pause. Once he had extricated himself from the Mexican debacle early in his career, he had been confident that he had avoided serious ethical dilemmas. In fact, he had made a point of doing so. The politicians he had worked for were generally admirable. The few who had not been had conveniently managed to avoid being elected.

At the same time, he relished the fact that he worked in the shadows. He had no desire to be exposed. He revelled in the acquisition and dispensation of hidden knowledge, of arcane lore, which few others appreciated but that moved events in ways outsiders could not hope to understand.

Here in British Columbia, however, he had helped set off a chain of events that was running out of control. Anne's motives might be pure, but her policy choices were triggering instability and violence. She seemed to have a boundless faith in the common sense of the electorate. She was committed, to a degree that James thought juvenile, to giving her constituents every opportunity to shape government decisions directly.

The upshot so far was a divided citizenry, heightened social tension, occasional death and injury, and precious little good public policy. James recalled a line from Vikram Seth's *A Suitable Boy*, an over-long, over-worthy book: "God save us from people who mean well."

Freighted with a collection of gloomy thoughts, James turned to one area where he knew he could act – investigating the possible role of de Groote in all this. Sitting in his car, he dialled the number of his NSA contact and began to describe de Groote and the recent sequence of events. He asked for any information his friend might have about the interim premier's less well-known activities. In particular, he wanted to know what connections de Groote might have with the Destiny Foundation.

* * *

The next day James was back in Victoria when the phone rang. After a short conversation, he stood up and booted his wastebasket across the office. His suspicions had been confirmed.

De Groote and JJ had known each other for years. The foundation's tentacles reached deeper into the government than he had ever imagined.

To a disturbingly long catalogue of new emotions, James was now able to add two more – guilt over his association with the foundation, an organization that had come close to taking Anne's life, and a desire for revenge so strong he could taste it.

CHAPTER 38

October 20, Chilliwack

The object of James' anger had wanted to be premier of British Columbia for some time – the dairy farmer from the Fraser Valley was patient and determined. Willem de Groote could never be accused of eloquence, but he was a serviceable speaker who was at his best in small groups. This was a setting where his sincerity shone through.

He was happy to talk for hours to a succession of his rural constituents, his powerful arms crossed over his barrel chest as he leaned back against the nearest wall. The secret of his popularity was a willingness to listen. He never seemed to be in a hurry. His commitment to giving everyone their say was the bane of his handlers. Somehow, de Groote could never make it to meetings on time. His tardiness had not detracted from his popularity, however, especially outside the main media markets.

His defeat for the party leadership by the upstart Anne Richardson rankled, but he was reasonably certain that the inexperienced new premier would engineer her own destruction. In the meantime, he continued building his credit within the party and acted in all things as a loyal lieutenant.

Then came the bombing,

With Richardson in hospital for an indefinite period of time, the party naturally turned to him as a safe pair of hands.

De Groote was gratified by this turn of events but, deep down, saw his ascension as an inevitable development. In a chaotic world, it was only right that the role of the godly would become more important.

In his first days in office, de Groote found the situation around the province to be even worse than he had thought. Despite the clear outcome of the referendum, the government's opponents were still active. Try as they might, local police forces could not damp down the recurrent civil disobedience, whether in the form of demonstrations or destruction of property. People seemed to have gotten into the habit of breaking the law, generally with impunity.

The federal government remained reluctant to commit significant numbers of troops to assist. The feds were no more effective dealing with the breakdown in public order than they were in providing meaningful assistance after the earthquake. With separatist pressures rising again in Quebec, federal attention was distracted from British Columbia. Ironically, the obvious federal unwillingness to move decisively to deal with unrest in BC simply gave the PQ a wonderful example of the incapacity of the central government to act credibly. When, two weeks later, the PQ government decided to announce the third Quebec independence referendum as a response to the demonstrable incompetence of the feds, Ottawa entered panic mode. British Columbia virtually disappeared as an item on the national agenda.

De Groote was baffled by the federal stupidity. He had spoken several times with Prime Minister Massey but to little effect. The conversations had been short. Each time, de Groote was left literally pounding his desk in frustration. The supercilious Massey obviously regarded the situation in BC as a sideshow precipitated by an incompetent government. He made clear his unwillingness to help the BC government extricate itself from a box of its own making. He would continue to send relief supplies and a limited amount of re-construction funding, but re-establishing law and order was a provincial responsibility. Once the news of the Quebec referendum broke, Massey would not even return de Groote's calls.

De Groote came to the conclusion that the people of BC had effectively been abandoned. He was also very aware that the level of violence around the province was increasing. The bombing that had injured Richardson was followed by a pause in protest activity but, within a week or two, the rhythm of arson and attacks on property picked up again.

De Groote's background included many links with the United States. The church he attended had received considerable assistance from a headquarters in Grand Rapids, Michigan. Co-religionists from Washington State had helped materially in the early 1950s, when the Dutch community was getting established in the Fraser Valley. In addition, since becoming an MLA, de Groote had met many times with American legislators from the Pacific Northwest region. Usually these discussions revolved around the routine practicalities of managing the common border and rivers such as the Nooksack that crossed it. Late at night over a drink, however, the talk turned to what the two countries had in common.

In the course of these meetings, it became clear to de Groote that in many ways he was at least as comfortable with his US counterparts as he was with his colleagues in the BC legislature. For one thing, the Americans obviously shared with him a worldview that assumed religious conviction was not only central to a man's private life but should be acted upon in his day-to-day career. He recognized that this sort of attitude would occasion eye-rolling from his more secular Canadian political allies so, at home, he generally kept his religious views under wraps. In the US, however, he felt no such compunction about speaking his mind.

After one particularly intense episode of late-night sharing at a trans-border legislators' group meeting, he had been approached from what to him was an unlikely quarter. De Groote was sitting quietly at breakfast, when a man dressed in western-casual garb limped up to his table and politely asked if he could sit down.

"Good morning, Mr. de Groote. My name is Jonathan Johnson – JJ to my friends. I was hoping I might have a quick word with you."

JJ settled into a chair and shuffled his cowboy-boot-clad feet. "I feel a bit awkward about intruding on your meal, but I just had to say that I've been very impressed with your contribution to the meetings here. And you should know that I'm not the only one."

De Groote was puzzled to hear about his newfound standing because, although he had participated in the meetings, he had not thought that he had played all that prominent a role. Truth be told, he was a bit suspicious about this man's approach and his soft southern drawl.

After a few minutes' chatting, however, he relaxed and started to enjoy JJ's pungent comments on the others at the meeting. There was a reassuring directness about the man's speech, the amusing anecdotes he recounted. JJ seemed to have a boundless network of contacts, each one with a set of personal idiosyncrasies that he was happy to describe.

De Groote had a morning appointment, but they agreed to meet for dinner later. When they did, over large steaks, JJ explained his involvement with the Destiny Foundation. He placed the organization in the broader sweep of North American history. He emphasized the importance that he and his foundation placed on the defence of the traditional values that had made the successful settlement of the continent possible. He was careful to acknowledge the differing experiences of Canada and the United States, but he pointed to the many commonalities he saw in their histories.

De Groote recounted his own experience as the offspring of recent immigrants and found himself sharing his frustration at the climate of cynicism and secularism that permeated the province's political culture. After dinner, JJ suggested that they remain in touch. De Groote left feeling that he had met a man he respected.

In the following years, de Groote and JJ met periodically, usually at trans-border regional legislators' meetings but once at the foundation's San Antonio offices. De Groote came to understand that JJ's network extended well into official Washington, D.C., as well as to the Pacific Northwest. Once or twice, JJ was able to sort out a problem that one of de Groote's constituents had run into and, after a while, the relationship seemed increasingly natural. De Groote had been flattered to receive a degree of financial support from the foundation when he made his run for the party leadership. JJ was on hand to commiserate when that attempt had fallen short.

When Premier Richardson had first floated the resource auction approach, de Groote touched base with JJ to get his take on the idea. He knew that the foundation might have problems with the extent to which the provincial government would be intruding in business affairs, but he was interested to discover that JJ had no objections to the auction itself as long as an American consortium were given a fair opportunity to win it. On that basis, somewhat to Richardson's surprise, de Groote was happy to throw his weight behind her.

When de Groote became premier, he received fulsome congratulations from San Antonio. And when the extent of civil disobedience across the province became evident, he had a brief conversation with JJ to see if he had any advice. The upshot was the Premier's Office making an appointment to see the US consul general in Vancouver.

CHAPTER 39

October 21, Vancouver

T he consul general was hardly a stranger. In the three years or so since he had been posted to Vancouver, Michael Jones had made a point of getting to know Willem de Groote.

Jones had been a soldier before he joined the State Department. As he advanced through the diplomatic ranks, he kept in touch with a man who had made a major impact on him as a young Special Forces officer, Jonathan Johnson. To Jones, JJ was the epitome of the gentleman soldier, committed to his country, concerned about the men under him, and possessed of a broad vision of America's place in history. Jones was appalled when JJ's career stalled and he left the military. When Jones himself moved on, he had no qualms about keeping Johnson informed on doings within State. Wherever Jones served, the Destiny Foundation was routinely copied on most of the reports he sent in to D.C.

Once established in his modest Vancouver office, Jones had followed up on a hint given him by JJ and quickly determined that de Groote was a major political player in the province. He was as startled as most other observers when Anne Richardson emerged successfully from the shadows to win the party leadership. Jones made a point of calling to sympathize with de Groote and to urge him not to give up in the longer term. As it happened, de Groote had no intention of giving up, but he had appreciated the call. Their monthly lunches at the Waterfront Hotel bar continued, as did Jones' reports to San Antonio.

Jones was not surprised, therefore, when de Groote's office called to set up a lunch after he had been interim premier for less than a month. Despite the new premier's best intentions and, in the absence of any meaningful federal help, the situation on the ground was getting out of hand. Jones assumed that de Groote would want to use him as a sounding board, as he had done several times before.

The small, trim African American rose from a table in a discreet alcove in the dining room of the Four Seasons Hotel to greet de Groote. The two men exchanged the usual enquiries about their respective families. Conversation was halting until the main course had been dispensed with. It wasn't until the dessert menus arrived that the premier began to explain himself in his characteristically cautious fashion. His flat delivery belied the unusual nature of his presentation.

"I assume you've been following developments," he began. "You'll know that we're having real difficulty dealing with some of the troublemakers out there. Between the huge task of reconstruction after the earthquake and the effort to kick-start the economy, the last thing we need is a situation where people feel unsafe and investors turn away." De Groote's broad face darkened.

"In addition, although it gives me no pleasure to say so, our federal government has just been going through the motions. We're getting all sorts of assistance short of real help. They're sending some money, but they're not really pitching in. They certainly aren't providing any extra manpower. And now that Quebec has become an issue again, I can't get the PM to focus on our requirements at all. He had an embarrassing time here during our referendum. I don't think he's ever gotten over it."

De Groote paused to scan the menu in a distracted fashion. "I was wondering how things were going in Washington and Oregon since the earthquake. We read the press accounts, of course, and I've talked to the two governors briefly since I became premier, but I was hoping you might fill me in on how much progress has been made since the disaster."

The consul general wondered where this conversation was heading. He liked the usually straightforward de Groote. The premier was obviously having some trouble this time getting to the point. The likelihood that de Groote wasn't well briefed on the situation across the border was fairly low, but he decided to let the exchange play itself out.

"Well, Mr. Premier, the earthquake and the tsunami hit us fairly hard, as you know, but not as hard as up here. We lost some folks on the Oregon beaches. Several communities there have been overwhelmed by the waves. But that looks to be under control, and we've started to rebuild already. None of our major urban areas was seriously damaged, although some freeways around Seattle collapsed. The worst problem we've had so far was with the dams and the transmission lines. We're only just getting regular power supplies back. Overall, we've been extremely fortunate. The casualty count has been very low, considering the size of the quake. Was there something in particular you wanted to know about?"

"I'm very glad to hear that there were relatively few people hurt," said de Groote. As you say, we weren't as lucky up here. We can always replace property, but people are another matter." He hesitated and then plunged ahead. "What I really wanted to talk about was the security situation."

Jones lifted an eyebrow.

De Groote rushed on. "The stress of the referendum overlaid on the shock of the earthquake has placed our society in a very delicate situation. If there is one thing I have come to understand since I became premier, it is how fragile our democracy is if you place it under enough pressure. Right now, I am very worried that we may be straining the ties that bind us past the point of no return. Unless we do something soon to bring the situation back under control, I am concerned that the damage will be irreparable. I know that there are many well-meaning people in the opposition, but the overall effect of the various acts they are undertaking is to shred the vital confidence which unites us."

Jones continued to look puzzled, so de Groote finally came to the point.

"I believe that the provincial government no longer possesses the resources by which it can successfully and permanently restore order," he said. "I have absolutely no confidence that the federal authorities are prepared to step in. This leaves me with only one credible alternative, and that is the United States. I realize that many will feel strongly that to approach the American government is to abdicate our national sovereignty but, frankly, at this stage I believe that not to take full advantage of whatever assistance the United States might be prepared to offer would amount to a dereliction of duty. I have no intention of presiding over the breakdown of British Columbia society."

By the end of this statement, de Groote looked as though he were about to leap to his feet and address the entire restaurant. His face was flushed. His voice had risen to the point that most of the other diners were turning to see what was going on at the corner table.

The consul general was startled by this outburst but retained his professional demeanour. He replied in a low voice.

"Mr. Premier, I know that it cannot have been easy to share your undeniably legitimate concerns about the current state of law and order in BC. We haven't had to contend with the same problems ourselves so far, but we also have every reason not to want to see instability north of the border. I've always regarded this part of the continent as a neighbourhood. I know that the governors next door look at things the same way. Keeping in mind the sensitivities up here around any hints of American interference, what exactly did you have in mind?"

De Groote had subsided somewhat, now that he had been able to broach a subject that he had been brooding about for weeks. He glanced around the restaurant and concluded that it might be advisable to continue this conversation behind closed doors. The two agreed to have coffee elsewhere. Shortly afterwards, they adjourned to the Consul General's Office nearby.

CHAPTER 40

October 21, Vancouver

Later that afternoon, de Groote summoned Indira Dhaliwal to his office overlooking Coal Harbour to brief her on the exchange with Michael Jones. The attorney general had difficulty believing what the premier was telling her. She glared at de Groote, trying to choose her words carefully, fighting the urge to hurl the nearest heavy object at him. The urbane attorney had never liked de Groote, but she had assumed that he would act predictably in his new role, one which Dhaliwal had always regarded as strictly temporary, just until Anne Richardson recovered.

"Let me make sure that I understand what you've just done," she began slowly. "Are you saying that you approached the US government for law enforcement assistance without having raised the matter with cabinet, and without even having given the province's chief law enforcement officer, that is to say, me, any heads-up at all? You are aware, are you not, that our own federal government might have something to say about all this? We may manage the RCMP in BC, but the last time I looked it was still a federal force. To say nothing of the fact that inviting foreign armed forces onto Canadian soil represents a significant abdication of national sovereignty, an act that many Canadians may find distasteful in the extreme, not to say, treasonous."

When Dhaliwal paused for breath, de Groote jumped in.

"Look, my discussion with the consul general was only exploratory. I just wanted to find out whether it was even feasible to imagine that we might be able to get some help from the Americans. How we might do that or even whether they'd be interested remain to be determined. I wanted to find out whether this was an option we could consider. In no way was I committing the government. Besides, even if American troops ever came in, their main task would be helping with the recovery effort, not keeping the peace. I certainly had no intention of going around you. Of course, you should be fully involved in all decisions related to law enforcement. And you will be," he concluded firmly.

"Premier, let me be clear about this," she said, her eyes flashing. "Either you agree to call a special meeting of cabinet to discuss this matter in detail, or I will tender my resignation right now. It's very simple. I have a practice to get back to, and I'm sure my family would appreciate seeing me once in a while, so it's not as though I will especially miss this job. It's for you to decide."

The attorney general waited for a reply. De Groote didn't bother to hide his annoyance.

"Of course, I will be calling on cabinet to discuss this matter. In fact, I was doing you the courtesy of briefing you before that meeting took place." De Groote's tone hardened. "I think it will be important for you to think seriously about your role in this government, however, if your view is that I am ignoring your statutory legal responsibilities. Given what is at stake for the province, I cannot afford to have a team that includes dissenting members. I respect what you have brought to government over the past few months, but I need to know that you are onside. The cabinet meeting you're calling for will be held the day after tomorrow in Victoria. Let me know by then where you stand."

The attorney general stared at de Groote with contempt. "Premier, you won't have to wait until that meeting for my position. I believe that the course of action you are pursuing is dangerous and probably illegal. It is not an approach I would be comfortable supporting. I have no confidence that you will be prepared to entertain reasoned alternatives to your plans. I suspect that cabinet will go along with your scheme, and I want no part of it. My letter of resignation will reach your desk within the hour. I wish I could say that serving with you has been a pleasure. I will consider my willingness to stay in caucus under the circumstances."

With that, Dhaliwal turned on her Blahniked heel and marched from the room.

CHAPTER 41

October 22, Washington, DC

While Premier de Groote was dealing with insubordination in his cabinet, the Destiny Foundation was preparing the way in Washington, DC. JJ and Alison Collette were working the halls in congress, bringing to the attention of key staffers the potential for instability just north of the US border. The staffs of the Washington and Oregon congressional delegations received carefully crafted material outlining the ways in which US interests might be harmed if the situation in British Columbia worsened.

They emphasized the possible vulnerability of key nearby military facilities, such as the Naval Station at Bremerton and the Submarine Base at Bangor. They pointed out that, taken together, these facilities constituted the third-largest navy base in the US. They were home to Trident nuclear submarines and Nimitz-class nuclear-powered super-carriers. Nearby was the Hanford Nuclear Reservation, the most contaminated nuclear site in the United States and an obvious target for saboteurs. In addition, if government opponents in BC attacked the extensive hydro-electric installations in the province, the entire power grid through the Pacific Northwest and down to California would be in jeopardy. The bottom line, according to the foundation reps, was that, if the local government was incapable of maintaining order, then it was clearly incumbent on the US to step in and help them out – on a temporary basis, of course.

JJ and Alison also ensured that their allies in the Department of Defense were made aware of this emerging danger. At the end of several days of concerted lobbying (judiciously leaked to friendly media and especially to the attack dogs of talk radio), pressure began to build on the administration. President Curry had not been having a very successful time lately putting out fires around the world. His advisers were extremely concerned that a growing threat right next door should not reveal the United States to be more of a stumbling giant than it already seemed.

As the exasperated National Security Advisor put it to the president as they drove to an appointment, "If we can't take care of a bunch of hippy bomb-throwers in the Pacific Northwest, why should folks like the North Koreans or the Iranians take us seriously?"

President Curry had been favourably impressed by Premier Richardson when they had met recently. In fact, he liked her. The flowers he sent to her hospital room after the bombing contained a personal message that went well beyond the pro forma words demanded by protocol. He had been told that the Canadian feds had been less than helpful, and he saw no reason to allow BC to go up in flames. The Canadian embassy in DC had, of course, got wind of the Destiny Foundation's campaign. The secretary of state had already received a "strong note" and a whiny personal intervention from the Canadian ambassador.

Curry was less than sympathetic, especially because he had never warmed to the stiff-necked Prime Minister Massey. He found the endless Canadian whittering on about Quebec separatism to be a major bore. He couldn't for the life of him understand why they wouldn't tell the Quebeckers once and for all to sit down and shut up.

As they emerged from the car, the president turned to his National Security Advisor and told him to contact his opposite number in Ottawa.

"You tell Massey's office that there are two options on the table right now. The first is that the Canadian government should be prepared to welcome US troops to BC on a temporary basis and pledge to combine the efforts of US and Canadian forces to restore order in British Columbia. The second is that we will go up there and do the job ourselves, with or without their permission. If Massey hesitates, remind him that our support for Canadian national unity might get re-examined in light of the convincing Quebec case for self-determination. That should focus the little twerp's mind."

CHAPTER 42

October 23, Victoria

The next day, Premier de Groote received a reassuring call from Michael Jones.

"I just thought you'd like to know that the alternative we discussed has been checked with the White House. They agree with your approach and have made sure that Ottawa will have no objections. I'm sure you'll be receiving a call from your feds shortly although, from what I hear, they may not be in a very good mood. The main thing is that they have decided not to object. Under the circumstances, you might want to think about making your own announcement soon about all this so that the people of British Columbia hear directly from you about the need for this unusual step. You might also want to emphasize the recovery aspects of the mission over the law-and-order aspects. Just a suggestion."

In fact, de Groote took this gratuitous advice. That evening he unilaterally announced that American troops would be joining with Canadian counterparts to assist with recovery efforts. He pointedly avoided references to the need for heightened security. As his former attorney general had predicted, he had managed to talk around a very nervous cabinet, the members of which turned out to be more concerned with arson and riots than they were with the niceties of national sovereignty. In the absence of Dhaliwal, there were no strong objecting voices. Despite this acquiescence, however, de Groote knew that, if this all went wrong, he would be left to take full responsibility.

The premier's musing about the general cowardice of most politicians was interrupted by a commotion in his outer office. He went to the door to find an outraged James Franklin demanding entry.

"You can come in for a moment, James," said de Groote. "I have a meeting in five minutes, so make it quick."

❋ ❋ ❋

James closed the door and wheeled around to confront the premier.

"I blame myself, you know," he began. "I should have trusted my instincts. I assumed you would make another attempt at the leadership, but I never thought you would go this far. You aren't the only one with friends in DC. I asked for a check on your communications traffic. It turned up some fascinating stuff. I had no idea that you talked to San Antonio as much as you do. I suppose it was the merest coincidence that you happened not to be in the room to celebrate the referendum outcome with the premier."

De Groote cut in furiously. "Mr. Franklin, if I were you, I'd be very careful about what you say next. There are libel laws, and I'd be more than happy to take every last penny you've got."

"You're nothing but a common murderer and a thief, de Groote. I intend to make it my business to prove it. I'm going to make sure that your American links become common knowledge. Your reputation will stink to high heaven. By the time I finish with you, your name will rank right up there with the great traitors. Quisling and Benedict Arnold will be nothing compared to you!"

De Groote stepped close to James. His thick body

loomed. The fury flowed off him in waves.

"Empty threats are childish," he said, clearly maintaining control with difficulty. "You're fired, of course. I expect you out of the office today. Just remember, there are people out there who know more about your past than even Anne Richardson does. Once you're out that door, you're fair game. Now, get out!"

CHAPTER 43

October 24, Vancouver

Late the next afternoon, relieved of his duties, James was sitting in Anne's hospital room. The former premier was making a remarkable recovery. Her rapidly improving health was reflected in her growing impatience with being bed-bound. Although she still tired easily, she was roaming the TV news-channels and demanding access to a laptop. So far, Katherine had managed to hold her off on that request, but she acknowledged that it was only a matter of time before Anne would be fully plugged back into the Net, despite her inability to get out of bed.

Katherine was not unhappy to see James. She and her mother got along better when one of them was unconscious. When she first arrived, Katherine had been terrified to find Anne covered in bandages and attached to multiple IVs. But with each passing day, Anne's resilience became more evident, a mixed blessing as far as her daughter was concerned. Without the distraction of the occasional visitor, Anne and Katherine were hard-pressed to keep from bickering.

On top of which, Katherine missed Robert and her colleagues in the EDF. From news reports, she knew that the EDF was active in the ongoing anti-government protests. She was keen to re-engage. She had not raised the subject with her mother yet, but her sense was that within a few days she could afford to leave Anne in the hands of friends like James and get back to a real life.

"I can't believe de Groote actually fired you," Anne said indignantly. "Those people are acting as if I'm dead, not just in hospital. There's no way I'm going to let that stand."

James was touched at her reaction but pointed out that she was in no position to do much about his severance. "And besides, I could do with a break," he said. "I used to have this incredibly demanding boss, you know. I never had a moment's peace. I haven't used my cell-phone for an hour or two today. It's quite relaxing not to be at someone else's beck and call."

Anne looked suitably chagrined but maintained that James had been hard-done-by. "If anyone should have the satisfaction of giving you your walking papers, it should be me. I'm the one who hired you, after all."

Katherine interjected to try to calm her mother down. "Why don't we watch the news? James, if you can't keep Mom from getting all worked up, you'll have to leave."

James and Anne looked at each other and grinned. For the moment, it was clear who ran this particular sick-room. The three of them turned to follow the early *CBC National*, which was just coming on.

Canadian news appeared only after the obligatory stories on Middle East carnage and African chaos. The next lead was the impact of the Quebec government's decision to hold a referendum on independence. The reporter in Quebec recited the information about the referendum wording (surprisingly direct) and the date of the vote (surprisingly soon). Several streeters in Montreal and Toronto followed. People in both cities seemed remarkably calm about the prospect. A person interviewed on the street in Calgary suggested that Quebeckers should just get on with separation so that the rest of Canada could plan for the future.

An excerpt from the prime minister's statement at the end of the piece hinted at "strong measures" to keep Quebec part of the country, but included few specifics. He emphasized the need for the Quebec government to respect the provisions of the *Canada Act*. The CBC reporter concluded the story with the rhetorical question: "Will this be the occasion when the people of Quebec make their final decision on whether they wish to remain Canadians?"

The next story concerned developments in BC. The trio in the hospital room paid closer attention. The report was quite short. It noted the continuing protests throughout the province and linked this with the expected arrival of American troops to help with recovery. The new premier was quoted as making reassuring noises about the temporary nature of US humanitarian assistance and pledging their departure as soon as possible.

The PM again appeared, this time to state that US soldiers were in the country with full federal support and under full federal control. He thanked President Curry for his willingness to facilitate the arrangement and praised the effort as a good example of bilateral cooperation between two old allies. Even the standard head-shaking objections of the leader of the Opposition were brief. The newscast moved on to a major flooding problem in northern New Brunswick.

Anne was dumbfounded. "That's it?" she eventually managed. "That's all the damn CBC sees fit to say about the day when this poor old country finally gives up its sovereignty? They make it look as though having American troops at Vancouver International Airport is standard operating procedure. I can't believe it. I realize that it's only happening out here in BC, but surely they're going to say something else!"

"Tonight is the Political Panel," said James. "You can bet that they'll talk about it then."

But in fact, when the panel came up, the BC story was subsumed in a lengthy discussion of the prospects for the Quebec referendum. The general theme was that the federal government was losing control of the national agenda. The Quebec vote illustrated that incapacity. Widespread alienation in BC after a major natural disaster barely rated a mention. One of the panelists characterized the Canadian government's decision to give permission for US troops to provide assistance as a canny fiscal move, a way of allowing it to focus on the more important question of national unity centred in Quebec.

"After all," another panelist said, "if Quebec leaves, technical issues of sovereignty will become largely moot. We won't have much of a country left, anyway." To which sentiment the whole panel gravely nodded their agreement, and that was that.

Anne fell back against her pillows and closed her eyes. "That is the saddest thing I've ever seen," she said eventually. "I've never really trusted de Groote, so I suppose I shouldn't be surprised at what he'd do, given half a chance. But I assumed, obviously naively, that somebody in Ottawa might give a damn. I guess I was wrong." She looked suddenly older and greyer.

Katherine was alarmed at her mother's reaction but determined to make a break for freedom.

"Mom, I was going to wait until you were a bit stronger, but I might as well tell you now. I got a call from Robert last night. The EDF could use some help. I know I can count on James and your friends to take care of you here, so I'm off to see if I can do something more than just moan about what governments aren't prepared to do. If we don't do something directly ourselves, it will never get done. I hope you understand."

James replied before a startled Anne could. "The fact that the Americans are going to be out there changes everything. I know that the provincial government will make a big deal about how the American troops will only act in a humanitarian support role, but I can tell you from direct personal experience that no US commander worth his salt will take orders from some foreigner. The situation on the ground there is about to get much more dangerous. The US troops might have some scruples about letting loose if they are in Washington or Oregon, but they are unlikely to care once they get on foreign soil. I have no idea what you and your EDF friends are planning, and I don't want to know. But you should recognize that the rules have just changed. It isn't just the RCMP and a bunch of dozy Canadian reservists you'll be running into; it'll be the 82nd Airborne, or whoever they've sent up."

Katherine's reaction was immediate. "Listen, this is a matter between me and my mother. Last time I looked, you weren't family. You should just butt out!"

James looked stricken, but held his tongue.

"James was just trying to point out some realities, darling," said Anne. "There's no need to be offensive. Besides, he's right about those EDF people. They have no idea what they're taking on."

"Oh sure," countered Katherine, "this from the woman who sleep-walked us into an American takeover. You should keep your advice for someone who respects it."

Anne stared at her daughter, clearly hurt. She knew they were moments away from another major fight. She also knew that now was not the time. She was tired. She had no desire to drive her daughter away again. She took a deep breath.

"Katherine, I can't stop you from going wherever you want and being with whomever you choose. I'm not even going to tell you to be careful. You'll do what you want anyway. So I'll just ask you to do one thing for me. Please check in regularly. And would you mind giving me your cell-phone number? It makes me nervous that we can't contact you if something important comes up."

Katherine looked uncertain. "Of course, I'll check in. You'll always have a good idea of where I am. I can give you my current cell-phone number, but I can't guarantee it will stay the same in the next few weeks. We'll just have to see." The tension in the room subsided.

Given her track record of secrecy, James assumed that Katherine's number would in fact change momentarily, whatever she might be saying to keep the peace. He wasn't inclined to call Katherine on it at this stage, however. He had no desire to set off another dispute.

James left to let mother and daughter say their good-byes. Out in the hall he ran into Indira, looking as stylish as usual. "Former Madam Attorney," James greeted her, "I gather that we are both hitting the unemployment lines. Someday when we have time for a debrief over a bottle of scotch, we should ruminate on the transitory nature of life."

"I don't know about the transitory nature of life, but I'd be happy to swap stories about how big a shit our new premier is. How is our old premier, by the way? I've brought grapes. My mother always brought grapes."

"She's on the mend," James said, "but your timing is impeccable. Her daughter is about to set off on yet another attempt to save the world. I know Anne isn't very happy about that. She can use some distraction other than me. Why don't you wait until Katherine leaves and then go on in. She may be quite tired, but I'm sure she'll welcome someone else who understands how difficult daughters can be."

James watched as Katherine left and Indira went in. He decided to make some calls. He wanted to make sure the police knew that the former premier's daughter was on the loose again and might need watching. He wondered as he did so whether he was being disloyal. Katherine's retort about his not being family had stung more than he would have expected. In some unspecified but uncomfortable way, he now felt responsible for her.

CHAPTER 44

October 28, Victoria

I t was Einstein who heard them first. James was fast asleep,
safely tucked up on *Shangri-la*. He seemed to sleep best in
the early morning, usually after a restless night of dreams
about blood-soaked rooms and earthquakes. When the cat
jumped down onto his chest, James started up just before
heavy knocking shook his float-home. He stumbled across to
the door, opened it and confronted several large policemen
and an array of cameras. His initial reaction was one of embarrassment; he knew he looked dishevelled in his night-shirt at
an hour when most good people had been up for hours. Anger
took over, however, as he realized that the new Premier's
threats had been far from empty.

James accepted a search warrant with bad grace and
stood aside as the police marched in. He was allowed to throw
on jeans and a shirt and was then led along the wharf and up
the gangway to the parking lot where a police cruiser waited.
He sat in the back seat for half an hour, feeling assaulted and
confused. Reporters shouted questions and camera crews focused in on the hunched figure. He refused to react to the mob
outside the car window.

He had no doubt that de Groote and the foundation
were behind the arrest. At their last encounter, de Groote
had been clear that there would be consequences for his ac-

cusations. James had been naive to dismiss the possibility of straightforward intimidation. The lesson was clear – the foundation and its allies played for keeps.

CHAPTER 45

October 30, Vancouver

Striding onto the airport tarmac, Premier de Groote was feeling triumphant. As he prepared to meet the first contingent of American troops at what was left of Vancouver International Airport, he reflected on how well matters had gone.

He had convinced the Americans that providing help in BC was in their own best interest. He had managed to mouse-trap the feds into agreeing to the US incursion. Admittedly he had had to sign a status-of-forces agreement with the Americans that included a commitment to defray certain US costs and established that US personnel could only be tried for alleged crimes "in country" by US courts. But, generally, the press coverage had been positive. Any concerns that were raised were directed at a Canadian government that was generally characterized as "spineless" and "out of touch." His friends at the Destiny Foundation were pleased and had congratulated him on a job well done. Moreover, no one seemed to miss Anne Richardson's presence. The "wet" wing of the party had been stunned into silence.

De Groote headed towards a reviewing stand flanked by Canadian, BC and American flags whipping in the wind. Not far away were a number of large, dark-green American transport planes disgorging a variety of men and equipment. He shook hands with a US Marine general. Together they watched as the troops formed up and, to the accompaniment of their own band, marched stiffly past. The general returned the salutes of his men.

Not for the first time de Groote was reminded how much more powerful and impressive Americans were, once they decided on a plan of action. So unlike their Canadian counterparts, who seemed trapped in analysis and best intentions. The premier had no trouble sincerely welcoming the men and women of US Northern Command to their new base at YVR. Their arrival would speed the process of making operational a key element of the province's shattered infrastructure. It could only be a matter of time before the naysayers and protesters were brought back into line. Then the job of full recovery could move ahead.

* * *

Despite these encouraging developments, the situation in the province stayed static over the following weeks. Most people in quake-affected areas concentrated on trying to put their lives back together. De Groote was frustrated by the time it took for the Americans to establish their post at the airport, although he knew that they had to work around serious earthquake damage. Up and down the coast, the slow task of clearing away debris and rebuilding whole communities inched ahead.

In the meantime, the protests continued around BC. The police seemed unable to do much beyond cleaning up sites after arson attacks and maintaining a modicum of control around the edges of demonstrations. Their size and frequency kept growing. The premier wanted the crowds deterred from gathering in the first place, not simply held in check. He hoped that once the US troops started to show up, potential rioters would think twice before getting together.

The media were unhelpful in their insistence on giving major publicity to every radical group that raised its head. De Groote was especially annoyed when BCTV interviewed a shadowy figure who spoke in an artificially distorted voice about plans to blow up dams on the Columbia River. The objective was to trigger floods aimed at damaging the Hanford Nuclear Reservation downstream.

The fact that this scheme was hare-brained and unlikely to generate any such result was less important, from the premier's point of view, than the impression it left. The interview conjured up visions of a province crawling with saboteurs and of a provincial government either unaware of the threats or incapable of dealing with them when they emerged. Immediately after seeing the report, de Groote was on the phone to the head of Northern Command, urging him to get his troops out of their base and into the countryside. The response was deferential but non-committal. Apparently the Marines had their own way of doing business. They would not be rushed.

Determined to act directly where he could, the premier moved to ensure that some of his most immediate and aggravating opponents were appropriately dealt with. He had been receiving regular reports about the police efforts to track down the people responsible for the bombing that had put Anne Richardson in hospital. Much to his amusement, a collection of wiretap evidence came to light that suggested James Franklin had been somehow involved with a local anarchist group immediately prior to the bombing.

Strictly speaking, the decision to prosecute should have been left entirely up to Crown counsel. This case was sufficiently sensitive that an informal indication had been given to the Premier's Office that Franklin was being investigated. De Groote was delighted to be able to respond to this feeler with a straight-faced injunction to the police and Crown that they should follow their leads wherever they led. They should not worry about the fact that one of the persons of interest might have had previous connections with the Premier's Office. As far as the current premier was concerned, justice must be seen to be done.

Shortly afterwards, a collection of uniformed and plain-clothed police arrived early in the morning at Fisherman's Wharf in Victoria. A bedraggled James appeared at the door. He stood by while his home was ransacked. Then he was hustled out of his float-home and into the back seat of a squad car, as his neighbours looked on in amazement. His discomfiture was made complete by a collection of cameras that duly recorded the scene. The local media had been tipped off in advance, so the Franklin perp-walk graced the evening news. De Groote enjoyed the scene from his office in Vancouver. News of the arrest reached as far away as Alamo Plaza in San Antonio.

The other satisfying tidbits of information de Groote had received since his elevation concerned his predecessor's daughter, Katherine. The Environmental Defence Force, of which Katherine was a longstanding member, had many linkages to radical organizations and cells, whether on the environmental or the aboriginal side. The EDF itself seemed to have kept its skirts relatively clean, but they belonged to an expanding alliance of disaffected groups. Some of these were quite capable of resorting to violence. Certainly Katherine's boyfriend, Robert Williams, was an outspoken advocate of greater First Nations autonomy. He required careful surveillance.

De Groote directed, more in sorrow than in anger, of course, that the RCMP and local authorities should keep an eye out for Katherine's activities. He was sure that in due course that annoying young woman would step over the line, and action could be taken against her. Meanwhile, it would do no harm to ensure that the public became aware of her questionable associations.

De Groote allowed himself a private chortle at the prospect that two people most closely associated with the former premier – James Franklin and her own daughter – would be swept up in public controversy. Until now, Richardson had managed to keep her personal reputation intact, despite her less-than-savoury antecedents. With the Franklin arrest and with newspaper stories appearing about Katherine's radical connections, however, some of the Richardson aura was bound to be diminished. It was important, de Groote thought, that the voters of British Columbia should begin to understand the true nature of the person in whom they had reposed such unconditional trust.

He had never understood the attraction of the woman, apart from her undoubted physical attributes. In fact, he had sometimes felt as though Richardson held the BC public under a sort of spell. He regarded these revelations about Franklin and Katherine as an overdue form of exorcism. Perhaps now the electorate would recognize Anne Richardson for what she was.

"Succubus," murmured de Groote, and then quickly looked around to make sure that no one had heard him.

VI. RESISTANCE

CHAPTER 46

November 15, Nelson

Eventually, Northern Command stockpiled sufficient troops and materiel. Joint patrols began across the province. The usual drill was for the local police, which outside the large cities meant the RCMP, to take the lead, whether in investigating an incident after the fact or in acting to contain and disperse demonstrations. In response to prompting from the provincial government, both police and military now tried to deal pre-emptively with protesters.

Drawing on the intelligence capacity of the Mounties and a heightened involvement of the Canadian Security Establishment and its US counterpart, the National Security Agency, combined teams descended on known activists, confiscated materials and tried to build cases in the absence of specific acts. Most of these prosecutions got nowhere. Judges across the province expressed concern about the behaviour of authorities. The government was apparently prepared to withstand this level of judicial discomfort provided it could maintain pressure on potential troublemakers. Media reaction to this approach was mixed, depending on the circumstances of the individual case.

Then, chatter on the web told of a major demonstration planned for the heart of counter-culture country, the lovely town of Nelson in the West Kootenays. Stretched across a hillside dropping down to Kootenay Lake, this community was home to a full spectrum of old hippies, deep ecologists, ancient draft-dodgers, entrepreneurial weed farmers and disgruntled lefties. The word was put out on social media that a historic gathering of the clans was planned in two weeks.

Triggered by the arrival of US troops, a "people's coalition" was coming together to challenge the government. NSA intercepts revealed that the coalition included representatives from the local Ktunaxa First Nation. They brought to the effort major organizing capabilities and a clear commitment to non-violence.

What concerned the interim premier when this news reached him was the evident respectability of the demonstrators. The coalition cut across ethnic and class lines. It even included a major contingent from the vocal Downtown Eastside Residents Association, as well as support from all the public- and private-sector unions in the province. When the eminently middle-class environmental groups were added to the mix, the threat to the provincial government's credibility became clear. De Groote let it be known that this was one event that would not be given any leeway. The law would be strictly enforced.

The Nelson demo was scheduled for mid-November. Saturday dawned a beautiful crisp fall day. The parade marshalled early at one end of Baker Street. As participants streamed to the start line, people began to marvel at the size and diversity of the gathering. Banner after banner billowed in the breeze.

At the head of the procession strode the Ktunaxa, strong and proud in full regalia, stepping steadily to a thunder of drums. After them came a remarkable assortment of groups bearing multicoloured banners – an array of environmentalists outraged at the resource auction; a collection of supporters for and/or participants in a bewildering variety of sexual preferences; the stern, old-fashioned representatives from unions large and small; contingents of military vets in formal and ragtag uniforms; a huge float built around a gigantic marijuana plant; a growling formation of motorcycles fronting the unlikely slogan *Bikers for social equality* – one after another, they streamed across the line and headed down the street in the bright sunshine.

After a couple of blocks, people at the front end of the procession started to notice that, in addition to the police cars that blocked off the side streets and the RCMP motorcycles that preceded the parade, soldiers were lining the side of the road. Even more disturbing, the soldiers were not the reassuringly scruffy Canadian Forces variety, but the more menacing US Marines in full battle gear carrying assault rifles. Elements of the demonstration started to yell at the soldiers. Some of the chants were direct and obscene; others involved suggestions that the soldiers attempt an assortment of physically taxing and imaginative sexual practices on themselves.

The Marines held their ground, although the level of their annoyance was clearly rising. Rocks and bottles began arcing out of the marching crowd. Word spread quickly back through the protesters that armed soldiers lay ahead. Some people slipped away at this, but the majority marched on.

By now, the front end of the march had reached the stage at which speeches were planned and music would be played. The space in front of the stage began to fill. The press of bodies from the back of the march was irresistible. The buzz of conversation filled the square, punctuated from time to time by chanting directed at the collection of soldiers and police surrounding the site on three sides.

From one flank came a sharp report. Few of the people in the march had ever heard a rifle shot in real life, so at first there was little reaction. The same was not true of the military, however, and most of them assumed defensive postures while rapidly searching the crowd for the source of the shot, if that was what it was.

Then a second report rang out, from fifty yards farther along. This time, the response of the police and soldiers was instantaneous. A volley of tear gas canisters flew through the air, landing in the midst of the crowd gathered in front of the stage. People panicked and evaporated outwards, leaving the centre of the square momentarily vacant. A third shot rang out, and this time the answer was gunfire. Brown and white smoke shrouded the stage and floated back along the parade route.

The crowd reacted in anger and fear. There was shrieking, and everyone ran in whatever direction seemed the safest, anywhere the tear gas seemed thinner or the volleys of gunfire farther away.

Ten minutes later, the smoke began to clear, driven by a cold wind. Shaken, the soldiers and police gazed at the street and the stage where, just moments before, a colourful crowd had milled and sung. Now the space contained bodies. Some were still twitching; one or two people had moved in to help others. And in place of chanting there was low moaning and the occasional cry.

The demonstration was over.

CHAPTER 47

November 16, Vancouver

For lack of a more meaningful label, commentators characterized the "Nelson massacre" as a game-changer. Not surprisingly, public reaction to a death toll that reached fifteen, plus forty or so wounded, was rather stronger. The Twitterverse exploded with first-hand accounts and hand-held phone pictures of the moments when the American troops opened fire. Three of the dead came from the local First Nation. Aboriginal leaders across the country joined the chorus of dismay.

In partial response, the Marines released overhead drone shots of the moments before the killing. The intent was to demonstrate that the shooting started from the crowd's side, but the overall effect was to add a level of high-tech unreality to a very disturbing event. Cable news outlets played and replayed the footage of the march. American stations in particular were fascinated by this tragedy in a country that generally took a pious position about guns.

The provincial and federal governments found themselves on the defensive, faced with almost universal condemnation. Both governments announced immediate investigations. Premier de Groote made a point of being seen meeting with US commanders, whom he defended as consummate professionals and good neighbours. Opposition parties in Ottawa and Victoria, however, demanded immediate repatriation of US troops.

De Groote was adamant that the fault lay in the first instance with the rioters. He expressed deep sorrow at the deaths but laid full responsibility at the feet of those he characterized as "radical anarchists" and "eco-terrorists." His position was that, although all British Columbians would rightly be shocked at the outcome of the Nelson march, the real blame lay with those using violence to challenge the duly elected government. He vowed to get to the bottom of the "so-called massacre" but, in the meantime, he remained convinced that most people in BC wanted a firm hand bringing stability and peace back to the province.

"It would be easy to hesitate after this horrible event," he stated in an address to the province after the evening TV news, "but that would play into the hands of the troublemakers. It would simply benefit those who share none of the values that British Columbians hold dear. I refuse to take a backward step faced with this direct challenge to our way of life. I know I can count on the calm majority of people in this province to support us. I ask you to remember me in your prayers as we confront these times of trial."

While de Groote was taking most of the heat, the prime minister contented himself with decrying the violence and calling into question the ability of the BC government to manage affairs. Parti Quebecois leaders took advantage of the situation to remind their electorate that an equivalent disaster could never occur in an independent Quebec. Within days, support for the Yes side in the referendum moved steadily upward. The federal governing party was paralyzed by a vicious internal debate between those who were desperate not to show weakness and those who felt that the US military presence in Canada had to be removed immediately. For the moment, the Massey government did little beyond handwringing.

CHAPTER 48

November 16, San Antonio

From the foundation offices in San Antonio, JJ and Alison watched this growing chaos with a degree of satisfaction. The activities of their agents in BC were having the desired effect. Triggering the shooting in Nelson had been easy to arrange, thanks to the presence of two former Green Berets, who blended into the crowd with no difficulty. Similarly, a sprinkling of ex–Special Forces soldiers attached themselves to activist groups across the province, bringing with them expertise in explosives and "monkey-wrenching." These operatives urged their new companions not to back down despite increasing pressure from the authorities. Their work had the dual benefit of keeping morale in these groups high while improving their efficiency.

"Well," came the honeyed drawl, "I think we've done a reasonable job of stirring the waters. The folks up there are just going to have to get used to the fact that, when a US Marine tells you to stop doing something, you do what he tells you. Those guys have dealt with much tougher opponents than a bunch of deep ecologists. It won't do any harm to bloody a few noses, if that's what it takes to restore order."

"You're right, on both counts," said Alison. "We want the situation to stay unstable for a while so that the government can eventually take control and give people a sense of security again. Speaking of which, I'm a bit worried about our friend de Groote. I guess he means well, but he sure isn't the most natural leader at a time of crisis. He comes across as God's instrument a little too much for my taste. He doesn't exactly have the common touch."

"I know he's not ideal," JJ replied, "but you can only work with what you've got, and he's all we've got. I want you to go up there and give him some strong advice, stiffen his backbone a little. The most important thing de Groote can do right now is to demonstrate that his government can still govern. For example, now would be the best time to finish up that auction thing of his. We need a completed process and we need an American group to win. And by the way, Mr. Franklin is a loose end. Let's tie that up as well. I think he has the makings of real hero, so let's give him a chance to be one.

"Of course," JJ added sadly, "sometimes heroes don't make it to the end of the story. Perhaps a dead legend is worth more than a live hero. See to it."

CHAPTER 49

November 17, Nelson/Vancouver

While Alison travelled to BC, US troops, stung by the backlash from the incident in Nelson, were going on the offensive. Communications intelligence suggested that the main opposition groups were using small rural communities as safe havens from which to launch their activities. The Marines determined that they needed to disrupt those cells at source. As a result, community after community in the Cariboo and the West Kootenays awoke to the rhythmic judder of helicopter rotors.

Doors were kicked in, often seemingly at random. Men, women and children were herded out into the street in their night clothes. There they stood in forlorn shivering groups as the troops stamped through their houses leaving wreckage behind. The Marines rarely discovered anyone who could be called an activist.

At the other end of the scale, small US units in plain clothes worked the alleys and darkened doorways of Vancouver's Downtown Eastside. The American command was convinced that key figures in the resistance were being sheltered in the East End. They coordinated closely with local police to increase the pressure on those who might be hiding them. Although these efforts had the unintended result of clearing the streets temporarily of the homeless, they had little other impact.

In the poorest parts of Vancouver and the smallest communities in the countryside, the determination to resist the foreign troops grew exponentially. Young men and women slipped away, only to turn up in the makeshift training camps for resisters. Not for the first time, military overreaction proved to be a potent recruiting tool for the opposition.

Among the young people swept up in the anti-government movement after Nelson were Katherine and Robert. The EDF had protested early against the resource auction plan. It had been fully engaged on the No side in the referendum campaign. Much of its impact derived from the deft use of social media. Katherine pioneered this work. She used a double-breasted approach to communication.

On the one hand, she developed a vibrant network of supporters through the use of social media such as Twitter and Facebook, while also building a generally respected blog called *Katherinewheel* and regularly posting short, quasi-documentaries on YouTube. The response to this outreach had been gratifying, especially among the young. Outraged older BCers started to join in after the government unjustifiably named the EDF as a purveyor of alarmist misinformation.

This following grew even larger when Katherine and the EDF went on the run, trying to avoid the American troops. It was certainly the case that the intensified focus on the part of the authorities made it almost impossible to devise protest actions. The EDF was too busy trying to avoid arrest to undertake operations. To that extent, the American approach was working. Katherine's ongoing use of social media made her and the organization even more popular, however. Her reports from the front were compelling reading and viewing, as she and Robert were chased from place to place by the US military.

The other part of Katherine's communication activities went on while this public campaign gained momentum. This involved using the darknet to establish a network that provided untraceable links among activists around the province. Through this friend-to-friend file-sharing, the broader "movement" was able to maintain contact, reasonably sure that the authorities were not listening in. The fact, if not the content, of this function, however, soon became known to Northern Command. The result was that finding Katherine became a higher military priority. The pressure on her and her immediate supporters continued to build.

One evening, after nights without sleep and days of clambering through the bush, an exhausted Katherine took a chance and made a quick call to her mother. The exchange was brief, because Katherine was worried about her cellphone being traced. Anne's voice was back to normal, but she was clearly very worried about her daughter. There was little Katherine could do to reassure her. She refused to give her a number to call. "It's just too dangerous, Mom, but I promise I'll call again soon." And with that, Katherine rang off.

She sat miserably in a gentle rain, looking across the green valley, wondering whether the whole thing was worth it. At least she knew that her mother was continuing to recover. After a few more minutes of staring damply into space, she clambered to her feet and went back to the fireless campsite Robert and her friends had cobbled together. The only compensation for this exhausting trek was the time she spent in Robert's arms.

CHAPTER 50

November 19, Vancouver

T he first thing Alison did when she reached Vancouver was to set up a quiet meeting with the premier. De Groote came by her hotel. They spent an hour or so in his car being driven around the city.

"Mr. Premier," she began, "I want you to know how impressed we are at your efforts to put the province back on the road to stability and order. What happened in Nelson was tragic, of course, but we all know that the activists are quite pleased at the loss of life. It really serves their purposes to try to label the police and the soldiers as out of control. The way you nailed that by pointing out where the real blame lay was masterful. We commissioned some polling, by the way, and you'll be pleased to know that your support among middle-class British Columbians, the bedrock of this society, is not just holding firm but climbing steadily. Our numbers clearly show that people are convinced that strong leadership is the only way out of this situation. You're providing that leadership. People recognize that."

De Groote reacted quietly to the praise. Ever since the Nelson "incident," it had become clear to him that a critical point had been reached. He was grateful that God had placed him in a position to be able to guide the province through its tribulation. He found Alison's words reassuring. Although he knew perfectly well that his ultimate success or failure would not be dependent on any human interventions, support from the foundation was welcome.

He glanced over at her, trying not to stare. He found her appealing in a disturbing sort of way. Entering the back seat, she had brought with her a waft of perfume and warmth. Under her raincoat, she wore boots and a short knit dress that clung to her body. "Thank you for saying that, Miss Collette. This has been a trying time for us all, but I'm convinced that we're on the right track. Once the current anti-activist sweep is over, I have no doubt that things will get back to normal. I should tell you that I admire the professionalism of the soldiers that your country was kind enough to send to help us. Their leaders are unfailingly polite. They're always happy to take my calls when something comes up. It's only a matter of time before that small group of trouble-makers is rounded up and we can get on with the job at hand. People tend to forget that the earthquake wasn't so long ago. We have a great deal of work to do, and very little time to do it in."

"You're absolutely right, Mr. Premier," Alison agreed. "It's vital that your government not be distracted by people with an agenda of their own that bears no resemblance to what the vast majority of British Columbians want and need."

She put her gloved hand on de Groote's arm and leaned slightly towards him. "We don't like to give you unsolicited advice, Mr. Premier. You know best what needs to be done. But all our sources in the US and abroad are indicating that there is real anticipation around the outcome of the resource auction. We can't think of anything that would demonstrate to your own people and the world that BC was back on track more than a successful completion of that process."

De Groote could feel the heat as Alison moved closer. He noticed the expensive silk scarf knotted around her slender neck. Her eyes were an unusual shade of green. He couldn't remember seeing that before. Perhaps it was the scarf that brought the colour out.

"It's funny that you should mention that, Miss Collette, because I was discussing the auction just the other day with a few of my colleagues. I think it's fair to say that we'll be moving forward on that file shortly. As you say, the demonstration effect should be considerable."

Alison smiled and settled back in her seat. "You know, I've had the privilege of working with a number of prominent leaders over the years. It always surprises me how the greatest of them seem instinctively connected to the people who elected them. If you don't mind my saying so, you have that gift as well."

De Groote flushed and stared straight ahead. "The truth is," he said, "I learn as much from a visit to Tim Hortons as I do from all the surveys our party keeps insisting on commissioning. My own view is that the primary duty of the politician is to keep as directly in touch with the people who elected him as possible. Those folks out there might not have very fashionable ideas, but they're the people who give us our jobs. It seems to me that the connection is pretty clear."

"Well, there's a revolutionary idea." Alison laughed warmly. "Actually listening to the electorate. I don't think you need much advice from people like me, Mr. Premier. You just stay the course. I have total confidence in your judgment. Now, if you wouldn't mind dropping me here, I have a number of other meetings before I catch my plane back to San Antonio. It's been an absolute pleasure. If you ever need me for anything, you have my number."

Alison looked across at de Groote as the car pulled over, halfway down Denman in the West End. She held his eyes for a moment, smiled a brilliant smile, opened the car door and was gone.

De Groote felt pinned to his seat. He could still catch the faint memory of her perfume. He watched as Alison made her way down the street, hips swaying, and into a nondescript office building. He sighed, and then he told the driver to take him back to the office.

* * *

Alison walked through a combination-locked door into a quiet, darkened room three floors up. The aluminum blinds cut down on the light coming through windows covered in a translucent film that provided electromagnetic shielding. Street noise penetrated only as a low hum. This might look like an ordinary room, but it was as impervious to eavesdropping as modern technology could make it. The five men Alison met here, however, looked anything but ordinary.

Although they ranged in age from forty to fifty-five, they shared an obviously high level of fitness, short cropped hair and a disciplined alertness reflective of years of purposeful waiting. They sat around a small boardroom table, each with some version of an electronic device open in front of them. These they closed as Alison joined them.

"Gentlemen," she began, "thank you for meeting me. I know you have been briefed for this assignment, but I wanted to make sure you were aware of the latest developments before you set off." She removed a single sheet of paper from a slim, stylish briefcase and placed it on the table.

"The target for this mission is James Dean Franklin. At the moment, he is being held on remand at the police station on Caledonia Street in Victoria. You have been sent floor plans for that building electronically. The first thing I would like to go over is your plan for removing Franklin from that building. The second item on the agenda is your facilitation of Franklin's journey from Victoria to the vicinity of Princeton on the mainland, where he is to rendezvous with elements of the Environmental Defence Force, and specifically with a member of that organization, Katherine Richardson, the daughter of the former premier. Thirdly, I want to discuss the specifics of how you plan to terminate Franklin in such a fashion as to implicate the American forces currently in the

Princeton area seeking to neutralize the EDF. I have an hour, gentlemen. Let's proceed."

Sixty minutes later, Alison left the building, comfortable that the foundation's team was well prepared for their task. Her own operational experience told her that success was not guaranteed, but this skilled group was extremely professional. She could find no weak points in their preparation. She stopped at a street corner to send a two-word confirmatory text to San Antonio, and then she hailed a cab. She would treat herself at a small, select lingerie shop on Robson before travelling out to the airport and taking the foundation's private jet on to Portland, where her next task awaited.

CHAPTER 51

November 19, Vancouver

Premier de Groote had a staff meeting of his own when he returned to the office. He wanted an update on the resource auction. Over the following half hour he was briefed.

The bottom line was that the bids that had been received by the due date were complete and had been analyzed. The three serious bids came from consortia of Chinese, Japanese and American companies. This was hardly surprising, nor was the fact that, in the end, the three were remarkably close in terms of their benefits to British Columbia. The provincial government's fiscal requirements looking outward a decade were well enough known. What was much less certain were the likely trajectory of international resource prices and the particular requirements of the much larger and more complex national economies of the three main bidding countries.

The senior public servants took the premier through a technical summary of the pros and cons of each bid. De Groote was able to follow most of the analysis, but some of the finer points eluded him. He was relieved to gather by the end of the quick briefing, however, that a reasonable decision could made in favour of each of the proponent's cases. The mix of benefits to BC would vary, but there was no runaway winner.

As the officials left his office, the premier called his

deputy minister over. Alessandra Barbieri waited for instructions.

"I thought that went well, didn't you?" de Groote said to her. "I think we are ready to talk to ministers about where we stand and what we should do next. This will be a critical decision for the government. I want to ensure that all ministers understand and agree with the course of action we undertake. I want a PowerPoint presentation prepared that lays out in bullet form the main points related to each of the three alternatives. This should be as non-technical and straightforward as possible – no slides entirely covered in writing that no one can understand."

The premier looked determined. "Officials can take us through the slideshow and answer any questions ministers have but, after that, I want the discussion to be in-camera. No tribe of twinkies around the walls, nobody typing away as we talk. At the end of the day, this is going to be a political decision in the best sense of the word political. We will have to take into account the full range of considerations. We can't be ruled by technicalities or limited by cautious bureaucrats. No offence meant to you or your colleagues, Miss Barbieri."

"None taken, Premier," responded the deputy minister. "I assume you will want a communications plan developed to go along with each of the three choices."

De Groote blanked for a second, and then said, "I'll be asking the head of the Government Communications Secretariat to take care of that personally. As you can imagine, everything related to this decision needs to be closely held. You don't need to worry about that side of it."

"With respect, this is one of the most important and complicated sets of policy decisions this government will take. I'm uncomfortable that we won't be staffing this out as thoroughly as we should," said Barbieri. "A bullet-point slideshow is hardly going to provide ministers with the background they need to make an informed judgment. And bolting a comm plan onto the back won't allow for the substance to be fully integrated into our public positions. In my view, we're headed for trouble here when the press starts asking detailed questions."

"I've told you what sorts of materials we will need in this case," responded the premier. "I appreciate your views may be different, but I've seen too many good ideas gutted by the bureaucracy. This isn't about to join that list. Have I made myself clear?"

Barbieri made a last attempt. "Yes, Premier. By the way, have the attorney and his staff had an opportunity to go through the outcome of the auction process? I know that the former attorney general had some concerns about existing rights-holders. Presumably we don't want to end up in the courts indefinitely."

"Absolutely he has, and I can assure you that he is entirely supportive of our course of action." The premier's cheeks were starting to flush, and he added, "I believe we are done for the moment. Thank you."

Barbieri hesitated, then turned and walked away. Moments later she was standing in front of Georgina's desk, outside what used to be James's office.

"Georgina, do you have any idea where James is? I saw the story about him being arrested. Do we know what that's about?"

Georgina looked up at her, distressed. "All I know is that he cleared out his desk and went home. Then I read the story in the papers about the arrest. I expected to hear from him, but I'm as puzzled as you are. All my contacts have dried up. Alessandra, people are scared. Nobody's talking, and I think I've reached the end. You're the closest person I can think of as a boss, so you'll be getting my resignation this afternoon. I wish there was more I could do, but this place has gone nuts ever since we lost the premier." Georgina's usually composed expression was crumbling.

It was Barbieri's turn to express concern. "I need you to stay here for the moment. Let me get to the bottom of things and try to find out what happened to James. If I have to, I'll go and visit Anne. She might know what's happened. But in the meantime, you've got to stay in place. I need someone here I can trust. Will you do that for me?"

Georgina took a breath. "I'll stay for the rest of the week but, if nothing changes soon, I'm out of here. And you take care who you talk to. I'm not hearing much, but what I do hear is a bit scary."

Barbieri thanked her and returned to her own office, where she stayed behind closed doors for the rest of the afternoon, working with a small team on the PowerPoint presentation commissioned by de Groote. As directed, she ensured that the next full cabinet meeting was attended by only a few staffers. It ended with a closed session that took the better part of an afternoon. Afterwards, the premier summoned his deputy minister.

"All right, Miss Barbieri, that went well. Thank you for your assistance. The Government Communications Secretariat will take it from here. They are drafting my address to the province. You should know that I will be on television tomorrow evening announcing the winner of the resource auction. Just for your information, and not for repetition outside this room, our American friends are going to be very happy."

Barbieri tried without much success to keep the contempt out of her voice. "I see, Premier, and what provision have you made with respect to the losing bidders? Who will be contacting the Chinese and Japanese? The Government Communications staff?"

The premier was annoyed. "The minister of Trade will be talking to the key Chinese and Japanese officials tonight. We have no doubt that they will react appropriately. We have extensive long-term relationships with companies in those two countries, and those will not be affected. It certainly isn't in their interest to question the outcome of this process."

"Really, I wouldn't have thought that they have much to lose. For the next few years they're going to be hard-pressed to do business directly with us at all. Perhaps they can work out some arrangement with the Americans, now that they are managing our resource base for us."

The premier's face froze. "That will be all for the moment, Miss Barbieri. After the address tomorrow, perhaps we should have a discussion about your future assignments in the government. I look forward to that chat."

Alessandra nodded briefly and left. She wondered where the latest version of her c.v. was housed. She would need it soon enough.

CHAPTER 52

November 25, Victoria

Alessandra watched her soon-to-be-ex boss on television with some distaste. In the course of her rapid rise up through the ranks, she had run across a fair number of people she disliked or distrusted. Usually she was able to work around or ignore the worst of these. It was difficult to disregard the premier of the province, however. In this case, it was particularly galling, because she did not actually disagree with the substance of the decision he was announcing to the public.

All factors taken into consideration, the outcome of the resource auction was not irrational, assuming the usefulness of such an exercise in the first place. Of the three most credible bids, the American consortium's was the most compelling. The match between the US companies' capabilities and the provincial resource base, the existing links between the BC and US economies, the cultural similarities among the main players, the willingness of the US corporations to enter partnerships with local firms, all of these mitigated in favour of the American bidders.

Nonetheless, Alessandra remained uncomfortable about the process. The senior Finance officials who had analyzed the bids were veterans who were unlikely to succumb to pressure, although they recognized the practical limits they worked within. The problem arose when the analysis reached ministers. At that point, the decision passed beyond even her view. That caused the premier's deputy minister considerable concern.

It had been unusual enough that she and two cabinet secretaries had prepared a summary PowerPoint that served as a virtual decision document. She had seen some other decision processes almost as closely held. But to base critical policy determination on such a simple document, with no more elaborate background pieces available for ministers to read, struck her as reckless.

Moreover, there seemed to be no implementation plan at all. The communications plan (assuming one actually existed beyond speaking notes for the premier's announcement) had been hived off to the government communications flacks to produce. That alone was enough to be an invitation to disaster. The effect of cementing relations with the Americans seemed quite likely to mean rupturing relations with the Japanese and Chinese at the same time. Little if any strategic thinking had gone into the aftermath of the decision itself.

Based on a number of conversations she had had with Anne Richardson before her departure, Alessandra knew that managing the province's external relations after the resource auction had been the former premier's consuming concern. Anne believed that it would be impossible to avoid a degree of hard-feeling on the part of the losing bidders, but she was determined to emphasize that opportunities for their ongoing involvement in the BC economy would remain.

Alessandra did not necessarily share Anne's optimism in this regard, but she agreed entirely that an effort needed to be made. The resource auction was always going to involve a sort of Faustian bargain – a higher, more predictable level of government revenue in return for a significant limitation of independence. At least Anne understood this and was determined to try to moderate the worst effects of the bargain. De Groote didn't seem to care that BC was becoming an extension of the US imperium. In fact, he apparently welcomed it. As for the relationship with the rest of Canada, including the federal government, that dimension didn't seem to have registered at all.

"My fellow British Columbians," the premier was saying, after a short introduction. "I realize that we have all been through a difficult time. The recent disaster has tested us as never before. At the same time, I have never been more inspired than by witnessing the determination of the ordinary men and women of this province to work together to repair the damage and move ahead.

"On top of the physical destruction, of course, I know that many of you have been very concerned about the political divisiveness that seems to have overtaken us. I share that concern. I believe that you also share with me a clear sense that this society must come together, must unite around the values that have allowed us to prosper in this beautiful land. In particular, violence at the level that we have seen in the past few months is simply unacceptable. It must end.

"On a more positive note, and as a clear indication that the province is moving ahead, today I am pleased to be able to announce the successful conclusion of the process that my predecessor began and which you supported by your votes in the recent referendum. The successful bidder in that process is the Liberty Consortium from the United States of America. We look forward to working with that group in the coming months. We congratulate them on the extremely high quality of their proposal.

"I would like to take a quick moment to compliment the other bidders in this process as well. They can be proud of the proposals they developed. We hope that they will continue to be active participants in a rapidly developing BC economy.

"In the days to come, we will be releasing additional details about the next stages of this important process. For the moment, I want you to know that British Columbia is back in business, that we have turned the corner and that we can look forward to better days ahead."

"It is in that spirit of hope and determination that I wish you all a good evening. May God bless British Columbia."

Alessandra was startled by this somewhat cryptic pre-recorded address, not least by the religious note the premier struck in concluding it. Whatever else the speech was, it was certainly not the standard issue announcement generated by officials. The thought occurred to her that the premier might have drafted most of the brief statement himself. Now there was an unusual occurrence. She wasn't sure whether she should be amused or disconcerted.

What was clear was that, in his current mood, the premier would be very unlikely to want to avail himself of her services for much longer. While she still had access to government communications and staff, she needed to make some enquiries.

First of all, she wanted to find out what had happened to James. To her surprise, when she consulted her Police Services contact, she was told that James had been released into the custody of the Sheriff's Service for transportation to a court hearing. This struck even her contact as a bit odd, since no date for a court appearance appeared on the records. Second, she needed to speak to Anne Richardson. Apart from wanting to check on her recovery, Alessandra thought that her former boss deserved an update on her successor's activities.

VII. FLIGHT

CHAPTER 53

November 25, Victoria/Langley

E arlier that same morning, James was taken from his cell and handed over to a pair of uniformed Sheriff's Services staff. He had not realized that he was scheduled to go anywhere that day, but he was well past being surprised by anything that happened to him. He had talked to a lawyer briefly after his arrest. Several days of dead air had followed.

Now, enquiries about his destination were greeted with surly silence, so he settled into the back of the Chevrolet Express van, as it headed out of Victoria down Highway 17. He assumed that they were bound to the ferry terminal but, two stops short, the van turned off and ended up in a small marina. James was bundled out of the van and onto a classic Chris-Craft moored at an out-of-the-way dock. James's cuffs were removed, and he was shoved down into a cabin below decks. Within minutes, the boat was underway. As the sheriffs left him, one of them turned with a grin and said, "JJ says 'hey' and wishes you a good trip." And with that they were gone, leaving James with a sick feeling. Once again his erstwhile mentor was manipulating his life.

Looking around the cabin, James saw a change of clothes and, sitting on top, a set of credit cards and a cell-phone. He had to admit that the foundation people were thorough. He was not about to demand to be turned back in. He did wonder how many years escaping from jail might add to whatever custodial sentence he was eventually given, but he decided for the moment to go along for the ride. After all, based on past performance, that seemed to be what James did best – go along.

Climbing up to the bridge, he found a cheerful fellow named Joe, or so he said. Joe was extremely uncommunicative about who he was working for and how this had all been arranged, but otherwise he was quite happy to pass the time of day and comment on the scenery as they motored along.

A couple of hours later, the boat sidled up to a dock at the Delta Hotel near the Vancouver airport. Joe reached into his pocket and produced a set of car keys, which turned out to belong to a nondescript Honda. When James reached the car-park, he turned around to wave, but Joe was already gone. JJ wasn't losing his touch, James thought. He was even more impressed when he checked the trunk and discovered camping equipment, a sturdy jacket and a serviceable pair of hiking boots.

The next order of business was to track down Katherine Richardson. James had spent most of the boat-trip from Vancouver Island trying to decide what to do next. His first instinct had been to go to Anne but, realistically, he would be picked up by police the moment he walked into the hospital. The last time he saw her, he had deliberately not shared his strong suspicions about the links between de Groote and the Destiny Foundation and his conviction that both had been complicit in the bombing in which she'd been injured. He had assumed that there would be time enough to talk this through with her later. He was unwilling to add to her stress while she was still so weak from her injuries. But before he'd had a chance to take this line of enquiry further, he had been arrested.

His jail time in Victoria, however, had given him a chance to think things through. He had concluded that, if the foundation was desperate enough to strike directly at the premier, it would have little compunction about attacking her daughter as well. At the very least, they might want to capture Katherine and use her as leverage. Alternatively, and this made James' blood run cold, they might simply want to remove her, knowing that killing the daughter would destroy her mother. What the foundation could not know was that Katherine's safety was now vital to James as well.

At last report, she was with her friends in the EDF, being chased across the countryside by US troops. He needed to catch up with her, explain the situation, and get her to shelter. Knowing Katherine, convincing her to leave her comrades would not be easy, but he owed it to Anne to make the attempt. And as a recently revealed father, he owed it to himself to take action, to stop being a cipher, an unthinking pawn on someone else's chess board. James reflected that his life of unattached freedom was apparently at an end. It seemed he had obligations to others after all. This included Einstein, of course, although he was sure Jenny would look out for the cat in his absence.

The last location he had for Katherine was somewhere near Princeton, so that was where he would start the search. Before he left the Vancouver area, however, he needed some idea of where the EDF might be. James decided to risk a telephone call. He was pleased to be able to reach one of the senior environmentalists who had befriended him when he first returned to BC and started working with Anne. Marta lived on a small farm outside Langley, so he could drop by on his way to the Interior. In addition to being one of Anne's key political supporters, she had known her and her daughter for years. Katherine had no grandparents, but Marta performed the role with devotion.

James drove slowly up the rutted, puddled lane leading to the small farmhouse. The front porch was framed by the tattered remains of a cloud of blue wisteria. The yard was unkempt, overgrown shrubs punctuating a scrubby lawn. As James walked up the path, he was greeted by a pair of kittens, bold and skittery.

"What are their names?" he called out to the figure on the porch.

"Alpha and Omega" came the reply. "They're the beginning and the end of my social life these days. I don't see many people. Who told you where I was?"

"Anne Richardson said that you were taking a break out here. A while ago she said that, if I ever needed it, you could give me good advice. She's the one who gave me your telephone number."

From out of the shadowed porch emerged Marta Poniatowska, a slender, fine-boned woman of pensionable years. Her snow-white hair was pulled straight back from a face dominated by a prominent nose and sharp grey eyes. She spoke with a slight accent, reminiscent of central Europe or the Middle East.

"Anne's a fine lady, but I've had some cause to doubt her judgement recently. Still, I wouldn't have wished on anyone what happened to her. I hope she is recovering. You and Katherine must have been very worried." She held out her hand. "Good to see you again, James. I don't normally like political operatives, but you always struck me as well-intentioned, if somewhat naive."

"Thanks. It's wonderful to see you again too." James let Marta's hand drop. "I'm not sure what Anne might have told you, but I've made a promise to her that I will try to look out for Katherine. Under the circumstances, with Anne in hospital and American troops roaming the province, I really need to track Katherine down. Unfortunately, I have no idea where she and her friends might be, and I was hoping that you could point me in the right direction."

"As it happens, Katherine passed through here several weeks ago. She mentioned that she and Robert might be using an abandoned copper mine up above Princeton as a sort of retreat, if things got too hot. I can give you directions, but I can't promise they'll be there." Marta looked carefully up at James, as if trying to reach some conclusion.

"It's a chilly day, isn't it?" she said. "I was about to have some hot chocolate. Would you care to join me?"

Despite his desire to be on his way, James found himself agreeing, and followed her inside. Marta fetched cups from the kitchen, and the two of them settled around a rough-hewn table opposite the stone fireplace that dominated the room. The log fire crackled and popped.

"I am a bit surprised to see you walking free," Marta said, after they had taken their first sips. "I had understood that the Cossacks had detained you. It was unclear to me whether the charges were justified, but the likelihood seemed low. Congratulations on your escape, if that is what it is."

"I appreciate your faith in me," said James, "or perhaps this is just a reflection of your general cynicism about the motives of the authorities, whoever they may be at any given time."

Marta nodded and added, "You shouldn't feel badly about your incarceration, you know. My father always said that, for any but the seriously poor, prison time was a badge of honour. And he should have known. He was thrown in jail by the Polish government, the Nazis and the Soviets. I sometimes thought that he regarded the time he had at home as simply an interlude between periods of his real job as an inmate. The biggest surprise he had when we finally reached Israel was their steadfast refusal to jail him. Maybe if he had lived longer, they might have lost patience with him too."

"Anne never told me about your background. How did you end up in BC, anyway?" James was anxious to get on with his search for Katherine, but he found this quiet, strong woman drawing him in.

Marta took another sip of hot chocolate. "Well, I'm not sure it has anything to do with why you're here, but I'll give you the short version, and then we can talk a bit about Katherine, and Anne . . . and you."

CHAPTER 54

November 25, Langley

After stirring up the fire, Marta came back to her battered chair. Her face was shadowed; her voice was low but distinct.

"My father was a young Socialist newspaper editor in Poland before the war, and he was a Jew. That was enough to make sure that the government of the day paid close attention to his activities. From time to time, this meant throwing him in jail for one offence or another. Then the war came. He and my mother survived the Germans and the destruction of the Warsaw Ghetto, but the eventual Communist government in Poland had as little time for them as its predecessor."

Marta stared for a few moments at the fire.

"My parents were brave. But even they could see that it was time to leave. They made *aliyah* to the Holy Land and fought once more, this time in the 1948 war of independence. In due course, the Jewish side won. The state of Israel was established. My father and mother settled on a kibbutz near the Golan Heights. My brother Ariel and I were born over the next few years.

"This should have meant a happy ending, should it not?" she went on. "But that would have been too straightforward. My father was never the same after the injuries he received in Poland, and later in Israel. He became depressed, and never fitted in to Israeli life. He thought the country too hot, too noisy and too new. He found Hebrew difficult and the traffic impossible. He died in 1956.

"My mother always claimed that the Suez crisis was the last straw for him. Although the Israelis won the war militarily, they lost it politically, because the Americans refused to support them. My father's view was that this proved that Jews would always be alone in the world. Even after all that had happened in Europe and the miracle of the founding of Israel, he saw no way forward for his people. One day, he turned his head to the wall, and that was that. It was just one betrayal too many."

James picked up Omega, who had chosen this moment to mount a serious attack on his shoe-laces. The kitten squirmed free. "So how did you get from Israel in 1956 to British Columbia in the nineteen sixties?"

"Well, my father may have given up on Israel, but Ariel was a true believer. He turned out to be one of those tough, brave *sabras* who were convinced that anything was possible. They simply assumed that they would inevitably come out on top of any battle they got into. In the years before the Six-Day War in 1967, he was desperate to join up, and he succeeded. He became a pilot; the best of the best. My mother was so proud and, God help me, so was I. The Air Force won the Six-Day War for Israel. They established absolute air supremacy by shattering the Egyptian, Jordanian and Syrian Air Forces in the first few hours. More than four hundred and fifty enemy aircraft were destroyed and only twenty-four Israeli pilots were killed."

Marta paused. "Unfortunately, Ariel was one of the twenty-four."

James spoke inadequately into the lengthening silence. "That was terrible bad luck."

"I didn't think it had anything to do with luck," said Marta. "I thought it was the final, irrevocable sign that my family was cursed. I had to get away. I didn't care what my mother thought. I was young, and I was angry. I wanted to go to a place with as little history as possible and lots of nature. I thought about Australia or New Zealand, but they were ridiculously far from anywhere. I even considered Argentina, but too many Germans had gone there. I settled on Canada because it seemed so dull and secure. I went to the West Coast because people told me it was so green. They were right. After the brown of the Israeli deserts, that seemed perfect.

"For many years, BC seemed both green and safe. I was happy to work to keep it that way. Early in the environmental movement, I became involved. As far as I was concerned, all of the important issues were interconnected. Poverty, feminism, environmentalism, peace – they could only be addressed effectively if the relationships among them could be understood. Most importantly, the people I met in BC seemed remarkably genuine and kind. Coming to this country was like being immersed in a warm, reassuring bath."

"Surely you didn't think that human nature was all that different on this side of the Atlantic?" asked James.

"Not after a couple of years. It soon became clear that the way people expressed themselves might be different, but the capacity for betrayal remained constant – especially on the part of governments. Until quite recently I thought we could make progress here that couldn't be made in the old world. It turns out that I shared more of my father's unwarranted optimism than I thought.

"In some ways, your old boss was the final straw. I got to know Anne at UBC, and of course I met her daughter as well. Katherine is sweet and smart, and it has been a privilege to watch her grow up. She often comes to stay with me here. We talk a lot, and I like to think that her love of nature was triggered by the walks we took near the cottage.

"When her mother first came to political prominence, I was attracted by the way she applied her intelligence and her evident sincerity. She usually appeared to say what she believed. Her willingness to lie to the electorate seemed limited. The simple fact is, however, that this scheme to auction off the province's resources is dangerous craziness. We'll be left with empty streams, huge clear-cuts and large holes where the open-pit mines used to be. And for what – a few front-end jobs and a trickle of revenue? Thank goodness for the First Nations, because they're the only ones who might be able to slow down the slide to oblivion."

James could think of little to say in response to this, so he focused on the reason for his visit. "Okay, I understand that you think that the government is headed in the wrong direction, Marta, but I've made a commitment to Anne. And that means I have to get on. Thank you for the warm fire, and for the history lesson."

Marta stood up, scattering Alpha and Omega off her lap. As James rose in response, Marta laid a hand on his arm. "Anne is not one to share confidences but, over the years, I always had the sense that there was someone out there she cared about, even if he wasn't a regular part of her life. I must tell you that since you returned to BC, she has seemed happier, in her own private way. For that, I think we have you to thank.

"But be careful in your quest, and remember – you can be as heroic as you like, but don't get tangled up in the relationship between a strong woman and her strong daughter. That way lies serious danger. Katherine and Anne still have major differences even though, as I tried to point out to Katherine, they have more in common than they think. In the meantime, by all means be supportive but, if you value your ties with either of them, don't get caught in the middle."

James nodded but said nothing. He wished that non-involvement was still an option.

A few minutes later, directions in hand, James expressed his thanks again for the hot chocolate and for the information. As he turned to go, he said, "I have to ask, Marta. You and your family were at the centre of many of the most important events of our time. Even when you came here to BC, you were a leader in the War in the Woods. You gave wisdom and courage to the people who challenged the corporate agenda that successive governments have supported. You've decided to retreat to the farm, but I get the distinct impression that under the right circumstances you'd be back in the battle. If you're so cynical about leaders and politics, whether in government or the private sector, why bother?"

Marta squinted into the setting sun and shook her head. "Young man, that is a particularly silly question. Almost as silly as the notion that any of us has much of a choice about how we conduct our lives. We do what we must. We will probably fail, but that has little to do with the effort itself. Now go off and see if you can help Katherine. I know that Anne is counting on you. Although she is in many ways a questionable politician, she and Katherine are dear to my heart. Get going."

With that, James ventured to give Marta a hug and headed back to the Honda. He bumped down the lane towards the main road watching Marta in the rear mirror. Her arms were full of kittens.

❊ ❊ ❊

It was full dark when he reached the outskirts of Princeton. He was having trouble keeping his eyes open. He pulled into a roadside campground, tilted back the seat and closed his eyes.

Before he drifted off, he thought about Marta's story. He wondered whose side he'd been on through all those campaigns he'd run. He had always prided himself on being one of the good guys, but maybe he'd just been tending the machine. Perhaps more disturbing, the events of the past few months seemed to confirm that even the good guys could help generate bad outcomes.

The next thing he knew, he woke up with the sun in his eyes and a stiff neck. He started the car and trundled on. The side road up into the hills was just where Marta had promised. The road turned from hardtop to gravel, from gravel to a track.

He stopped at the end and saw where a trail led uphill.

Before setting off with as much of the camping equipment as he could carry, he waited by the car for half an hour, listening. It didn't seem likely that he was being followed, but you could never tell. Time passed. James let the crisp air and the multi-coloured, boulder-strewn mountains seep into his bones. All he saw, though, was the occasional bird. All he heard was the wind. Clearly he had inhaled some of Marta's paranoia. He shrugged on the pack, took a slug of water and set off up the trail.

CHAPTER 55

November 26, Copper Queen Mine

In a nondescript motel room twenty miles away, three men watched Franklin's progress across the landscape. The task was almost laughably easy. Not only was there a GPS tracking device in the Honda, but there was a second in Franklin's new cell-phone and a third sewn into the collar of his shirt. The signal from the car was stationary, but the other two moved on as Franklin climbed steadily.

"I assume you aren't going to alert the Marines until we're reasonably sure that Franklin has met up with Katherine Richardson," said the thick-set man named Joe.

"Relax," responded a taller, former Special Forces sergeant. "We've got to give them time to settle before we call in the cavalry. I want to know which direction they're going to run. Then we'll be waiting for them."

* * *

James was soon starting to feel the effects of the hike. Recently he had run less and less. He hated to admit it, but the years were taking their toll as well. Every half hour or so, he stopped to take a drink of water and to look back down towards the valley floor. He had come a long way up through the pines and, as he stood straining to catch any sounds of pursuit, he was glad of the jacket. The air was crisp in the shadow of the trees.

He emerged past the tree-line into full sun and followed the dusty trail across a slope and along to a ridge. From here, he looked ahead to see the path snaking across the far hill and out of sight up to the left. He checked to see if anyone was following him, but the path was empty. The fact he could see no one did nothing to reduce his level of anxiety.

All he could see was an eagle circling lazily on the thermals. He was surprised at how much height he had gained in the last two hours. He started down and across the saddle before heading farther up.

When he reached the point at which the path disappeared, he was able to look up and ahead towards a tumbledown collection of mismatched wooden structures perched precariously on the spur of a mountain. That must be the abandoned mine site.

An hour later, he walked up to the first building, the former terminus for a tramline that had taken men and ore down to the valley. The platform and the buildings above it were made of weathered grey wood. None of it looked very stable, but he clambered cautiously up onto the catwalk, which led to a rickety flight of stairs. From there he looked back down for thousands of feet and across at a range of mountains capped with snow. The sun might be bright, but the air was cold.

Looking upward, he could see the head-frame capping the mineshaft outlined against the deep blue sky. From somewhere inside his storehouse of useless facts came the less-than-reassuring recollection that this piece of machinery was also known as a gallows frame. He climbed the steps until he reached a small dusty plaza with the mine entrance on one side and a series of decaying wooden structures hanging off the cliff on the other side. Except for his footsteps and the sound of the wind whistling through rusting cables, the place was silent.

Marta had told him that this deserted mine was the

bolt-hole used by the Environmental Defense Force when they were under pressure. She also told him that Katherine had joined up with the EDF several weeks previously. On her way up, Katherine had visited Marta.

Marta had no idea when, or even if, Katherine would turn up at the mine. Given the way in which the EDF and their allies were being harried across the countryside, however, it seemed likely that they would appear sooner rather than later.

So far as James could tell, he was alone on this windswept ridge. He opened the splintered doors in the buildings near the mineshaft one by one, but they were filled with dust and old rubbish. If people had spent time here recently, they had made a point of cleaning up after themselves.

As the sun sank behind a neighbouring mountain and the temperature dropped, James made camp in a small shed that seemed marginally less porous than the rest. Darkness fell early, and he was tired. He laid out the tarp and the sleeping bag after a cold meal. He was fast asleep within minutes.

He awoke to a painful jab in the ribs from a gun barrel. Momentarily he could make out several shadowy figures standing over him. Then a large boot descended on his chest. His ribs cracked and the air left his chest in a rush. A light shone directly into his eyes. He couldn't speak and he couldn't move – he was trapped!

"You have exactly thirty seconds to tell us who you are and what you're doing here" came a low voice. "If we don't find your explanations convincing, you're going back down this mountain a whole shitload faster than you came up it." The matter-of-fact tone was more threatening than a shout.

The words came out painfully. "My name is James Franklin, and I'm looking for Katherine Richardson." James tried without much success to match the calm tone adopted by the owner of the large boot. He hesitated to say more, because he had no idea who these people were. So far as he knew, they might be soldiers as easily as activists. Certainly they seemed disciplined and alert. He waited, but the boot stayed where it was. The gun barrel didn't move an inch.

There was a bustle at the door. Somebody pushed through the ring. "James, is that you? What the hell are you doing here? Is my mother all right?"

The pressure on his chest eased. There was Katherine herself, dressed in camo and with a blacked face.

"I don't suppose you could convince your friend here to let me up. Your mother's fine. She's still in hospital, but she's fine."

"So what's the story?" Katherine asked. "This is not the sort of place you just happen to pass by. And my friend's name is Derek. He's tired and he's hungry, so be polite."

The man with the boot let James sit up but showed no sign of moving away. "Katherine's right," he said. "We need to know how you found us and what your business here is. We've been moving for the last two days straight. The army's still on our tail. They seem to have more luck finding us than they should. As far as we know, you're part of that problem."

James tried to think of a way of explaining his presence that didn't sound stupidly condescending. He gave up and decided to tell the truth or, at least, most of it.

"It's personal," he began, but knowing that this was not going to wash, he continued. "Okay, I know, there's nothing I can say that your colleagues can't hear. I get it. All right then, the last time I saw your mother, she asked me to keep tabs on you. It wasn't that she didn't trust your judgment. It's just that she was in no position to do it herself, and she was worried. And now that I'm here, I can see what she was talking about. Do you have any idea what you people are up against? The Marines don't kid around."

As James spoke, Katherine flushed in embarrassment. One or two of the others smiled. Derek, however, remained grim-faced.

"We know all about the damn Marines, old man. What I want to know is whether you're working with them. Let's see your cell-phone."

James passed it over, and without even looking at it, Derek smashed it under his heel. "We can't take chances. Now if you have something to say to Katherine, say it and get on your way."

"In the middle of the night? Get serious," James said. "All I was looking for was a chance to talk to Katherine. Nothing more. I'll leave at dawn. How about that?"

By this time James was on his feet, surrounded by twenty or so young people dressed in assorted forms of out-door clothing or quasi-combat gear. He recognized Robert among the group, but no one else. Few of the others looked armed, but they were all grubby and tired. Derek was clearly the leader, but the rest of the group seemed disposed to let James stay, at least for the rest of the night.

Now that the excitement was over, they began drift-ing away to other buildings. Soon James was left with Derek, Katherine and Robert.

Derek was obviously still uncertain about James, but he turned to Katherine and said, "Fine, if you want your cozy lit-tle chat, you can have it. Come on, Robert, let's see if we can or-ganize some food."

As they left, Katherine rounded on James. "Thanks a lot. That was really great. Do you have any idea how long it's taken me to establish any kind of credibility with these people? Well, you've just managed to blow all that away in two minutes!"

James blinked and absorbed the anger. "I know I am probably the last person you wanted to see right now, but I told your mother I would check up on you occasionally, so here I am."

Katherine looked at him incredulously. "I presume she meant a phone call from time to time, not a cross-country trek."

"Point taken, but I had a reason to talk to you face to face, which I have not shared with your mother. I know my appearance may be a pain in the ass, but give me ten minutes, and you'll see why I had to track you down."

Katherine continued to look doubtful, but said, "Okay, ten minutes, and then I have to get some sleep. I'm dying on my feet."

CHAPTER 56

November 26, Copper Queen Mine

K atherine and James sat down together at the top of the steps leading to the dusty square beside the pit-head. They could feel the wind gusting up from the valley, but they were looking out into an inky blackness. No lights could be seen on the valley floor. James paused, trying to decide how much to tell Katherine and where to start the story. The beginning might be best.

"Your mother must have told you that she and I knew each other in grad school. She may also have told you that at the end of the last semester I simply vanished. One day I was attending classes, and the next I was nowhere to be found."

"Mom didn't spend a lot of time talking about you, but she told me that much, yeah."

"What she probably didn't tell you, because I'm fairly sure she never knew, was that, thanks to one of my profs who'd seen my analytic work, I was recruited by a small American intelligence agency."

Katherine's eyes widened.

"I know, I know," James said, "as far as you're concerned I'm just a middle-aged political hack who looks as though he'd have trouble running around the block. Hardly Bond mater-ial."

"Boy, are you out of date," Katherine laughed. "Nowadays it's Jason Bourne, not James Bond. You're right, though. I wouldn't have seen you as a man of international mystery and intrigue."

James felt slightly disappointed. "Well, I was younger then, and I'll have you know that I run regularly to keep in shape. I even have very trendy low-impact running shoes."

"You have Vibrams?" Katherine asked. "I hear they're quite cool, although I'm not certain I could stand having my toes separated, and don't they really smell?"

"It's like anything," James replied stiffly, "it takes a while to adjust."

"Okay, so we've established that you were a junior spy and that you jog occasionally. What has that got to do with your interfering in my life?"

"I didn't actually stay all that long with the US feds, although I got some useful training and travelled a lot."

"Does this mean you can hot-wire a car and field-strip an AK-47?" Katherine asked innocently.

"As a matter of fact, yes, although I could hot-wire a car long before I made it to grad school," he retorted. "Actually, most of the time, I rode a desk. Most of what I did was related to signals intelligence and content analysis. We left the wet ops to others."

"So, what happened next? And what does this have to do with me?"

"I was on an operation in the southern States, and I got recruited by an outfit called the Destiny Foundation. They told me that I could do all the interesting things I was doing without any of the bureaucracy and with a much bigger salary."

"Didn't that strike you as being too good to be true?"

"It seemed like a good idea at the time. The foundation people were very convincing, and anyway I was younger then."

Katherine looked at James with disbelief. "And this is the guy who chases me all over the countryside so he can tell me to be careful about who *I* associate with? Really?"

"I would have thought that my experience would give me more, not less, credibility," said James defensively. "Anyway, I was part of a foundation operation in Mexico that went badly wrong. A guy I was working with was slaughtered by cartel killers in a way I still have nightmares about. I was being chased by the *federales*, and the foundation had to get me out of there pronto. At that point, I'd had enough of the foundation and their kind of work, so I quit. After wandering around a bit, I joined a political campaign out of curiosity and that was it. I got the bug, and I've been working around the edges of politics ever since. I don't usually stick around long and, in fact, the job I was doing for your mother was the first permanent gig I've had in years. I thought I'd found a place to settle. I've even been adopted by a cat."

Katherine looked at him steadily. "You don't strike me as the settle-down type. And don't bother with animals. You'd never be at home to feed them."

James looked guilty, and Katherine said, "So obviously the story doesn't end there, or you wouldn't be sitting on a mountaintop in the middle of the night, on the run from the police and consorting with a bunch of eco-terrorists."

James was startled. "You heard about my arrest? I didn't think that would reach you way out here."

"We check the news on WiFi occasionally, and you're a big deal. According to the police, you escaped custody. You're wanted in connection with the bombing that injured my mother." Katherine stopped, and her eyes narrowed. "So exactly what did you have to do with putting Mom in hospital? And if I don't get a convincing answer, I'll hand you over to Derek. He's quite expert at extracting information, by the way."

James' voice climbed. "Let's get one thing straight – I would never harm your mother, whatever the police say! I care about her very much – and, regrettably, I can't think of many others I would say that about."

He registered Katherine's skeptical glance and took a deep breath. "Just let me finish. From the time I left Mexico I had no contact with the Destiny Foundation. I'd even managed to forget I ever had anything to do with them. Then, right after the government decided to go ahead with the resource auction idea, who should give me a call but the foundation's executive director. She wanted me to come to San Antonio for a chat. When those guys make a suggestion, it's unwise to ignore them totally, so down I went. The chat turned out to be an ultimatum. I was supposed to make sure that an American consortium they supported won the resource auction. I tried to explain that I was hardly in a position to guarantee any specific outcome, but they were less than understanding. I left without making a commitment one way or the other. I assumed that would be that." The wind from the valley was getting colder. James huddled into his jacket.

"When your mom was hurt, I was sitting on my houseboat in Victoria, drinking and watching TV with my cat. I got over to Vancouver as soon as I could but, while I was travelling, I thought about what I'd seen. The one prominent person who wasn't at the post-election rally was the deputy premier, Willem de Groote. That didn't seem to be a coincidence to me, so I checked with a couple of friends in the NSA. It turns out that de Groote has a long history of contact with the foundation. In effect, it looks as though he was the foundation's man in the BC government. All of a sudden, the pieces started to come together. Clearly, the foundation wanted to make sure that their consortium won the auction. It's all part of a longer-term plan to pull BC away from the rest of Canada and start the break-up of the country. The foundation obviously didn't think that your mom would be easy to manipulate, so they decided it would be safer to have their own guy in charge. Hence the bombing, de Groote takes over, and I get thrown in jail."

Katherine's face was hard. "I assume you never told my mother about the approach from the foundation. You never warned her that she might be in danger."

James looked away. "I thought the foundation call to me was a one-off. I had no idea that they would follow up with an attempt on your mother's life. If I had thought for a minute that that was a possibility, I would have told her and gone straight to the police. I thought I had time to let this play itself out. I thought I had things under control."

James turned to look Katherine in the face. "I know I don't come off as much except an incompetent, bloodless mercenary, but there have been a few people in my life who have been important to me. Right at the top of that list is your mom. I would do anything to keep her safe. After I'd seen Anne in hospital the first time, and I knew she was out of danger, I went to see de Groote and confronted him. He basically blew me off and reminded me that the foundation had a very long reach. I found that out the next day, when I landed up in jail."

Katherine was unimpressed. "So I'm supposed to be pleased that, after endangering my mother's life, you make a feeble effort to protect her and totally fail? Sounds symbolic of your entire career to me – pointless and ineffective."

"I don't blame you for being angry, but you can't be any harder on me than I am on myself. The reason I'm here is that I'm convinced that the foundation won't stop with your mom and me. I think that they're going to take a run at you. I don't know how or when, but I'm sure they'll make an attempt. I'm not sure they'll try to kill you, but they are going to want to maintain leverage over your mother. The best way of doing that is through you. If I can find you, then you can be sure that the foundation can. As long as you're with the EDF folks, you might as well be carrying around a large sign saying *Kidnap Me*. You've got to get down off this mountain and take cover – at least for a little while, until we see how things are working out."

Katherine stood up and glared at James. "For someone who is supposed to be this great political genius, you are the stupidest man I've ever met. Just exactly how did you manage to break out of jail? Did you get a file in the mail?"

James stared back, puzzled. "No, I think the foundation had something to do with it."

"No kidding, Sherlock. And how convenient do you think it is for them that you managed to find me so quickly? You've succeeded in bringing the foundation, the police and the army down on our heads! Asshole!"

And she ran back towards the buildings where Derek, Robert and the rest of the EDF were waiting.

* * *

The trio in the motel room were packing their bags and moving out. They had let their Marine contact know the location of the EDF cell and alerted the two foundation agents near the deserted mine site to move in. Shortly, the whole EDF group would be on the move. Franklin would be with them, probably with Richardson nearby.

Once the trap was sprung, the five foundation operatives could make sure that Franklin and Richardson were taken care of, unfortunate collateral damage of a well-conceived government raid on a nest of dangerous ecological radicals. A useful lesson to all concerned and a loose end successfully tidied up.

Neither JJ nor Alison much liked loose ends. They'd be pleased.

* * *

James sat numbly contemplating his own ineptitude. Katherine was probably right. His whole escape had seemed strangely straightforward. So much for looking out for Katherine. All he'd managed was to lead her enemies right to her. Now what was he going to do?

Behind him he heard a commotion. All pretense at secrecy gone, the EDF group were noisily gathering their belong-

ings and arguing about what to do next. And then, in the distance, the sound of helicopters.

CHAPTER 57

November 26, Copper Queen Mine

T he squabbling group of activists froze as they heard the rhythmic thunk of chopper blades. Eerily, the noise was coming from below. The helicopters were coming up the valley and would be overhead in minutes.

Derek gathered his followers around him. "Right," he rapped out, "you all know the drill. Don't stay too close together. Move in small groups of two or three. You know where the next rendezvous point is. Keep moving as long as you can. We'll try to delay the pursuit here. Good luck. See you soon!"

And with that, most of the young people moved into the shadows, while eight or ten scattered into the buildings near the pit-head.

Just as the EDF unit scattered, a volley of blinding white flares exploded over the hillside. The clearing in front of the mineshaft was flooded in dazzling white light. The shadowed buildings stood out in bold relief against the jet black night. The engine noise from the helicopters became deafening. Searchlights speared down, sweeping the open space for targets. From several windows around the clearing, sporadic gunfire broke out, answered almost immediately with heavy machine-gun fire from above.

Into the midst of this chaos, James ran looking for Katherine. Just as he reached the clearing, a figure barrelled into him, knocking him onto the ground back into the dark. James struggled to catch his breath and twisted round, trying to break free.

"It's no skin off my nose, but Katherine seems to want you alive. Stay out of the light! Let's go!" Robert dragged James to his feet and pulled him across to the staircase, where Katherine was waiting.

The three of them clattered down the rickety steps, James remembering the sheer drop that awaited under the elderly wooden staircase. Behind them, shots continued. One of the helicopters settled onto the roof of a building opposite the mine entrance.

"Come on, old man," urged Robert. "Keep up! We need to clear the area."

James needed little prompting.

For the next hour or so, he focused on keeping Katherine and Robert in view as they all ran, slid and fell down the ridge leading up to the mine. Several times he thought he heard people close behind, but the noise from the mine-site slowly faded. After half an hour, all he could hear was his own laboured breathing and the noise of their boots scrabbling across the shifting surface.

Finally, just as James was wondering whether he could continue to keep up the pace, Robert called a halt.

"Okay," he said, "we've put some distance between us and them. I don't want to blunder on too much farther in the dark. One of us could get seriously hurt." He rounded on James. "Just so you know, if it turns out that you had any connection with those American cowboys, you're dead meat."

James turned to Katherine, who was retying a bootlace. "You can't really believe that I would intentionally bring those troops down on us," he asked. "I was trying to get you out of there."

Katherine looked up. "Let's be clear about this. I only asked Robert to bring you along because of my mother. For some reason I don't understand, she seems to like you. There's no accounting for taste. Anyway, apart from anything else, I look forward to telling her that it was me keeping you alive, as opposed to the other way around."

Katherine contempt rankled, but James decided not to pursue the matter and looked to Robert for advice. "Where do we go from here? Those folks aren't going to give up. My car is a long way away. Actually I have no idea where the car is from here, in any event. So what do we do?"

"I don't see why I should be making the decisions. It may surprise you to know that First Nations folks aren't all instinctively at home in the woods. I was brought up in Kitsilano. My traditional territory runs mostly up and down Fourth Avenue. For what it's worth, I think we should tuck in for what's left of the night and take stock at first light. Old man, do you have any water in that pack?"

James rummaged around and came up with a bottle, which they shared. Then Katherine and Robert snuggled up together at the base of a tree. James sat opposite, sore, cold and tired – and appalled at what he had unleashed. Within minutes they were all asleep.

* * *

Some distance away, over the brow of a hill, two foundation agents spoke quietly together and then called in to the rest of their team.

"The three of them have stopped running. I reckon they'll wait until daybreak before they move any farther. So far they're moving roughly west. They don't know it, but they'll run into the highway soon. At that point they'll probably try to get a lift back to Hope. What's your ETA?"

Joe responded. "We should be closing on your position in the next hour. We'll set up between them and the highway. When we're ready, you start them in our direction, and we'll take care of business. Remember, our preference is to take

Richardson alive but, if it gets messy, the last thing we need is witnesses, so act accordingly. And be careful. You never know, one of them may decide to be a hero. Franklin isn't packing, but I wouldn't assume the other guy isn't."

The exchange completed, the two agents sat back and took the opportunity to check and clean their weapons.

CHAPTER 58

November 27, Near Princeton

At daybreak, Robert shook James awake, and the little party started off downhill. A branch snapped somewhere close behind them, and they ran, bolting from tree to tree, falling through bushes and trying in vain to stay upright. Ten frantic minutes later, they tumbled through a last line of trees and looked up to see with two large men in fatigues pointing Glock 18C machine pistols at them.

"Ms. Richardson, it's good to see you. We were getting a bit worried that you might get lost in the hills. There are dangerous people out there, you know. It's just as well we're here to ensure your safety."

Katherine slowly got to her feet and stared at them. "Who are you, and what do you want?"

The man who spoke smiled briefly and lowered his gun. "Sorry, ma'am, we're paid to be careful. You can never tell who you might meet in the woods this early in the morning." He looked over Katherine's shoulder at two more figures emerging from the bushes. These two were carrying rifles. So, they had been followed.

"See what I mean? You just can't tell. Did you have any trouble keeping up with them?" He addressed the last two to arrive.

"Actually, they were very considerate" came the reply.

"I suppose they could have made more noise, but I don't know how. You know, you'll find that you can move faster if you don't keep falling down and running into trees." The four uniformed men were clearly amused.

"Fine, you've had your little joke," said Robert. "What happens now? Are you working for the Americans?"

"Actually, we *are* the Americans," said the first man, and the other three nodded, relaxed, their guns still at the ready. "I think it would be accurate to say, however, that we are less official than the Americans you are thinking of. Quite a bit less official."

"Enough already, Carl, we've got a schedule to meet. Let's get on with it."

"What do you mean, a schedule?" said James. Carl turned to James with no good humour in his eyes at all. "We've been asked to safeguard Ms. Richardson here, so she'll be coming with us. We don't have any instructions about you two, however. We've got a camp nearby. The best thing would be if you went with Chuck and Allen here to wait until we can make arrangements for you as well. Okay?"

Robert responded angrily. "No, it would not be okay, Carl, or whoever you are. I am not leaving Katherine with you, and I am not going off to some camp!"

"Well now, that is not really up to you," said Carl, "so I'd suggest that you shut up and do what you're told."

Chuck and Allen had by this time closed in on Robert and James. Their guns were aimed directly at them. Katherine was obviously alarmed.

"Robert, do what they ask. They won't harm me. When I can get to a phone, I'll let people know where you are and you can be picked up."

"Right," Carl grunted approvingly. "I think you should take your lady-friend's advice, Robert. It'll be better for all concerned."

With that, Carl and his companion led Katherine down the hill and were soon lost to sight.

"Get your hands where I can see them," Chuck ordered James and Robert. He patted Robert down and removed a small pistol from his pocket. "Nice little item," he said, "but you won't be needing that where you're going." He performed the same search on James and found nothing.

"Okay, let's go," said Chuck. He directed James and Robert down a path that led across the hillside. They soon came to a cave with a mossy clearing in front.

"Put your hands behind your head and kneel down," ordered Chuck.

"No, you can't," shouted James, as he realized what was about to happen.

Before he could protect himself, he felt a blow from a rifle butt and a searing pain in the side of his head. He fell face-down into the mud. He felt rather than heard Robert turn on their captors. There was a volley of shots, and then, silence. As he lay there, James couldn't understand why he wasn't dead. His head was splitting. He felt nauseous, couldn't move. After what seemed an age, he felt hands on his shoulders, rolling him over.

"Are you all right?"

James opened his eyes. In the middle of a swirling world, he saw the concerned face of Robert.

"That was quite a blow you took. You must have a very hard head."

James closed his eyes again in a vain attempt to slow the world down. He opened them again and tried to sit up. He looked around and saw for the first time four other people. And two bodies, splayed awkwardly off to one side.

"I thought they were going to shoot us," James began unsteadily. He explored his skull and found a large lump.

"They were," said Robert, "but these gentlemen intervened."

James recognized Derek and several other EDF members. "We always seem to start our conversations with me lying on the ground," said James. "But thank you. I thought you were otherwise engaged."

Derek grinned. "We managed to delay the Marines and then took off. It looked as though you and Katherine could use some help, so we tracked you down. You weren't too hard to follow."

"Everyone keeps telling us that," said James. "So those guys obviously weren't with the soldiers. I have an idea about who they are, but I can't be sure. I doubt they're Canadians, somehow."

Derek shook his head. "I have no idea how they fit in, but they were just about to finish you off when we arrived. Seemed like a good idea to stop them."

James made feeble efforts to get up. "But we've got to find Katherine. If they were prepared to shoot us, God knows what they have in mind for her."

"Not to make you feel bad, but I think they regard Katherine as a good deal more valuable than us," said Robert. "I'm sure they won't harm her, at least in the short term. Still, if you can walk, we should catch up with them if we can."

"We left a couple of people to follow Katherine when we came after you," said Derek. "It sounded as though they were headed to the highway, though, so we need to get after her before they load her in a car and take off."

James struggled to his feet and stood for a moment, willing the sky to stop whirling around. "Lead on," he said to Derek. "I'll let you know if I'm about to collapse."

CHAPTER 59

November 27, Near Princeton

J ames was sure he was concussed. Just staying on his feet took a massive effort. After the first few steps, he vomited all over his shoes. He knew he had to keep up, however, so he staggered on, stabilized by Robert's hand on his shoulder. The EDF crew maintained a steady pace downhill. Then a figure emerged from the trees ahead, and the procession stopped abruptly. There was a whispered conversation, and then the group moved on, this time at a slower pace. James assumed they were getting close.

Finally, Derek turned around and motioned them to get down. He crawled forward ten yards or so and looked down over a bank. He waved James and Robert forward. James saw they were twenty feet or so above the level of the hard shoulder of a highway. To their left was a white panel van with people gathered around it. One of them was Katherine.

Although they were too far away to make out the words, there was obviously a loud argument going on. Katherine was making some points and so was one of three armed men. They were both trying to convince a stocky individual, whom James recognized as Joe from the Chris-Craft. James's suspicions were confirmed – the foundation was running the whole operation. The organization's power seemed boundless.

His head still hurt, and he was having trouble focusing,

but his main anguish derived from the realization of how simple-minded he had been and how much danger this had placed Katherine in. The foundation had played him like a violin, but Katherine was about to pay the price.

Derek whispered in James' ear. "If we're going to stop them and rescue Katherine, we're going to have to get a lot closer. You're in no shape to help, so you stay put and keep quiet..."

Robert cut in and hissed, "You're not leaving me here!"

Derek looked amused but simply nodded.

A moment later, James found himself alone, once again a spectator rather than an actor. He had a grandstand view of what happened next. Down by the van, the debate, if that was what it was, looked to be winding up. Joe was clearly eager to be on his way. Katherine was staring around desperately and edging away. Then everything exploded into action.

Katherine sprinted around the other side of the van, prompting two foundation agents to leap after her with guns drawn. Robert broke cover and yelled Katherine's name. She skidded to a stop and changed direction towards him.

One of the agents dropped to a knee and double-tapped Robert, hitting him in the chest. The young man pitched forward onto the gravel. Katherine screamed and dove on top of his still body. Shots rang out from the trees. The two agents fell, leaving Joe standing uncertainly by the van.

Moving quickly for a heavy man, he jumped into the driver's seat and gunned the vehicle away in a hail of bullets from the EDFers, who were breaking from the trees.

As quickly as the violence had erupted, it was over.

James scrambled down the bank and ran to Katherine. She was weeping and calling Robert's name. She had rolled him over and was clutching him to her chest. Derek had already reached him and felt for a pulse. As James came up, Derek looked over and shook his head.

James sat down heavily. He desperately wanted to give Katherine some comfort, but she was rocking Robert's inert body, moaning. James was suddenly aware of his fatigue and his injuries. In the course of escaping from the mine-site, he had fallen countless times. His clothes had been reduced to filthy rags. His head was pounding. He was still having trouble focusing.

Sitting there next to a sobbing Katherine, he assumed he should be taking charge and issuing orders, but he was absolutely drained. Lifting a hand seemed like an insurmountable task. His arms and legs were sacks of cement. Even talking required a huge effort.

Derek saved him the trouble. "We can't stay here. This is a main highway. There are bound to be cars passing soon. We can't afford to be caught out in the open. You and Katherine need to get back to Vancouver. You've got to tell people what's really going on out here. You have to get the word out, or these bastards will win."

Turning to Katherine, he spoke gently. "Katherine, Robert's gone. You can't help him anymore. He wouldn't want you to get caught again. You and James have to get out of here. We'll take care of Robert and make sure that he gets back to his family."

He turned back to James. "I've called some friends nearby. They should be here soon with a car. I think your best bet might be to go back to Marta's, although it's up to you. She was the one who told you where you could find us, wasn't she?"

James nodded. Coherent speech was too difficult.

"She contacted me just before you arrived at the mine," Derek went on. "Otherwise, you really would have ended up at the bottom of that cliff. As it was, we decided to take a chance on you. I'm not sure you were worth the trouble, but there you are. Strange bedfellows, eh?"

Derek looked around at the bodies. "In the meantime, we've all got to move back into the tree-line. We'll take care of these two and the others back in the woods. No one will ever find them. Let's go, everybody!"

And with Derek firmly in charge, some organization returned to the group. Within minutes, the side of the highway was cleared. Everyone waited in the trees. Katherine was clearly suffering from shock. Leaning against a tree, she stared blankly ahead, unresponsive to any questions. James sat down beside her. He tried to put his arms round her, but she stiffened and turned away. He stood awkwardly, trapped in sadness. He tried not to fall asleep, but the effort to stay awake was increasingly difficult. Eventually, he lay down and drifted off.

After a wait that stretched interminably, a beaten-up SUV slowed and then turned off in response to Derek's wave. Katherine and James were bundled in the back seat and driven off. The young girl driving turned around and looked worriedly at her passengers.

"Are you two okay for the moment? We should probably get you checked out by a doctor, but I want to put some miles between us and this area. There's some water in the back seat and blankets to keep you warm. Once we get to Hope, we can look for a clinic. Sit tight."

The ride back to Hope was uneventful, although James noticed that there seemed to be more police cars on the road than usual. Luckily, they weren't pulled over. By noon, the three of them were sitting in a small restaurant on the town's main drag.

Katherine was slowly starting to come back to life, but James' head had not stopped pounding. They had decided that he should visit a clinic. He had emerged with a diagnosis of a mild concussion, a prescription for painkillers and the advice to take it easy. As if he could. The one reassuring factor from his point of view was the return of his appetite. Hence, the restaurant.

"I can take you anywhere you want to go," said the girl, whose name was Poppy, "but, James, your picture is all over the newspapers. If you walk straight in the main door of a public place like a big hospital, the chances of your being recognized are really high."

Katherine was starting to take in her surroundings. "That's fine, but I want to see my mother. Isn't there somewhere in Vancouver where we can drop you off, James, and you can lie low for a while?"

This was directed at James, who was wolfing down a sandwich and feeling much better since the meds had kicked in. James paused and thought for a moment.

"You're probably right about the police looking for me. Poppy, this is what I think we should do. We need to get back to the coast. We don't have time to check in with Marta, and, anyway, the more we have to do with her, the worse trouble she'll be in. Once we get closer to Vancouver, we'll call Indira Dhaliwal. She can get a message through to Anne. Assuming Anne's well enough to travel, we'll set up a time and a place to meet. Then we'll get off the main roads and work our way slowly into town.

"Together, we can figure out what to do next. We can't let these buggers get away with all this. There's got to be a way we can rain on de Groote's parade and counter the foundation."

Katherine looked dubious, but at least they had the beginning of a plan. Poppy clearly had no idea who de Groote and the foundation were, but she seemed content to go along with James' suggestion. After they ate, they were back in the SUV headed for Vancouver.

* * *

Not far away, Marta sat motionless on her porch, slumped over to one side. The kittens, Alpha and Omega, played at her feet. That night, there would be no one to feed them.

VIII. RECOVERY

CHAPTER 60

November 28, Vancouver

A nne looked out across a manicured garden and over a carefully clipped hedge out towards the Fraser River and the sea beyond. The traffic noise from Southwest Marine Drive was muted. Every five minutes or so a large aircraft lifted off from Vancouver Airport and disappeared into the clouds.

After the weeks in hospital, simply sitting here in the watery winter sun, wrapped in a blanket, felt like a luxury. The fresh wind stirred her hair and cooled her cheek. Bruised all down one side of her body from the bomb blast, she still found movement uncomfortable, but she was on the mend. She had reached the boring part of recovery – almost no anxiety, but plenty of frustration.

The terrace she was sitting on extended from the living room of Indira's modern South Vancouver home. Where once a standard, ivy-covered family home for the rich and staid had stood, there now stretched a stone and glass shoe-box that embraced the view down onto Southlands and absorbed all the sun the southern exposure could generate.

The homeowner herself stepped out onto the terrace with a steaming cup of tea. She placed it carefully beside Anne and checked to ensure that her friend was appropriately bundled up against the late-afternoon breeze.

"Every time I see you, you look stronger. You're developing some colour in your cheeks," said Indira, sitting down beside her on the other side of a low table. "At least the rain has stopped long enough for you to be able to see something. There's nothing more annoying than knowing that there's a view out there and being unable to see it."

"Frankly, I'd be happy to sit out here in the pouring rain, just to get out of that damn hospital room. You'll never know how much I look forward to these visits. They're like parole. I know that the folks at the General mean well, and they've done a wonderful job getting me better, but I hate the place! I can't wait to get back to my own bed." Anne sipped her tea. "The single thing I'm most looking forward to – apart from seeing Katherine again, of course – is being able to go through my front door, closing it behind me, and just standing there enjoying the silence. Entirely alone!"

You'll be able to do that soon enough," said Indira. "The doctors tell me that you should be an out-patient by next week. Have you made any arrangements for nursing staff to look in on you for a while?"

"Oh, I didn't have to do that. Jeff, bless his little compulsive soul, has everything arranged. If he weren't such a good doctor, I'd tell him to take a hike. Also, he's not that hard on the eyes."

Anne and Indira smiled at the thought of the fit young physician who was coordinating the former premier's care. He had a pretty young wife, but there was no harm in appreciating the doctor's strong hands and warm grey eyes.

"Have you given any thought to what you plan to do next?" asked Indira. "Not to put any pressure on you, but you may have noticed that politics in BC have gone to hell in a hand-basket since you left. I don't think most people can believe that we have American troops roaming the countryside or that we've given the most important sectors in our economy over to US companies."

"I know that you weren't the most enthusiastic supporter of the resource auction plan, but this wasn't the way it was supposed to turn out," Anne said morosely. "The question to my mind is not whether we made some mistakes in the past? Obviously, we did. The question, is what do we do now? Apart from anything else, we need more information. That's what I'm hoping James can provide this afternoon."

"I just hope that he can make it through all the police roadblocks," said Indira. "When he called to set up this meeting, he was coming in on back roads in the Fraser Valley, but at some point he's going to have to go through a tunnel or cross a bridge. It's those choke-points that will be hardest to get through. Anyway, I'm sure Katherine will have some ideas. She seems to specialize in moving from place to place in a surreptitious manner. It will be great to see her again, won't it?"

"That's an understatement" came the anxious reply. "James said she was all right, but I'll believe it when I see it."

The two friends settled down with their tea and waited. The sun was low on the horizon, when there was a knock on the back door. Indira leapt to her feet and went to answer.

Moments later she brought James and Katherine out onto the terrace. Katherine rushed to embrace her mother and fell to her knees, the two engulfed in tears. James stood a bit awkwardly at the French doors. Anne hadn't heard from Katherine for weeks. Once the news of James' escape had hit the media, she had assumed that he might try to track down her daughter, *their* daughter, but she couldn't be sure. Then the stories had come in about the abortive raid on the EDF campsite. Anne had been terrified. As for Katherine, the combination of grief over Robert's death and overwhelming exhaustion from the trek into Vancouver had left her completely unstrung. She sobbed with her head in her mother's lap, Anne stroking her hair and trying to reassure her.

"We should let them be for a while," suggested Indira, as she drew James back into the house. They sat down in the modern but comfortable living room.

"I didn't hear a car. How did you manage to get here?"

James gave a brief smile. "Actually, the last bit was on the Forty-First Avenue bus, after which we walked. We ditched the car in Surrey, bought a change of clothes, climbed on the SkyTrain and then took buses. I don't think we were followed, but you never know. There are a lot of people out there looking for us. I can't stay long – and I don't want to put you and Anne in jeopardy. All I wanted to do was deliver Katherine to her mother, and then move on. I'm an escaped criminal, you know," he finished up, with some satisfaction, but major underlying anxiety.

"Was that on your bucket list?" said Indira. "Just as well I'm not the AG any more. I'm sure harbouring you breaks any number of oaths. I agree that you are something of a police magnet, though. Anne and Katherine don't need any more attention than they'll get in any event, once the press realizes Katherine's back and Anne's much closer to recovery. I'll get you something to eat, then you can put your head down for a while before you leave. In the meantime, the four of us need to talk seriously about where we go from here."

James nodded, happy to have someone else take over for a moment. He leaned back, and then, before he knew it, Indira was shaking him back to wakefulness. She led him to a table on which were steaming bowls of soup and assorted sandwiches. Katherine and Anne sat on the other side, looking tired but less emotional.

Sliding easily into the role of chair, Indira began the conversation while the others ate. "Considering the circumstances, it's almost miraculous to be sitting together like this. I know this might be temporary, but it's wonderful to see you all again. Before you arrived so dramatically on my back porch, Anne and I were starting to consider what we should do next. The two of you have a great deal of information that could help us make some decisions. Between gulps, James, could you bring us up to speed about what you've found out?"

James's story came out slowly, around mouthfuls of food.

CHAPTER 61

November 28, Vancouver

"**K**atherine, you feel free to interrupt any time, but it seems to me that the crucial point we've uncovered is the role of the Destiny Foundation," said James. "We can argue forever about the decisions the government has made since the election, but the key fact now is that the premier of British Columbia is being ordered around by a foreign organization. That group has the goal of breaking up Canada, absorbing its constituent parts and suppressing any dissent, by violent means if necessary, as it goes along."

Katherine nodded, content to let James summarize.

"So, what do we know, or think we know, about what the foundation has done?" he continued. "From the beginning, the foundation was intrigued by the resource auction idea we were so proud of. It was keen to take advantage of the openings it might offer. From their perspective, they had a couple of advantages. They had come to know de Groote through their patronage of regional groupings, and they knew me from an earlier movie. With de Groote as deputy premier and me in the Premier's Office, they thought they had some leverage."

James ladled soup into his bowl energetically and then went on. "Their objective was simple enough. After they concluded that we were actually serious about the auction, they wanted to generate a credible bid from a consortium of

American companies. Of course, they wanted to ensure that this bid won the competition. In addition, they wanted to take advantage of several circumstances they could not have predicted to generate instability across the province. The massive earthquake spread a useful degree of chaos along the coast, to start with. Your determination, Anne, to consult the people through a referendum made sure that an already split electorate would have weeks to battle around not just the very divisive auction idea, but the whole question of provincial autonomy as well. With all due respect, it is hard to imagine a more toxic brew. And we carefully stoked the fires under it. In retrospect, the foundation hardly had to do much more than add the occasional log to the fire."

Anne looked contrite and Katherine angry. Indira maintained a discreet silence.

"If this was the outline of the foundation's plan," James continued, "they took a number of specific steps to bring matters to a head. Once the referendum campaign started, they sent teams of specialists into the province to contact local groups that might be receptive to suggestions for direct action. These teams provided training, tactics and equipment. Throughout the campaign they kept raising the ante. Your friends in the EDF, Katherine, might have been content to chant and throw green paint, but the foundation guys wanted more impact than that. They encouraged and managed arson and bombings. They kept the level of paranoia within the First Nations and environmental movements high, and they generally ratcheted up the tension.

"The foundation's most spectacular coup came on the night of the vote itself. They blew up the premier. This had several benefits. It got you out of the way, Anne, and it made it likely that their man, de Groote, would ascend to the premier's chair. With you and your Far East connections sidelined, an American victory in the resource auction would be that much more likely. It also provided them with an opportunity to lay a trail of false clues that led to me. I was a detail they wanted to deal with, because I knew too much about the foundation already. Finally, all of this gave a marvellous impression that the province was on the verge of anarchy and virtually ungovernable. Once de Groote was installed, he was able to supplement that line and call in the 82nd Airborne – or in actuality, the US Marines. Not content with this, the foundation, I suspect, also had a hand in triggering the Nelson shootings. The Marines have always claimed that they were fired on first. In this case they were probably right."

James stopped his account to grab another sandwich.

Katherine finally spoke. "This whole thing makes me crazy. Why none of you could see that this damned auction was a loser idea, I don't know. Even without the foundation horning in, it made absolutely no sense! Didn't it register when just about every single First Nation, environmental or progressive group in the province dumped on the auction from a great height? Didn't any of you care? Do you realize how many lives have been destroyed by this stupidity?" She slumped into silence.

Anne looked stricken but chose to say nothing. The effort to remain silent was clearly costing her.

James took up the story. "The last actions by the foundation have been aimed at consolidating their gains. They arranged for me to be sprung from jail, assuming that I would try to help Katherine. The attack at the mine-site was intended to result in both of us being removed from play. And except for Robert's sacrifice" – James paused – "and the EDF's intervention, it would probably have worked. So here we are, with a bit of breathing room, but not much. I'm still on the run from the police. I wouldn't be surprised if the foundation tries again to kill Anne or Katherine, or both. The last thing they want is for opposition to coalesce around credible political figures. Both of you fall into that category."

Indira had been listening carefully to James's account and occasionally re-filling soup bowls. Now she came back to the table and looked across at a bereft Anne.

"I think that the key to this situation is Anne," she pronounced firmly. "You've never resigned your seat; you remain a member of caucus; and de Groote can just as easily be removed as he was promoted. He's only the premier because you were injured by a bomb-blast that he was complicit in planning. Now that we know about the foundation and his connections to it, it is simply outrageous that he should remain in power a minute longer! In point of fact, Willem de Groote should be in jail."

Anne raised her head and stared back at her friend. "I contributed sufficiently to the mess we're in. Even if the party accepted me back – which I don't see as a foregone conclusion, I might add – I am not sure what the public reaction might be. Do you really think they'd be prepared to give me another chance?"

"Let's take one thing at a time," responded Indira. "Are you prepared to join me in going back to caucus, revealing de Groote's connections to the foundation and demanding his removal? The rest of it will sort itself out, but unless we get rid of de Groote, we can't make progress at all. What do you say?"

Anne turned to Katherine, who was watching the exchange with not much enthusiasm.

"You can't lay this on me, Mom. You didn't pay any attention to my views when you invented the stupid resource auction in the first place, so why should you care what I think now? For what it's worth, I absolutely agree that the necessary first step is to get rid of that religious bigot, de Groote. But I also think that Indira's wrong. You can't simply march in and take over again without thinking through where you want to end up. It wouldn't be fair to the party, the people – or me, for that matter." Katherine subsided again, but she was now more engaged in the conversation.

Anne thought for a moment. "Okay, I agree that trying to become premier again for its own sake isn't a good enough reason. And I can't say that right this second I have a clear program I want to implement. I can tell you two or three things I want to see happen, though. First, in the largest sense, we need to take our province back. That means getting rid of the foundation-puppet de Groote and asking the US Marines politely but firmly to leave. Second, we need to put the emphasis back where it belongs, on rebuilding the province after that horrible earthquake. I know we won the referendum, but we need peace and quiet to rebuild, not more disorienting change. So, third, and please don't scream I told you so, Katherine, I think we need to re-build our international credibility by parking the resource auction."

"Yes!" shouted Katherine, jumping to her feet and punching the air.

"All right, all right," said her mother. "The fact is that the bidding process turned out to be rigged, and not even the Americans will be able to complain once we tell them and everyone else about the foundation's activities. What the province needs now is a retreat from radical departures and a focus on the bread-and-butter issues. I know what my daughter thinks. What about you two?"

Indira was the first to respond. "Well, obviously, going back to caucus will take a bit of stage-managing but, faced with the alternatives of you or de Groote, I don't think there's much doubt who they'll choose. We need to talk about exactly what we do with de Groote once he's no longer premier, but perhaps your new attorney general can provide the appropriate advice. And as for your three points, they sound sensible to me."

They all turned to James, who had been remarkably still throughout the discussion.

"You know," he began, "I can remember when the work I did mostly involved reading memos, writing questionnaires and talking to people – not running around the countryside, being shot at and getting arrested. So I've been giving serious thought to changing my line of work to something a bit more peaceful. And besides, as you all know, I have some unfinished business in the United States that I want to take care of. The foundation's based down there and it can't be allowed to act unchallenged. All that to one side, however, perhaps I can give you a last piece of political advice, before I move off into the sunset.

"Anne, I don't think there is any question that you should return to government. The fact is that a lot of this stuff is your fault. It's up to you to help clean it up. I agree with Indira that you'll probably be able to pull it off and, anyway, I think you owe it to the electorate to try." James paused.

"There are two provisos, though, and the second may cause you grief. The first one is easy. I think you should blame a lot of the problems on me. From the outside, it's me who looks like your closest political adviser. I believe that you should indicate that much of the advice about the resource auction came from me, that I was the one who allowed the foundation to become involved, that there are reasons to believe that both de Groote and I were party to the bombing that put you in hospital, and that therefore you are firing me with immediate effect. In order to make this all credible, you need a believable scapegoat, and that's me. You can indicate that an extensive search is underway, but that so far my whereabouts are unknown. And, in fact, that last part will be true, because if I can make it through the roadblocks I will be off to visit my friends in Washington and San Antonio."

The reaction was immediate. Although she was clearly shocked, Indira slowly nodded and reached across the table to take James' hand. Katherine was taken aback as well, but something approaching respect was washing across her face.

"James," Anne said softly, "I can't do that. It would destroy your reputation and everything you've built up over thirty years. You're asking me to lie about someone I care about deeply, who has been my closest adviser ever since I got into this crazy game. I can't do that to you."

"Yes you can," said James, having trouble keeping his voice level. "You need to have someone else to blame apart from de Groote and the foundation. I'm the logical choice. If people are to accept you as premier again, we have to direct blame as far away from you as we can. And besides, you haven't heard my second proviso ... and this will be harder for you to agree to than dumping me."

James focused on the eyes he found so hard to resist. "I believe that the only way your return will work is if you pledge right up front that you will *not* seek re-election. You have to commit to serving only until your successor is chosen by the party. You have to pledge that in the intervening time you will work day and night to undo any harm that you may have done. I don't expect you to take responsibility for the earthquake, but everything else is on you. People have to understand that you are brave enough and honest enough and honourable enough to act on that belief. British Columbians deserve a fresh start. You are the only person who can give it to them."

Silence fell over the room. Then Katherine and Indira began crying. Anne got up and came around the table to embrace James.

She looked oddly relaxed, even relieved. "Of course, you're right, James. A fresh start."

CHAPTER 62

December 1, Vancouver

T he reunion in Indira's kitchen had some immediate consequences. Anne went back to hospital for a last few days of convalescence but then returned home, much to her great relief. Now that she knew she wanted to take one last run at politics, the prospect of the coming battle gave her a jolt of energy.

Once Anne was an out-patient, Katherine stayed with her to settle her in. She and Anne had long conversations about the activities of the EDF. They also spent some time working together on ways in which social media might be mobilized against de Groote and the foundation, when the time was right. Katherine was relieved to be treated for hours at a time as a colleague rather than a daughter. She found her stress levels diminishing daily, although Robert was never far from her thoughts. The work with her mother helped her to deal in unexpected ways with her loss.

As for James, his primary short-term concern was to stay out of the hands of authorities. A friend of Georgina's loaned him a room in a small house near the Burrard Street Bridge. He spent several days catching up on sleep and taking stock.

Most days he stayed indoors, but in the evening he would walk over to Kits beach. Sitting on a bench with an unobstructed view of the sea and the mountains, he would count the freighters riding at anchor. He was not sure why this was worth his time, but it seemed almost as important as the number of cats he counted in the course of his walk. The more freighters and cats he found, the better he felt. He came to know where the cats lived on his usual route and, when he returned to his room he was able to say to himself, "A three-cat walk, not bad." And "I haven't seen the orange tabby on the corner for a couple of days; I hope he's fine." Einstein would understand, even if most humans wouldn't.

Most of the time, of course, he just sat and stared at the sea, letting his mind wander. The impact of recent events had stripped away his usual equanimity. He had almost died twice, in the earthquake and then at the hands of foundation thugs. His career was in tatters. He was on the run from police. More unsettling was a series of shocks to the foundations of his beliefs about himself. For years, especially since the bloody events in Mexico, James had tried quite successfully to insulate himself from situations involving physical or emotional risk. He had determined that life was simpler without unnecessary attachments or commitments. His reconnection with Anne, coupled with the astonishing revelation about Katherine, seemed to call into question the virtues of this level of detachment.

James' friendship with Alastair had also formed part of what he could only feel as a form of awakening. He had a high regard for Alastair's hard-won wisdom. After talking to the crusty former librarian, issues in his personal and professional life seemed easier to place in perspective, if not easier to resolve. He admired Alastair's commitment to the underdog, his refusal to accept unfairness. Most of all, he craved Alastair's respect, and he had little doubt that the older man would find his foundation connections unsavoury at best. Sometime soon he would need to confess to Alastair about that link.

Similarly, he thought about another elder, Marta, and the hour he had spent in her warm cottage in Langley. Her compelling personality had touched him in ways he found unexpected. He was awed by her bravery, envious of her certainty. And now Marta was dead – and it was his fault. His mind squirmed away from images of Marta and her kittens.

And, finally, he remembered Robert, the man his daughter loved, the man who had given his life so his daughter could escape. James tried to face down the gnawing realization that he was complicit in Robert's death. He had brought the foundation down on the EDF. He had been content to lie there while Robert and others had acted to save Katherine. He had been instrumental in bringing grief into his daughter's life.

So as he walked along the beach or sat by the sea for hours at a time, James juggled conflicting emotions. All his instincts urged him to disengage, to let others take the risks. For much of his life he had achieved a degree of peace through this tactic.

But now he had new commitments to people he cared about, living and dead. In some cases he had debts to repay, in others, he had obligations to discharge. With each passing day he came to recognize that he could no longer simply walk away. The prospect of taking on unconditional responsibility scared him – but the alternative seemed to be an arid existence bereft of meaning. In the end, perhaps the key lay in Marta's words – "We do what we must."

James knew that he still had unfinished business with JJ and his foundation minions. That might take years, and it was unlikely he could do much alone. In the meantime, he needed time, space and quiet to collect his thoughts. The small Oregon cottage had never seemed so necessary to his well-being. He would be there soon. He would be safe again soon.

CHAPTER 63

December 12, Vancouver

While Anne and Katherine and James focused on healing and planning, each in her or his own way, Indira was carefully reaching out to her friends and supporters in the party. It was vital not to tip off de Groote about the coming storm. It was equally necessary to prepare the way for Anne's return.

What Indira discovered was that the new premier had hardly endeared himself to the caucus in the weeks since his elevation. The call for American assistance had almost provoked a revolt, but the usual political cowardice prevailed.

More personally, however, a growing number of government members were finding de Groote's directive style hard to take. De Groote had always tended to sprinkle his comments with biblical references, but this habit was becoming alarming. The premier apparently saw Divine Providence acting directly through him to shape events in the province. Most of his colleagues found this unsettling.

In the end, the factors that dislodged him were decidedly mundane.

Two weeks after the kitchen conference, word spread that Anne Richardson might be returning to caucus. The columnists picked up the rumours. Expectations were running high by the time caucus met in Vancouver for their usual monthly meeting. Reporters approached the premier before-hand, but he seemed remarkably serene.

Standing in the offices outside the cabinet chambers, responding to a question about his continued leadership, he said, "You know, I was called to this position by my colleagues. If they have issues they wish to discuss with me, I am always prepared to talk, and . . ."

Just then, Anne appeared, rolling through the door in a wheelchair propelled by a beaming Indira. The press scrum instantly deserted de Groote and descended on the two women. Anne was crisply dressed in a black pant suit and, apart from being in a chair, gave no evidence of her injuries.

A chorus sang out, "How are you feeling?" "Are you back for good?" "Do you expect to be premier again?"

Anne smiled and held up a hand to try to answer over the hubbub.

"I know you will have many questions. I have every intention of answering them. Right now, though, my priority is to meet with my colleagues and talk with them about what happens next. I'll be available right after the caucus meeting. I'd be happy to talk to you all then. In the meantime, you should know that I'm well on the way to full health. I look forward to coming back to work hard for the people of British Columbia. Thank you for your interest!"

Then she moved through the doors of the cabinet chamber, leaving a buzz behind her. De Groote followed quietly in her wake.

The press were ushered out of the office suite. They had to wait two hours in the hallway before anything more happened. At that point, the doors were flung open. They shuffled through to find a pleased-looking Anne Richardson. As her colleagues slipped out around the scrum, she squared up to reporters.

"I am very pleased to tell you," she said, "that my colleagues have done me the great honour of asking me to become premier again. I have accepted. I will meet the lieutenant governor this afternoon and the House soon afterwards. At that time, one or two other adjustments will be made to the composition of cabinet. I don't think I am breaking caucus confidentiality to tell you that my colleague and friend Indira Dhaliwal will be returning to play an important role.

"Before I take any questions, I would like to make two points. First, I know that recent weeks have seen events that have worried and concerned all British Columbians. Coming on the heels of the terrible earthquake that struck so many families and caused so much damage, the confusion and controversy in our political life have added unnecessarily to people's anxiety, at a time when steady, predictable leadership is vital. Now that I am back on my feet, so to speak, I hope to provide that leadership. I will be reporting to the House shortly on our plans for the coming months.

"The second point follows from the first. Although I have been thrilled to be your premier and am content to take up the job again, I will not be running in the next election. I feel strongly that it is vital at this critical time that the government be led by a person who can make the tough decisions with no regard for short-term electoral considerations. Accordingly, I will serve as party leader and premier only until a convention can be arranged.

"Given the circumstances, and subject to discussion with the party executive and members generally, I would not expect that convention to occur much before the middle of next year. This timing will give some immediate stability to the government and provide potential leadership candidates with the opportunity to make up their minds and canvass support.

"Now, I am happy to take questions, although I gather I have to be out of here in half an hour."

Out of the deluge of questions that followed, little additional information was extracted. The reinstated premier pronounced herself in good health. She said she'd be out of the wheelchair in a day or two. She expressed no doubt about her ability to stand up to the physical demands of the job. She refused to disclose details of the discussion behind closed doors but made it clear that the sentiment of the meeting had been nearly unanimous.

The one question she was repeatedly asked, and which she repeatedly refused to answer, concerned the future of Willem de Groote. She referred all enquiries to de Groote himself, who had left unseen down a back stairway. She pointedly refused to offer the usual thanks for de Groote's work in her absence. When pressed, she indicated that the attorney general would be undertaking an investigation of a number of issues related to de Groote's tenure. Soon afterwards, pleading the need to get back to work, Richardson ended the press conference, leaving behind considerable confusion.

Safely back in her personal office, Anne sagged in her chair. She turned a tired face to a small group that included James, Indira and Georgina Ho. James was poised to head to the United States, thanks to arrangements organized surreptitiously by his NSA contacts, but he couldn't resist the temptation to witness the premier's return.

"Well, that's over with. Georgina, could you make the arrangements for going over to see the LG this afternoon? I'll be staying in Victoria tonight. I'm not sure I could face another flight today. Thanks."

Georgina bustled out of the room.

"What did you think of de Groote's reaction, Indira?" asked Anne.

"I thought he was suspiciously quiet," said Indira. "But then, I can never predict how he's going to act, anyway. He's one peculiar person, is our friend Willem. I assume you want my folks to move on him. My suggestion is appointing a special prosecutor. That insulates us all and makes it clear to de Groote that we're serious."

"De Groote isn't likely to disappear without a fight," warned James. "At the very least, he'll want to take me out, and he'll do everything he can to discredit you, Premier."

"Well, sadly, we'll be pre-empting him about you, James. I think that my announcement about not running will reduce his ability to take me on," replied Anne. "In the meantime, you have to get out of here. Fortunately, Indira isn't the attorney general yet. Otherwise, she would be required to ensure your detention."

With a smile, James made for the door.

* * *

Meanwhile, the subject of these speculations was slowly making his way back to the Fraser Valley. The roads had not been completely repaired since the earthquake, so the trip took longer than usual. De Groote sat in traffic, barely seeing the car ahead of him. He also blanked out the earthquake devastation on either side of the highway. It was remarkable how familiar and ordinary the shattered landscape had become.

De Groote was not particularly surprised that Richardson had tried to take her job back, although he was amazed at how well she looked. What had stunned him was the speed with which his caucus colleagues had welcomed her, especially since Richardson had not mentioned anything directly about his connections with the foundation. On the other hand, he had noticed that some of the members refused to meet his eyes. Only one or two had shaken his hand at the end of the meeting. No doubt Richardson and her acolyte, the Dhaliwal woman, had been spreading poison behind the scenes. Typical.

In the event, publicly Richardson had been all sweetness and light, thanking him for his work and taking back her position as if by right. For a second or two, de Groote had considered taking a stand and refusing to relinquish the premiership. But as he looked around the room, it was clear that his support was minimal. An open breach would be futile. Once again, de Groote decided to cede the field and walk away. But this time, it left bitterness in his mouth and a mounting anger. His big hands clenched the wheel as he bulled his way through traffic.

It was time to make a virtue out of necessity. If he was to be attacked for connections with the Destiny Foundation, he might as well take advantage of those links. As he pulled into the driveway leading to his house, he thought about how he would couch his report to JJ. The foundation had a great deal invested in him. He could not believe that they would write that investment off without a struggle.

CHAPTER 64

December 16, Victoria

As reinstated premier, Anne returned to Vancouver after seeing the lieutenant governor. She left the day-to-day business of government to others and focused on the speech she would give shortly in the House. The party could simply have bought time on the main television channels, but Anne felt that it was important to emphasize parliamentary traditions, even if the effect was to give the Opposition a free platform as well. Some degree of normalcy had to be re-established.

When she rose in the Legislative Assembly a few days later, expectations were high. Anne's earlier scrum had whetted the media's appetites, but more details were required. The House was silent and the galleries packed as the premier rose in her place. The Edwardian grandeur of the chamber lent solemnity to the occasion.

She began with a standard, if heartfelt, expression of appreciation for the support she had received since her injury. She went on to say that her hospital stay had given her time to reflect on the state of the province and the steps that needed to be taken to get British Columbia back on track. She acknowledged that, in the midst of the political game that obsessed elected officials, it was all too easy to lose track of the things people outside politics most valued in their everyday lives.

Chief among these were a general sense of predictability and the related conviction that the government could be relied on to manage the public interest efficiently. The need for this reassurance was especially high, in her view, after a disaster on the scale of the recent earthquake. In these circumstances, people had every right to assume that rapid recovery was the government's main focus, well ahead of any potential partisan advantage.

"So it is in this spirit," the premier went on, "that I want to give the people of British Columbia an account of recent events and our government's initial plans for moving the province forward from here."

Everyone in the House leaned forward to listen.

"Central to the story is an American organization called the Destiny Foundation. This group is based in San Antonio, Texas. It has almost unlimited funds and considerable influence in Washington, DC, as well as regionally. It also has a clear objective – to bring those parts of North America that are not currently United States territory under its direct control. Although this goal sounds like something out of the plot of a B-movie, we have learned to our cost that it would be a mistake to underestimate the power and determination of this organization."

At this point in the premier's speech, MLAs and visitors alike were turning to one another in disbelief. A buzz broke out around the chamber, and the Speaker called for order.

Anne continued. "It is no exaggeration to say that this foundation is prepared to stop at nothing, including murder, to achieve its ends. Most of the time, however, it makes use of its significant financial resources and the gullibility of a variety of 'useful idiots' on both sides of the border. Perhaps most importantly, the foundation is playing the long game.

"It has been active for many decades. It is prepared to persevere for many more. It seeks influence in local, state and federal governments in the United States and in many of their counterparts here in Canada. Its agents and associates operate for years at a time in perfectly normal ways. Then, when the time is right, they act to undermine governments and achieve foundation aims. We have posted on the provincial government's website a dossier outlining their activities. I would urge all of you to take a look at this information when you can."

There was a bustle in the Press Gallery as reporters grabbed their iPads to bring up the government site. Most spectators remained riveted to their seats, as the premier continued her extraordinary speech.

"So, how has this foundation affected the political life of British Columbia? The House will know that this government developed a plan to stabilize and increase the province's revenue base through the judicious mobilization of its valuable store of natural resources. Although my cabinet colleagues and I have been fully engaged in the decision-making around this innovative initiative, I think it is fair to say that its foremost champion was an adviser in my office, James Dean Franklin."

Anne took a deep breath before continuing. Those closest to her could see the strain on her face. "I regret to tell you now that a painstaking internal investigation has revealed that James Franklin systematically abused his position of trust to twist this program to the purposes of the Destiny Foundation. He was instrumental in ensuring that the resource auction was won by a US consortium. More importantly, he worked with foundation agents to foment unrest and generate instability during the recent referendum. Among the operations he helped plan were the provocations that led to the shootings in Nelson and the bombing that occurred at the end of the referendum campaign.

"Through his actions, James Franklin has seriously undermined the province's international reputation. More to the point, he has threatened the democratic process here in British Columbia. The law enforcement agencies of the province are currently seeking to arrest him. We hope to bring him to justice shortly."

Amid rustling, listeners seemed to be digesting the information she was presenting. The premier took a sip of water, shuffled her papers and went on.

"Unfortunately, James Franklin was not the highest ranking BC official to be involved with the Destiny Foundation. Within the last few days I have been saddened to discover that my former colleague, Mr. Willem de Groote, has also had connections with the foundation for many years. So far, we have been unable to determine the extent of these links. Perhaps only Mr. de Groote will ever know the degree to which the foundation directly influenced his actions as a member of this House and later as interim premier. Suffice it to say that Mr. de Groote has left cabinet and caucus. He will have to decide for himself whether to give the voters of his constituency the opportunity to pass judgment on his conduct."

A ripple of exclamations greeted these revelations. The premier had to wait several moments while the Speaker called for order and the chamber quieted.

"The events of the past months constitute a sorry chapter in the history of British Columbia. Coupled with the disastrous earthquake that ravaged our communities, they remind us forcibly how important it is to maintain the integrity and effectiveness of our institutions. With this in mind, I am announcing today three important steps that my government is taking to set the province on the road to recovery."

Two of those steps were predictable, albeit major. First, she had contacted the US government through its consulate general in Vancouver to ask that all American troops be withdrawn from British Columbia immediately. She had also provided US authorities with a detailed account of the Destiny Foundation's illegal schemes and expected that appropriate action would be taken within their own jurisdiction.

Second, in the interest of focusing completely on economic recovery, she announced that the government would discontinue its resource management initiative until further notice.

The third step was less foreseen and, despite the premier's earlier comments to reporters, still caused an audible gasp in the galleries.

"Finally, I want to confirm that I will not run in the next provincial election. I feel very strongly that elected officials must take full responsibility for what occurs during their time in office. Under the circumstances, I believe that it is time for new leadership to step forward and move the province ahead. In the time remaining to me as premier, however, I promise to work day and night to rebuild the province and restore its relations with the rest of Canada and with our international partners."

And with that, the premier sat down, having delivered one of the most unusual addresses the Parliament of British Columbia had ever heard.

CHAPTER 65

December 17, Vancouver

Reaction to Anne Richardson's speech was broadly positive among the public at large. The prospect of a period of relative calm amounted to a reprieve to a population still trying to deal with a recent catastrophe. In addition, the premier retained a measure of respect as an individual from her tireless work during and after the earthquake.

Expert opinion was less kind. The consensus among the pundits was that a new government headed by an inexperienced leader had lost its way. It had then fastened on an ill-conceived revenue-generating scheme that would have ruined the province's economy, and which had provoked needless social conflict. Some commentators wondered how it was possible that such a hare-brained plan could make it through a professional public service. The conclusion was that most of the checks and balances within the government system had been eroded to the point that a sufficiently determined premier could push almost anything through it.

Even among her supporters, Richardson's promise to resign was accepted as inevitable. The government's track record taken as a whole was decidedly uninspiring. It was entirely unclear that it had the competence to manage the enormous task of recovery in the wake of the earthquake. The electorate didn't seem to want Richardson to resign in disgrace, but it had probably lost confidence in her capacity to govern effectively. On the other hand, Katherine Richardson's friends on the left and in the environmental movement chimed in on the internet to attack the Destiny Foundation and to applaud the premier's honourable decision not to run again.

As for Anne, she left the chamber in a high state of relief. She had taken on the party leader's job in the first place convinced that finding a new way of doing politics was vital. Beyond that general conviction, however, she had brought few specific proposals to government when she won her unexpected victory.

The resource auction idea had emerged at a time when the economy was stagnating and people were desperate for change. It was fashionable to condemn the government in retrospect, but the element of risk had been part of the scheme's original attraction. Bored and frustrated, people were prepared to take a flyer. Anne's personality had acted as a catalyst, but conditions had been ripe for a collective high-stakes gamble. Even after the shock of the earthquake, voters had confirmed through the referendum that they still supported a new and exciting way forward.

Anne acknowledged to herself that the excitement had dissipated quickly as the province descended into chaos. The foundation's role obviously contributed, but Anne recognized, even if she would never say so publicly, that her government's actions had made the intervention of an outside force much easier.

The next step had to be left to James. It was up to him to try to take on the foundation in its own territory. She knew he was grimly determined to hold the foundation to account for Marta's and Robert's murders, to say nothing of their attempt to blow her up.

She was worried about that, worried for him. She wished she knew what that meant about their relationship. With a sigh, she parked that thought for another time. For now, she just wanted James safe.

CHAPTER 66

December 18, San Antonio

While the premier was taking up the reins again, the head of the Destiny Foundation was less than pleased. He much preferred to operate out of the public eye. The sudden departure of de Groote and the revelations about the foundation's role were extremely unwelcome developments.

He was not surprised when de Groote called with a demand that he do something on his behalf. JJ was his usual courtly self, but he gave absolutely no indication that the man should expect immediate action from him. He did take some time to calm de Groote down.

After hanging up, he called Alison in. "You heard the news from BC?" he asked her.

"Yes. Not the outcome we were looking for. A pity. That was a great opportunity," she observed.

"Not every operation we undertake will turn out well," JJ replied soothingly. "The trick is to minimize the damage when we fall short. I think de Groote is going to be a problem, incidentally. It may be preferable that he not be available to the press any more. Can you arrange for him to withdraw from public life?"

Alison smiled. "I'm sure something can be worked out. He may not care about himself, but he'll be sensitive about his family. Don't worry, JJ, we'll see to it."

"Good," responded JJ. "I know I can count on you. My real concern, though, is not de Groote, but Franklin. He has turned out to be more resilient than we thought. I have a suspicion that he will use his contacts down here to try to do us some harm. Do your people know where he is right now?"

Alison looked a little uncomfortable. "We tracked him to Dhaliwal's house, but after he met with Richardson and her daughter, we lost him. He's shed his tail, and he's dropped off the grid as well."

"We've known Franklin for a good long time, now," said JJ. "He always struck me as being a very determined man. We have to assume that he's going to try something drastic. And you know, the timing might not be so bad for us anyway."

Her expression puzzled, Alison waited for JJ to continue.

"Over the years," JJ went on, "we've talked about the future of this organization, about our obligation to maintain our capability in the long term." Alison nodded. "Well, I think we've reached a critical point. If I'm reading our friend Franklin correctly, he's headed this way, and he's bringing the feds with him. If that happens, there may be a limit to how effectively we can hold them off. So, we need to do two things. First, we need to ensure continuity. That will be your job, Alison. Whatever happens here or to me, you have to be in a position to carry on. The Destiny Foundation is bigger than one person or one location. Your job is to lead the next stage in the foundation's life."

Alison's eyes filled. "You know I will do whatever you ask of me. You can count on me."

"I know I can, child," replied JJ warmly. "I've always been proud of you, Alison. I know that won't stop now."

"What's the second thing?" asked Alison, after a moment.

"The second thing," said JJ, with a glint in his eyes, "is to arrange for a reception for Franklin and his friends that no one

Peter Charles Heap

will ever forget."

CHAPTER 67

December 20, Fort Meade, Maryland

T he meeting room in Fort Meade, not far from Baltimore, had most of the features of the other meeting rooms James had inhabited over the years. Perhaps the only exception was the lack of windows and the related, claustrophobia-inducing fact that this room lay deep in the interior of a large black building. This was the National Security Agency. Its premises were shielded in every way conceivable.

James had arrived at Baltimore–Washington International Airport the evening before. His NSA contact had helped him to disappear from Vancouver. A collection of American security organizations had decided that a thorough face-to-face debriefing was warranted. James sipped his government-issue coffee. He went on with his account of the various ways the Destiny Foundation had intervened, sometimes violently, in the politics of British Columbia.

The roomful of officials seemed interested enough. For once, the story involved a country remarkably similar to the US and quite close by. James continued his rehearsal of the reasons why American authorities might wish to consider whether to allow the foundation to continue to exist.

"To make the most obvious point, the Destiny Foundation is subverting the foreign policy of the United States.

It may be that at some future date you decide that the constituent parts of your nearest democratic neighbour should be hoovered into the Union, but so far that does not seem to be your country's stated goal. And in the meantime, if word gets out that the United States actively seeks to undermine a close ally, the number of other close allies you have around the world may shrink alarmingly. Leaving aside the impact on relations with Canada, which is bound to be serious after this episode, your country will never be trusted again, unless steps are taken to remedy the situation."

The representative of the intelligence branch of the State Department intervened through pursed lips. She was simply dressed in tailored black slacks and an expensive-looking white silk blouse. This was clearly not her first meeting of the day; she exuded a certain tired resignation. "Mr. Franklin, the reputation of the United States has survived many more egregious acts than the mischief caused by a two-bit foundation from Texas. That being said, I take your point that the US should clean up its own messes. Do you have any other issues you wish to raise, other than worrying about the long-term state of American foreign policy?"

"I would suggest that the overriding American interest is simply to keep peace in the neighbourhood," James replied. "The foundation has helped to seriously destabilize the province and call into question the viability of the Canadian federation as a whole. Sending Marines into BC entails unnecessary expense. It also represents a distraction from the many more important issues your country faces globally. In addition, presumably you have no interest in leaving the impression with other paramilitary groups in this country that the US government can be manipulated for their own ends. My overall recommendation is that some combination of the agencies in this room take upon themselves the task of closing down the Destiny Foundation permanently. In my view, people on both sides of the border will sleep easier if that organization ceases to exist."

The senior FBI representative, a bespectacled reed-thin individual in the Bureau's standard-issue grey suit and plain blue tie, spoke up. "The question of how to deal with this foundation is purely a domestic matter, Mr. Franklin. Our friends in the NSA may have been kind enough to provide the venue for this meeting, but the responsibility for further action clearly rests with us. Unless others around the table have additional questions, I think you can leave this issue in our hands. Thank you for bringing it to our attention."

* * *

The next day, James received a call from the FBI in his motel room on the nearby highway strip. There followed an extended wrangle during which James pressed his case for being present when the Bureau moved against the foundation. His main argument was that he knew the key figures in the organization and might be of assistance. The FBI was very resistant to having a foreigner in the vicinity of an operation but, in the end, they told him his presence in San Antonio as an observer would be possible.

James hung up the phone, his thoughts churning. He was determined to witness the eventual destruction of the foundation, but he had no illusions about JJ's willingness to put up a fight. To his way of thinking, the Bureau's officials seemed a good deal too confident.

CHAPTER 68

December 20, Vancouver

Meanwhile, the foundation's executive director was engaged in one of her favourite activities – tidying up. Alison prided herself on the fact that the foundation's interventions rarely came to public light. Obviously, the recent speech by Anne Richardson flew in the face of that record, but that did not mean that JJ's direction to limit the damage should not be followed to the letter. There was little Alison could do directly about Richardson for the moment, although in due course, that person would discover that the foundation had a very long memory. The continued existence of de Groote, however, was an affront that Alison was happy to remove.

De Groote had not turned out to be a useful ally. In the short time he had been premier, he had demonstrated few leadership abilities. He had also begun to show disturbing tendencies towards messianism. Alison had no problem with associates mistaking JJ for the Messiah, but she drew the line at self-identification. From the foundation's perspective, De Groote's belief that he was the direct beneficiary of divine instructions significantly reduced his efficacy. It was time to finish him off as a factor in BC politics.

After some consideration, Alison decided that another of the former premier's foibles would serve nicely as the instrument of his destruction. She had a short conversation with the foundation's remaining senior operative in the province and was rewarded with quick obedience coupled with a gurgle of appreciative laughter.

* * *

De Groote was gratified when Alison subsequently called to follow up on his earlier conversation with JJ. He had found Alison to be intelligent and generally helpful. Indeed he had caught himself wondering just how far that willingness to help might go. So it was with a mixture of excitement and alarm that he agreed to Alison's suggestion that they meet at a small out-of-the-way motel on the Trans-Canada Highway. He could feel a knot of anticipation grow in his stomach as he pulled into the gravel parking lot. He got out of the car and knocked on the door. There stood Alison, resplendent in a form-fitting concoction that hinted at intimacies to come.

Half an hour later, Alison emerged alone. She stepped into an undistinguished Honda that took her quickly to nearby Langley Airport, where a private plane awaited.

* * *

The insistent ringing of his cell-phone eventually penetrated the pain and fog encasing de Groote's consciousness. He located the phone with difficulty and encountered a highly agitated constituency assistant.

"Mr. de Groote, thank God I've found you. We've been looking everywhere. You must have had your phone off."

De Groote struggled to clear his throat, not to mention the fog in his mind. Where was Alison? What had happened?

"Well, I'm here now. What is so important?"

The aide began slowly. "I think you should look at the BCTV Newschannel. They're running a feature on you, and they've been calling here for hours trying to get a quote from you. They claim to have received an anonymous e-mail attaching some video that appears to involve you." She paused. "They have played parts of the video on air already, Mr. de Groote. It doesn't look good. Perhaps you should contact them and clear this up. Here's their number." And with that, a very embarrassed-sounding assistant rang off.

De Groote grabbed for his iPhone and looked up the BCTV website. There, to his horror, he found a story that began with a clip of a naked person who looked astonishingly like him. He was clearly not alone. The other person, of indeterminate gender, was naked as well. The clip was short, but long enough to show that the two naked people were engaged in a mutually enjoyable activity.

Now de Groote looked around. The motel room was in disarray. Most of the blankets and sheets from the bed were on the floor. His jacket and tie were thrown over the back of a chair. He looked down and discovered to his horror that his shirt was lipstick-stained. His trousers were loosely zipped, and his feet were bare. Most unnerving of all, his boxers were on the floor beside the bed. Why were his pants on, but his underwear off? In that moment, his world collapsed.

As his eyes darted frantically between the news report and the wreckage of the motel room around him, he felt a terrible pain ripple across his chest and down his arm, and he toppled to the floor.

IX. RECKONING

CHAPTER 69

December 21, San Antonio

J ames was back in Alamo Plaza. Down at the other end from where he stood in the shadows, just beyond the little church that held such symbolic power, especially for Texans, loomed the Emily Morgan Hotel, with its distinctive tower at one corner. On the top two floors of the hotel were the offices of the Destiny Foundation.

It was late afternoon. The heat was dissipating along with the crowds of tourists. Although he could not see them, James knew that the whole area was awash with FBI agents. He spotted several black vans parked near the hotel and assumed they were full of equipment and armed officers.

He had been told to stay out of the way, and he would. He retreated round the corner, recognizing that he would be of little use if gunfire broke out. He fully expected that JJ would relish a showdown. The FBI had told him that they would be moving in at 5:30. Checking his watch, he saw that the deadline had passed. Nothing had happened. He paced nervously, out of sight of the Plaza.

Suddenly a panel van drew up alongside him, the door opened, and the gaunt FBI agent from the Fort Meade meeting ordered him to get in. James hesitated, but the agent's grim expression strongly suggested he was being given no choice. Fifteen minutes later, he was walking through the main doors of the Morgan, straight to the elevators. The lobby was empty. Why was he here?

James stepped off the elevator into the foundation's reception area, which led to the boardroom. Heavily armed agents lined the way into the larger room, the one with the low, beige-based pieces of furniture and the occasional kitschy but expensive examples of western frontier art – the room where James had so memorably burned his bridges with the foundation. At the far end sat Jonathan Johnson, looking remarkably relaxed, considering the circumstances. Three agents in FBI-marked combat gear stood nearby, weapons at the ready.

The agent from the Fort Meade meeting turned to him, open anger now on his face.

"He asked specifically for you, Franklin. I don't suppose that comes as any surprise."

"Actually, I'm amazed," James responded. "The last time I was here, we were hardly on friendly terms. Didn't he resist when you showed up?"

"No, he just sat there looking smug. Everyone on his staff had already left. We read him his rights, and then he asked for you. We want this to go as smoothly as possible, so let's get on with it. You've got five minutes."

JJ got up and offered his hand as James approached. "It's good to see you again. You look like you could use some sleep." The southern accent gave a courtly tone to the slightly insulting remark.

James ignored his hand. "What do you want, JJ? Isn't it enough that you've tried to kill a person I care about, destroy the government I work for, and then had me chased across the countryside? Now you drag me into this mess."

"Well now, there's no reason to get all worked up. You and I have always understood each other. I knew you'd want to hear directly from me what's going to happen next. Aren't you the least bit curious?" JJ's smile was wintery as he retreated to his desk.

The FBI agent interrupted, furious. "Cut the bullshit, Johnson! Say what you're going to say. Then we're taking you to prison where you belong."

"I see that the Bureau has retained its customary commitment to legal due process. All right then, for your benefit, and James', this is where we're headed. Your timing is exemplary, actually, because, when you burst in here, I was just putting on the finishing touches."

JJ stretched his leg in a habitual effort to ease his pain, but he seemed otherwise relaxed. "To begin, as my friend James here can tell you, the Destiny Foundation believes that the United States is fated to be the ultimate force for good in the world. We believe that America's 'manifest destiny' extends to global as well as hemispheric leadership. Unfortunately" – JJ looked downcast – "the so-called political elite are convinced that the right course of action is to lead America in a strategic retreat. This approach would be catastrophic, not just for America but for the world."

"Enough crap, Johnson," the agent closest to JJ shouted, "get to the point or you're out of here, now!" The agents took several steps forward.

JJ looked directly at James and went on. "The rapidly evolving situation in British Columbia attracted our attention, both because it presented a valuable opportunity to encourage the absorption of Canada's regions into the US, and because we happened to have a number of assets already in place in the province. Not only did these circumstances cry out for creative intervention, we could be absolutely certain that our inattentive, weak-kneed US authorities would never act themselves to take full advantage."

At this point, James could contain himself no longer. JJ's soft-spoken rationale for barbaric behaviour was too much to bear. He leapt towards Johnson and grabbed for his throat. JJ easily knocked his hands aside and pushed him onto the floor. The agents quickly stepped in to haul James back. James shrugged them off and stood up but didn't move towards JJ again. Trying to attack a trained special forces soldier, even an elderly one, was probably a waste of effort.

"Those were real people who died in BC thanks to your philosophical attachment to the American empire," James sputtered, panting. "I hope these guys throw you in the darkest cell in the oldest prison in America!"

JJ went on as if nothing had happened. "In the larger scheme of things, the BC operation was just a side-show for us. We've got bigger fish to fry. Above all, we have to educate the American people and bring them face to face with their responsibilities in an era of conflict between civilizations. The one thing that will drive that change is fear. Americans must re-learn the lesson of 9/11 and realize just how vulnerable they are. So, while you little folks up in BC have been squabbling away, we've been busy arranging for a crisis that will make the break-up of Canada look like a walk in the park.

"Despite your steadfast refusal to recognize your own self-interest, I've always liked you, James. I regretted your decision to leave us, and I held out hope that you'd eventually come home. That didn't come to pass, however, so I wanted the next best thing – a chance to show you what you're missing. James, this is what real power looks like!"

JJ pivoted to the desk beside him and punched a key on his computer. As he moved, the agents lunged towards him.

"Hands in the air!" shouted one. They hauled JJ away from the desk into the centre of the room.

The lights in the room flickered and dimmed; the air conditioning wheezed to a stop. A shout came from the reception area next door.

"Boss, the elevators have gone down!"

James turned on JJ, who was standing quietly in the grip of two of the agents with a satisfied expression on his face. "What have you done?"

JJ's voice came back strangely blurred and a bit indistinct, his words jumbled together. James saw that the agents who had grabbed JJ's arms were being forced to hold him up.

"I think you'll find that the entire western power grid has just gone off-line. When the FBI and its associates investigate, they'll discover clear evidence of a foreign plot. This information is being relayed to the major networks and websites as we speak. They will find absolutely no indication that the foundation was involved at all. What they will find is hard evidence of an ISIS-led plot to cripple this country. A blackout on this scale should grab the attention of even the most supine administration." JJ's breathing became laboured. "The American people are going to demand action. They won't be satisfied until the United States takes back the international role it should never have given up. No show-trial for me, though."

Just then, JJ's body slumped to the floor, convulsing. The agents had lost their grip on his arms. James started towards him, too late to catch him. JJ twitched one last time and was still.

The agents rushed to the foundation computer and tried to gain entry, but apparently JJ's single keystroke had frozen the machine after sending a last command to initiate the attack on the power grid. They grabbed for their cellphones seeking information, briefing superiors, calling for back-up, bringing the great lumbering beast of an intelligence system into play.

At first James stood there as the FBI tried to take control of the situation. He stared at the inert body of a man he had once idolized and later came to despise. Instead of satisfaction he felt emptiness. JJ might be dead, but his organization lived on. In a very limited way Marta and Robert had been avenged, but nothing had really changed. British Columbia might no longer be in the foundation's crosshairs but, as JJ had said, the province and its people had only ever been a sideshow. The dogs barked and the caravan moved on.

The heat rose steadily in the darkened boardroom. Looking out the windows to Alamo Plaza, James watched in disbelief as the lights of the city winked out, blocks at a time.

Outside the hotel, with no traffic lights operating, the cars on San Antonio's streets began competing for rapidly disappearing space. Collisions occurred across the city. In their wake, gunfire broke out as Texans exercised their constitutional right to self-defence. Along the shopping streets plate glass windows were shattered. Looting took moments to metastasize from neighbourhood to neighbourhood.

Consumed with trying to deal with a situation spiralling out of control, the growing crowd of FBI agents, Texas Rangers and city policemen barely noticed as James left the room and began the long trek down the stairs to street level. Once there, he would probably have to walk to nearby Fort Sam Houston, but his intelligence contact had assured him that if he reached the base he could count on transport out of San Antonio. Under the circumstances, though, even the US Army might take a while to get him home. And he would have to be careful – in Canada he was still a wanted fugitive.

As he clumped down the stairs into the gloom, he knew that soon he would have to disappear. But before he did that, he needed to say some farewells, face to face.

CHAPTER 70

January 5, Vancouver

Two weeks later, James sat drinking coffee at the kitchen table in Anne's house in Point Grey. His car was at the curb, waiting for a run to the border.

Despite the premier's speech, the authorities had been informed that it would be easier for all concerned if James were allowed to leave the jurisdiction – no detailed explanations, no revelation of sources, no public trial. Accordingly, the police were not pressing their attempts to arrest him, and he felt reasonably relaxed. So far as he knew, even JJ's minions had lost track of him in the chaos that the foundation had unleashed. James was under no illusion that his invisibility would last forever, however, and he felt the need to keep moving.

He gave Anne a full account of events in San Antonio. The massive blackout that had paralyzed the entire western US meant that it had taken him days to get back to Canada, despite the good offices of several US agencies. Heroic efforts by BC Hydro had managed to limit the damage in the province, but the economic and social impact of the cascading blackouts in the western states was enormous.

Civil order had completely broken down in several American cities. Large sections of Los Angeles were still no-go zones, even for the National Guard. Richer towns and neighbourhoods retreated behind walls. Intruders were shot on sight. Communications were crippled as cell-phone towers lost power. Irrigation failures in key areas like California's Imperial Valley were destroying crops and limiting the food supply. Hospitals generally had backup generators, but they would soon run out of fuel. Distribution of diesel had ground to a halt as pipelines shut down. Soon, most of the American west would be under martial law.

Recovery of the grid itself would take months, because the saboteurs had destroyed a number of large high-voltage sub-stations. Those installations had key components that were extremely expensive and difficult to replace. The transformer parts were no longer even made in the US. Coupled with the disruptive cyber-attacks on the western grid's system control centres and the levelling of a key series of adjacent transmission towers, prospects for a swift return to normalcy were zero. And, of course, the collateral damage was horrendous.

Rumours swirled about groups responsible for the disaster. The popular view adopted by most of the media was that a new Middle Eastern terrorist organization had come on the scene. This seemed to be confirmed when just such a group posted an elaborate manifesto taking full responsibility. US authorities cast doubt on the authenticity of this claim but stopped short of blaming domestic plotters.

"That Jonathan Johnson was a very strange man," Anne observed mildly. "It's a wonder that he ever found anyone to work with him."

"That never seemed to be a problem," said James. "After all, he had almost unlimited access to funds. He was supported by one or two billionaires and a Mexican drug cartel. Working for the foundation was very lucrative. In fact, the really worrying thing is that, by the time the FBI reached JJ's office, the place was deserted except for him. JJ may have moved on to the great nuthouse in the sky, but his followers are still out there. The man had undeniable charisma – I know that from painful personal experience. In effect, the Destiny Foundation lives on, largely unharmed. I can't say that makes me feel very secure."

"Well, I'm glad to see that you're okay so far," said Anne. She looked across at James speculatively. Outside the office, dressed in jeans and a work-shirt, she seemed softer, more approachable. "I guess now that we've painted you as the arch villain of the piece, your coming back to work with me is a non-starter." She reached over to touch him; he responded, and they sat side by side at the table, holding hands.

James hesitated before replying, revelling in the moment. "I'm still a wanted man." He gazed into Anne's face as if trying to memorize her features.

"Anyway, I've had some time to think about my so-called career. I can't say that I'm all that impressed. There's got to be a reason why my life has been shaken up over the past few years. Who knows, maybe that earthquake was some kind of cosmic wake-up call, not just for me, but for all of us. In any event, I need to try something new. I'm not sure what, but something new."

The silence grew between them. "You'll be missed, you know," Anne said quietly. "Even Katherine seems to have warmed up. Running around in the woods must have improved your image."

"No doubt," James responded absently. In his mind, once again he was watching Katherine in danger, with no way of helping her. He had come so close to losing her.

"Incidentally," he went on, with more focus, "about Katherine. I will always be very proud of her and of the extremely minor part I've played in her life so far. But don't you think it would be simpler if we left the details of her parentage the way they are? Why complicate things unnecessarily? You know that, if there was ever anything I could do to help her or you, I would come running. Why not keep things simple?"

Anne seemed sad, though not surprised. "I was rather hoping that Katherine might give you a reason to come visit us occasionally," she said. "You realize that you will always be welcome here."

James gently released Anne's hand. He was finding this conversation increasingly difficult. And it was not simply that Anne was the loveliest woman he had ever met and the most interesting person he had ever known. Between them, Anne and Katherine had touched a part of him that he had forgotten even existed. If he didn't leave now, he never would.

Yet he must. He still had some work to do. The foundation was out there somewhere, perhaps not in its old form, but out there. He owed it to a number of people to do something about that.

* * *

Katherine walked in a few minutes later and asked where James had gone.

Anne found it hard to reply calmly. She wondered if her daughter saw her emotions in her face – her uncertainty, her feeling of loss.

"I'm not sure, darling, probably his place in Oregon. He told me he had some things to look after. I'm sure he'll visit when he can."

"That's a pity," Katherine said, somewhat to Anne's surprise. "I was just getting used to having him around."

CHAPTER 71

January 7, Vancouver/Victoria

Before he left Vancouver, James drove through piles of rubble to Matt's house in Kitsilano. He was greeted with hugs and a marvellous lunch that Matt's wife magically conjured up from their very limited supplies. Not a word was said about the premier's speech naming James as a guilty party. Afterwards Matt walked James out to his car.

"You know, I called the premier after that address in the House," Matt said. "I wanted her to know that we were proud of the way she was leading us through the disaster and that I admired her willingness to change course when change was called for. I also told her I thought that scapegoating you was outrageous and uncalled for."

James smiled his thanks. "What did she say?"

"Not much. I think she was a bit embarrassed."

"Well, cut her some slack. As someone I once knew said – *we do what we must.*"

Matt looked unconvinced but nodded. "Travel safely . . . and don't be a stranger."

* * *

On the ferry over to Vancouver Island, James tried the latest number he had for Johnny Chen. Johnny picked up on the first ring.

"You really shouldn't be allowed out alone" came the clipped tone. "If you don't have someone older and wiser looking out for you, you seem to get into all sorts of trouble."

"In that case, you'll be pleased to hear that I'll be out of circulation for a while. I've got some thinking to do."

"That's fine," Johnny responded," but take care. My sources tell me that these foundation people don't take kindly to being thwarted. I'll be keeping watch, and you never know, I might find my way across to Oregon one of these days. I believe that I have a cousin or two in Portland. I probably owe them a visit."

"Don't worry about me. I'll keep in touch."

"Well, don't overdo the introspection," said Johnny. "In my experience a little drinking and gambling often does the trick – gazing into space is highly over-rated. And remember, when you eventually determine the meaning of life, you can always come over to Happy Valley and we can celebrate. As I recall, you're not bad at picking winners. Good luck, James." And he rang off.

James knew he would be taking Johnny up on his invitation, and in the meantime looked forward to meeting one of his many cousins.

❊ ❊ ❊

James had one last stop to make before he left British Columbia. It was one he dreaded.

The sun was setting when he drove up to Alastair's comfortable house in Victoria overlooking the Straits. An exasperated nurse ushered him in the direction of the refurbished library. She warned him that her patient had only recently come out of hospital.

"He likes to think he's cured, but he's got a long way to go," she said. "Don't let him get too tired." She paused just inside the library door. Alastair sat in his wheelchair near the leaded windows at the other end of the room.

"Actually, don't tell him I said so, but he's getting better faster than the doctors thought he would. He was badly hurt, but he's pretty tough. Mr. Reid, you've got a visitor," she said as she left.

Alastair turned to face the door. His face was in shadow. He was making an obvious but unsuccessful effort to sit up straight. He looked at James, seeking out his eyes.

"I don't remember much about all those weeks in hospital, but I do recall that you were often there when I woke up. Thank you for visiting. I'm sorry I wasn't more chatty. Take a seat."

"Well, that's hardly surprising. You weren't conscious much," James responded as he subsided into his usual wing-back. "I see that your shelving is back where it belongs."

"It's tidier that way," said Alastair.

The silence between them was not quite companionable.

"I saw the premier's speech. You're quite a pair, the two of you." The lines on Alastair's face deepened. Even this much conversation seemed to be exhausting him. "Why haven't you been arrested?" he asked. "She made it sound as though you deserve to be."

"It's a long story," said James.

"I've got all evening," said Alastair. "If I drop off occasionally, give me a nudge."

James launched into his tale, starting with the way in which he'd joined the Destiny Foundation and holding nothing back, not even the fate of young Roland Barker in Mexico. By the time he'd recounted JJ's death in San Antonio, night had fallen. The few lamps in Alastair's library left most of the room in darkness.

"So, what do you think?" James said, not entirely sure that Alastair was still awake.

"I think you were very fortunate to make it through.

You certainly can't ascribe your survival to consistent good judgment, however." Alastair roused himself and rolled across to the chair James sat in. "The main thing is that you eventually worked out for yourself what was important to you and what you believed in. Even in your case, that's the first step along the road to wisdom."

Alastair smiled and looked over to the sideboard by the door. "Now, why don't you find that bottle of single malt before the harpy comes back and puts me to bed."

CHAPTER 72

January 14, Depoe Bay

James drove into Depoe Bay a week later. He turned off the highway just before he reached the tiny harbour and took the side road up the hill to the bluff where his cottage stood. He had called down in June to find out whether he still had a home. The report was reassuring. The cottage was intact even if the contents were shaken up. Despite this, he held his breath as he drove around the last corner before reaching the house.

And then there it was. The sturdy grey clapboard bungalow stood welcoming in the late-afternoon winter sun, seemingly unchanged. James parked the car and walked inside hefting a large wicker cat-carrier. After checking to make sure that all the doors and windows were secure, he raised the top of the case.

For a moment, nothing happened. Then an outraged yowl announced the slow emergence of a large grey, orange-eyed tomcat. Einstein had arrived at his new home – and he was none too pleased. Riding for several days in a box in a car was far from his favourite pastime. In fact, at various points in the painful journey, James had toyed with the idea of dumping the outraged cat by the roadside. Instead he had gritted his teeth and pressed on. As Einstein began exploring the cottage, James could see that it would be nice to have another creature around after all. Besides, Jenny had made it clear on pain of condign punishment that she expected James to live up to his parental responsibilities with respect to Einstein.

He and Alastair had made peace after a long conversation punctuated by occasional naps on Alastair's part. He had said goodbye to Jenny, Georgina and a few others from work and then he had slipped out of town. The houseboat in Victoria was sold. He made his way down the Washington and Oregon coasts, skirting the earthquake damage as he went, headed for Depoe Bay and safety.

Minutes later James sat on the porch, beer in hand, watching the sunset. Einstein crept out behind him, suspicious but apparently reconciled to a new setting for his food bowl.

James had no immediate plans. He relished the prospect of simply reading and watching the seabirds for days at a time. He had no desire for company, not right now, and yet he found himself thinking about the people he had left behind. It had been only a few days, but already he was wondering how they were getting along.

Anne and Katherine in particular populated his thoughts. He was fairly sure that the decision not to tell Katherine she was his daughter was the right one; but he felt a lingering sadness about what might have been. Or not – Katherine was as stubborn as her mother, and he had not even had the courage to say goodbye. And as for Anne, her face and her voice rarely left him. They brought harmony to his days and comfort during the long nights.

Once again James was alone.

But possibly for the first time since he was a teenager, he was also lonely.

Although maybe that was not such a bad thing – after all, loneliness meant having people to miss.

CHAPTER 73

January 30, Depoe Bay

Down the hill from James' cottage, just off the main highway, Alison stood by the car as she took a call.

"I'm glad to hear that the de Groote matter is settled," she said. "I never liked the man. But then, neither did you – right, Indira?" She hung up without waiting for an answer.

Then she turned to walk up the road towards James' cottage overlooking the sea.

Now for the last piece of tidying up.

Acknowledgements

The title *Full Rip Nine* comes from a description of a major West Coast earthquake quoted in an article by Bruce Barcott that appeared in Outdoor Magazine on August 25, 2011.

The main plot elements of *FR9* were developed during a screenwriting course taught by Brian Paisley, who suggested that the subject matter might fit a novel more comfortably than a screenplay.

Many of the geo-political ideas underlying the story emerged from regular lunches in years past with colleagues at the Centre for Global Studies at the University of Victoria, notably Gordon Smith, Barry Carin and Rod Dobell. The current Director of the Centre, Oliver Schmidtke, and his Director of Operations, Jodie Walsh, were kind enough to provide workspace at the Centre as the first drafts of *FR9* were beaten into shape.

Warm appreciation is due my editor, Allyson Latta, who took a scattered and plot-heavy manuscript and gave it focus and a degree of humanity. Allyson has taught me how far I need to travel on the road to effective story-telling, but she was kind and insightful in the process.

Finally, and most importantly, I would like to thank my partner in life, Lynda Cronin – my first reader, devoted critic and consistent inspiration. Without Lynda, this story would be half-finished and neglected in some bottom drawer.

About the Author

After education at the University of British Columbia (BA) and Yale University (MPhil, PhD), Mr Heap joined the Department of External Affairs in 1974 as a Foreign Service Officer. After seven years with the Department, most of them in the field of Canada-US relations, he subsequently filled senior positions with the federal government (Federal-Provincial Relations Office, now part of the Privy Council Office) and the British Columbia Government (Intergovernmental Relations Office, Ministry of Aboriginal Affairs). His work with the BC Government involved the management of relations with the federal government, neighbouring US states, and countries around the Pacific Rim. His last assignment was as a Senior Treaty Negotiator engaged in the treaty process with BC First Nations. Upon retirement from the BC Government in 2002, he was awarded the Queen's Golden Jubilee Medal in recognition of his public service.

In addition to his government activities, Mr Heap has worked in a think-tank setting. Between 1990 and 1992, he was the Director of the Governability Research Program in the Institute for Research on Public Policy. From 2003 to 2013, he was a Senior Research Associate with the Centre for Global Studies at the University of Victoria, a group with which he remains an Associate Fellow. In both organizations, he worked on public policy-oriented projects intended to bridge the gaps separating the public sector, the private sector, academia and the general public.

Mr Heap has a number of non-fiction credits – a variety of articles on public policy, and a book on the G-20, *Globalization and Summit Reform, An Experiment in International Governance*, published jointly by Springer and the International Development Research Centre, subsequently re-issued in French and Spanish.

Peter Heap lives with his wife and cat in Victoria, British Columbia.

Made in the USA
San Bernardino, CA
17 November 2019

60010920R00210